BELLE AMI

RANSOM

TIP OF THE SPEAR
THRILLER SERIES

BELLE AMI

RANSOM

TIP OF THE SPEAR
THRILLER SERIES

www.belleamiauthor.com

Published Internationally by Tema N. Merback
Newbury Park, CA USA
belleamiauthor.com
Copyright © 2020 Tema N. Merback

Previously published as Ransom © 2018 by The Hartwood Publishing Group, LLC

Revised and Re-Released by Tema N. Merback © 2020

Exclusive cover © 2020 Fiona Jayde Media
Interior design by Tamara Cribley, The Deliberate Page

PRINT ISBN 978-1-7322071-9-6
EBOOK ISBN 978-1-7322071-8-9

ALSO AVAILABLE

ACKNOWLEDGMENT

Thank you to my parents Dina & Leo, my husband Joe, my children Natasha & Benjamin, my siblings Sarah, Joel, and Josh, my other children Julianna & Mitch, and my brother-in-law Steve.

A special thank you to Joanna D'Angelo, my editor, advisor, coach, and dear friend, without you there would be no books. Thank you, Fiona Jayde of Fiona Jayde Media for creating the most beautiful covers for the Tip of the Spear Series. Thank you, Tamara Cribley of Deliberate Page for your beautiful interior book designs.

To the men and women who serve and protect us in the United States and Israel. May the bonds between our nations remain strong and enduring forever.

PROLOGUE

Beirut, Lebanon
December 24
4 p.m.

Some people are born to be doctors, lawyers, or Indian chiefs, but Aryeh was born to be a spy. He had twenty different identities that ran the gamut from Orthodox Jewish diamond dealer to sophisticated Swiss banker, and he could switch from one to the other in less time than it took to fry an egg. Approaching the customs official at the Beirut Airport, he handed him his passport. The official gave it a cursory glance, asked him the usual questions, and handed it back to him. He thanked the customs official—they were well acquainted, given they were both Mossad. Aryeh slipped the passport back inside the pocket of his jacket, well aware that the customs official had slipped a note into it before handing it back to him. A small slip of paper with an address. His destination.

He needed a break, even a veteran spy like him, who reveled in the constant ever-changing excitement of the job—needed to stop and reevaluate his life at some point. He promised himself this would be his final mission for a while. Maybe he would take his cue from his friend Cyrus Hassani, that lucky bastard. Beautiful loving wife, cute little girl, and another baby on the way. Aryeh would even put up with a boring desk job like Cyrus had if it meant he could go home to a woman like Layla.

He strode confidently to the nearest taxi, taking his time, even though he'd already spotted the spooks the moment he cleared passport control. Like any operative worth his salt, he was always on alert.

One of the goons had made the classic mistake of meeting his eye. Aryeh held the man's gaze and smiled, but the fool averted his eyes and confirmed Aryeh's instinct that the men were watching him. His identity on his passport read Franz Stark. He'd made countless trips to Beirut under the guise of a Swiss banker from Zurich, a foolproof false identity. But this time was different. This time seventy-five million in rough-cut diamonds had been stolen from Mossad and were rumored to be on their way to Beirut by a Mossad agent gone rogue. Hezbollah would, of course, take notice. Swiss bankers were not above suspicion.

He rolled his carry-on to the curb and hailed a taxi. He focused on the passenger side-mirror and saw the Hezbollah tag team jump into a Mercedes following a safe distance behind. He'd have to lose them, but for now, leading his tails along for a joyride would pass the time.

The drive from Rafic-Hariri International Airport into the city took a little less than thirty minutes. When they passed the giant sentinels in the sea, Pigeon Rocks, Aryeh told the driver to slow down so he could get a photo with his cell phone. It also gave him a chance to snag a peek of the Mercedes tailing them.

Once past the massive rock formations, the traffic grew heavy, and the taxi wended its way along the Rue de Paris, passing hotels, cafes, restaurants, and clothing boutiques. To the left, the Mediterranean Sea glittered, a turquoise jewel in the afternoon sunlight. The wide street bordered the Corniche where locals and tourists rollerbladed, jogged, and strolled; children rode bikes, artists painted on easels, and musicians gathered. Aryeh enjoyed the meeting of worlds where traditionally veiled women walked alongside girls in miniskirts along sidewalks. Outside beneath colorful umbrellas sat men and women playing backgammon and drinking coffee.

He checked his watch. It was several hours before his hook-up with Zara. He needed a shower and a shave before his rendezvous with the beautiful DGSE agent.

The Mercedes was several cars behind. He leaned toward the partition that separated him from the driver. "There's a hundred-seventy-five-thousand-pound tip for you if you can lose that blue Mercedes behind us." Aryeh's Arabic was accent-free.

The driver checked his rear-view mirror. He nodded and smiled. Ahead, a streetlight turned yellow, and the cab braked as if to stop. At the last second, the driver hit the gas pedal, and the cab shot through the red light with screeching tires. He was barely through the intersection when the side traffic merged, their horns blaring. The taxi rocketed up the street veering in and out of traffic, barely avoiding a collision. Aryeh watched through the rear window as a delivery truck cut off the Mercedes at the intersection. He blew out a breath, in relief for the precious extra seconds as his driver took a hard right onto a side street and raced away, leaving the avenue behind. Not taking any chances and clearly enjoying his moment as James Bond, the driver made several more turns racing a path down tree-lined streets.

Shooting another glance over his shoulder, Aryeh could see no sign of the Mercedes. A minute later, he spied a neon sign boasting a martini glass and the name *After Hours*. "Pull over." The driver screeched to a halt at the curb that sent Aryeh's briefcase flying over the seat. He grabbed the case before the driver had even budged. Handing the driver a wad of pounds, he slapped him on the back and thanked him. "Just in case they catch up, I'd appreciate it if you ditched them again and take the rest of the day off. Here's an extra two hundred for your trouble." Aryeh ducked in the bar as the cab raced away. No questions asked. *Welcome to Beirut*. He grinned.

Walking into the bar, he chose a corner table, ordered an espresso, and kept an eye out the window.

The Mercedes drove by just as he'd downed his second espresso.

Hezbollah knew he was here.

Counting to sixty, he left the bar and grabbed another cab, giving the driver the address on the slip of paper in his passport of a small boutique hotel on the other side of the city.

He leaned his head back against the seat and let out a deep breath. Yes, he needed a break and soon, if he didn't get killed that is.

CHAPTER 1

Tel Aviv, Israel
December 25
8:00 a.m.

"*Ima,* when is the baby going to get here? I want a sister. Can't you order one of those?" Cerise, declared from her perch in her pink booster seat at the kitchen table. She blew away the red curls that kept tumbling in front of her eyes as she twisted and turned the colored rows of the Rubik's cube in her pudgy hands.

Cyrus Hassani and his wife Layla exchanged amused glances. Their precocious four-year-old daughter was focused on proving to her father that she could solve the puzzle as fast as he had. It was a wonder she had time to pepper them with questions about the coming baby.

Cyrus stood at the counter, dicing Persian cucumber, and tossed it into the bowl of red onion, tomato, mint, and lemon juice already marinating for the Persian Shirazi salad they would have for breakfast. "Eshgham, my love." He winked at Layla. "Do you want to take this one?" He always reverted to his first language, Farsi, when using terms of endearment.

Layla laughed as she stirred scrambled eggs in a skillet on the stove. "Cerise, it's not like going to the ice cream shop. You can't pick your favorite flavor. You have to accept what God gives you."

"I think we should give it back if it's a boy." Cerise wrinkled her nose.

"Whoa, what do you mean, give him back? What's wrong with boys? I thought you loved your *Aba.* I'm a boy." Cyrus huffed in playful dismay. "I'll show you what boys are good for." He pounced on Cerise, tickling her until her giggles rang out.

"Daddy, stop tickling me. You're the only boy I like."

"I see." He brushed her wayward curls out of her eyes. "And what about the boy at preschool? What's his name?"

Cerise's dimple in her chin, so much like his, deepened with her smile. "Jacob—his name is Jacob. I forgot he's a boy." She shrugged a delicate shoulder.

"You forgot because he's your friend. That's what matters anyway." Cyrus tapped her nose. "I think you'll make a wonderful big sister to a baby brother. Think of all the things you'll be able to teach him—like the Rubik's cube."

"Daddy, he'll be a little baby. Too small for a puzzle."

Cyrus kissed the top of her head and reached for the salt, throwing a pinch onto the salad followed by a healthy dose of freshly ground pepper. A quick toss and he set it on the table, grinning at his daughter's adorable face scrunched up in deep concentration as she worked on completing the white side. This child of his heart was growing up. That thought was scarier to him than going into battle. He tucked the wayward curl behind her ear, only to have it fall forward again.

"There's a butterfly clip in that little glass bowl beside the microwave," Layla commented from the stove as Cyrus tried to tame his daughter's curly locks into submission.

"She has your hair." He chuckled as he grabbed the clip and gathered Cerise's hair on top of her head.

The little girl gave a triumphant yell as she finished the white side.

"Maybe, but she has your ability to tune everything out when she's working on something," Layla threw over her shoulder, making her thick auburn ponytail swing back and forth in its high ponytail. She winced, her hand going to her lower back. She was in the last bloom of her pregnancy, and her back had begun to trouble her.

Cyrus joined Layla at the stove, encircling her waist, he rubbed her back with one hand and caressed her belly with the other. When he kissed her neck, she leaned back into his shoulder and sighed.

I'm the luckiest man in the world to be so blessed. Somehow, this broken man and former spy has found true happiness.

The man who'd never aspired to marriage and children had been lucky to be gifted with both. Layla looked up at him with those incredible turquoise eyes that never failed to send a tremor through his body. In his estimation, he was married to the most beautiful woman he'd ever known. Proof enough for him there was a God. He continued to massage Layla's aching back as she explained the concept of patience to their four-year-old. He almost chuckled, like him, patience was not one of her virtues.

Cyrus's phone vibrated in his pocket. He took it out and frowned at the caller ID, then slipped it back into his pocket.

Layla waddled to the table with the frying pan and set it down.

"Mommy, what will we name him?" Cerise set the Rubik's cube down, her attention now on the eggs, her mother was dishing onto a plate for her.

Layla set the plate in front of Cerise, sat beside her, and caressed her hair. "Maybe we'll call him Rubik if he's a boy."

Cerise giggled as she picked up her spoon and scooped up a bite of egg.

Cyrus's phone hummed once again. He ignored it as he sat across from his wife and child. He dished a heaping amount of eggs onto his plate and beside it an equal amount of salad.

Layla lifted a finely defined arched brow at him as she sipped her coffee.

"It's the office." He frowned at the phone's continued vibration, weighing whether or not to answer.

He could always say he'd been in the shower and missed the call.

"It could be important," Layla said.

"Everything's important to them."

"You have to answer it, Daddy."

Cyrus traced Cerise's delicate furrowed brows and tried to keep a straight face at his daughter's admonishment. Looking into her Nile green eyes was like staring into a mirror.

Yes, she certainly is my daughter.

The phone stopped buzzing. "Too late," he said. "If it's important, they'll call back."

A few moments later, the phone vibrated again. Cyrus sighed, knowing they would keep calling until he answered. "I'd better take this." He slipped out the sliding glass doors to the porch as he swiped the phone. "Hassani here."

Layla's conversation with Cerise faded into the background as he concentrated on what the man was saying.

"Aryeh disappeared a few days ago in Beirut," his supervisor on the Iran desk growled.

"Newsflash, Saul. That's what spies do. They go off the radar when necessary."

"Not with seventy-five million in diamonds belonging to Mossad," Saul countered. "The Ramsad wants to see you. Now."

"He promised me this leave of absence. He knows damn well what Layla and I have been through—how close we came to losing everything. Fuck, I nearly lost my child."

"Things change. Cyrus, this isn't a request; it's an order. He's waiting for you at headquarters."

Cyrus hung up and scratched at the stubble on his face. *Dammit, Aryeh, what the hell have you gotten yourself into?*

He returned to the kitchen and sat back down. Layla reached across the table and covered his hand with hers.

"You have to go, don't you?" she whispered.

He sighed as he watched his daughter. Cerise was munching on a slice of toast with her tablet in front of her, watching her favorite Disney movie, *Frozen*, for the tenth time he was sure.

"Yes."

Layla set his hand on her belly. "I thought we had another week before you had to go back."

"I did too…but something's come up." He gently rubbed circles on her abdomen.

"Can you talk about it?"

"Aryeh's gone missing in Beirut."

Layla shrugged. "That seems pretty ordinary to me. I mean, he's an intelligence agent. Disappearing is par for the course, isn't it?"

"Normally, I'd say yes, but this might be a little more complicated." He leaned back and scraped his fingers through his black hair in frustration. "The Ramsad wants to talk to me. I have to go."

"The Ramsad? Will you be gone long?"

Cerise's laughter rang out, and he smiled, distracted.

"Do you think you'll be home for dinner?" Layla smiled tantalizingly at him. "I'm making your favorite."

He chuckled. "My favorite, eh?"

She nodded, her eyes gleaming with sensuous promise.

"I'll call you and let you know if the meeting goes long." He pulled her into his arms and brushed his lips over hers. "I can hardly stand leaving you. You know that, don't you?"

The call couldn't have come at a more unwelcome time. He and Layla had just reconciled, and things were still fragile between them. Whatever it was, it better not take him away from Layla and Cerise.

She gazed into his eyes. "Yes, I know," she said softly, "I can't bear to be without you, either, but duty calls."

CHAPTER 2

He cursed under his breath as he cleared security at Mossad headquarters. The Ramsad, Noam Levi, was known to those inside Mossad as *Hashu'al*, The Fox. He was sly and cunning and believed the less known about an operation, the better. He was also known to single out certain individuals for stardom. If they succeeded, they joined an exclusive club of insiders. If they didn't, they were rarely heard from again.

He took a deep breath and entered the Ramsad's office. The blinds on the windows were down. The light filtering in stippled across the Ramsad's heavily lined face. The head of Israel's most secretive intelligence agency waved him in, indicating a seat.

"Cyrus, I can imagine you're wondering what the hell is going on," he said, folding his hands on the glass-topped desk. "I know I encouraged you to take time with your family, and now I'm ordering you back. How are Layla and Cerise doing?"

"They're fine, sir." Cyrus unbuttoned his jacket and crossed his legs. "We had some hurdles to overcome, but things have returned to a semblance of normalcy. Cerise is still clinging to Layla—doesn't let her out of her sight. From what the doctors have told us, children bounce back—and patience is all that is required. I am thankful for that, but patience is not something I possess in abundance."

"Keeping all of Israel's children safe is why you and I do what we do. We can't afford to be patient when it comes to their safety."

"That is true, sir." He knew he'd do anything to keep Cerise safe.

"We are facing an unusual situation. Something no nation on the planet is prepared to confront, but we've always dealt with the impossible, have we not?"

Cyrus nodded.

"No dream was ever more impossible than the birth and survival of Israel," said the Ramsad.

Cyrus stared unwaveringly into the eyes of the man who could coax water from a stone. "Yes, sir." Something was going on. Something big. But he'd be damned before he'd show the Ramsad any weakness.

"I think you could be of tremendous help in remedying what has gone awry."

"Whatever is needed, sir. You can count on me."

The Ramsad nodded his approval. "Other than Aryeh's team, you were the last person to see him, and now Aryeh has disappeared in Beirut with a great deal of treasure." He cleared his throat. "It's hard to imagine, but it appears Aryeh may have gone rogue on us."

Cyrus didn't flinch. "I don't believe it, sir. The man I met, the man who saved my family could never be a traitor."

The Ramsad drummed his fingers on the table. "I'm glad you don't believe it…" he leaned forward, "because it isn't true."

Cyrus breathed a sigh of relief.

"However, this is a secret between you and me. No one else is to know."

"May I ask why, sir?"

"I've chosen you to lead the operation to find Aryeh."

"I'm honored, sir." But he was also torn. This would take him away from Layla and Cerise. What if Layla went into labor while he was on assignment and he couldn't get back in time?

"With Aryeh gone, the team is lacking a head. I want you to assume leadership. On paper, your mission is to find the traitor Aryeh. You will extract him and the seventy-five-million in diamonds he stole and return him to Israel for trial."

The Ramsad was asking him to lead Aryeh's Kidon team, a secret unit answering only to the Ramsad and the prime minister. The thought made his head spin. The secret team known as the Tip of the Spear was a covert group specializing in assassinations, extractions, and operations never mentioned aloud by anyone in government or defense.

"If Aryeh isn't a traitor or a thief, what is true?"

"Truth can be a slippery slope. No one knows, and no one can know, but I sent Aryeh to Beirut. Are you familiar with EMP?"

"Yes, sir. An electromagnetic pulse is a burst of electromagnetic radiation created by a nuclear explosion above the Earth's surface that disrupts electronics, communications, defense systems, and could potentially shut down the electric grid of a nation and its military," he replied smoothly.

The Ramsad nodded. "Call me Noam, Cyrus. You and I will be communicating in secret, and the less formality between us, the better."

Using the Ramsad's first name was going to take effort on his part. He forced himself to comply. "Yes, Noam."

"Our cyber experts picked up a failed encrypted communication between Hezbollah's counter-espionage chief and officials in the Hermit Kingdom."

Cooperation between the terrorist group and the fledging nuclear-armed rogue nation, North Korea wasn't a promising situation. Cyrus considered the possibilities. "My guess is Iran has to be invisibly brokering this liaison."

"That's what my people tell me, Cyrus. Arms have been flowing between the two nations for years but have escalated since the disastrous American deal with Tehran. Iran has purchased long-range ballistic missiles from Pyongyang and Russia, and the Iranians and North Koreans are cooperating in developing a miniaturized nuclear implosion device. I have new Intel indicating they may have reached an unacceptable tipping point.

"The Mullahs in Tehran aren't ready to blatantly show their hand, but, through their surrogates, they might attempt an attack." The Ramsad picked up a remote and turned on the big screen monitor on the wall. A video showed a large cargo vessel with a smaller defense escort plowing through rough seas. "Stowed in that vessel are long-range ballistic missiles headed to Beirut. We could sink it, but it won't stop the next shipment or the one after that. We need to cut off the head of the snake, just like we did in Syria when we took out the nuclear reactor at the Al-Kibar military facility."

The video cut to a delegation of North Koreans arriving at Rafic-Hariri International airport in Beirut.

"Who are they?" Cyrus asked.

"North Korean diplomatic officials and two nuclear physicists from Pyongyang being picked up by Hezbollah operatives."

"What does this have to do with Aryeh and the diamonds?"

"We have an unidentified mole. We haven't confirmed it yet, but we believe the traitor is working at Mossad. The mission diverges from here. It's the reason I sent Aryeh to Beirut."

"Aryeh is on a dual mission?"

"Yes. I sent Aryeh with no one else's knowledge to Lebanon to make contact with Hezbollah."

"Why would Hezbollah take the bait and do business with Aryeh?"

"Aryeh's nephew was kidnapped on the Lebanese Israeli border and is being held hostage by Hezbollah. Hezbollah refuses to negotiate his release. It's provided the perfect alibi for an agent to go rogue. Once he gains Hezbollah's trust, he will communicate only with you and me."

"You set Aryeh up as a traitor based on his desire to rescue his nephew? Are the diamonds even in Beirut?"

"No, they're in my safe, but no one knows that either."

"What makes you think they're planning an EMP? And why now?"

"That's where the intercepted encrypted message comes in. Hezbollah named this operation "*Nihayat alealam. Alqishat al'akhirat.*"

Cyrus whispered the translation under his breath. "The end of the world. The last straw."

The Ramsad nodded. "The last straw was the United States recognition of Jerusalem as our capital."

"The interception also mentioned a one-time opportunity to do away with the big and little Satans—the United States and Israel." The Ramsad's eyes narrowed. They looked as if they could pierce armored steel. "I've chosen you and Aryeh to stop this from happening."

Cyrus shook his head. "Sir—Noam, I've been working with Intel on the inside of Mossad for four years. To work in the field again—as an agent—a team leader—I'm out of practice."

"Don't be ridiculous. You've just returned from a successful mission in the US. The reports from the FBI on you were glowing. Once an assassin, always an assassin. Once a spy, forever a spy."

Cyrus stared at the photos on the screen of the ship and its deadly cargo. Everything he held dear might not survive such an attack.

The Ramsad continued. "They tell me an EMP strategically imploded high over the Negev and simultaneously over Kansas would leave both the US and Israel completely helpless and open to attack without any ability to respond. Armageddon."

"Have you enlisted America's help?"

"No, I can't trust anyone. With a mole embedded among us, we must deal with this alone."

Cyrus knew two American's who could be trusted—Cass Saladino and David Weiss. The FBI agents he'd worked with in Pennsylvania on his mad quest to track down Layla and stop an explosion that would have decimated Washington and millions of people. He'd trust them with his life. Covertly enlisting them would give him access to a lot more intelligence and back up.

"Cyrus, I know you're thinking about the FBI agents you worked with in America. However, I forbid you from taking them into your confidence. This operation will be kept to a small circle of the need-to-knows."

Damn! Going against the Ramsad's wishes would be suicide. "Why me, sir?" Cyrus didn't bother correcting himself and using the Ramsad's first name.

"You must have known the day would come when your unique services would be called upon once more. I would think you'd be relieved to use those exceptional skills again."

He hated to admit it, but what the Ramsad said was true. Rescuing Layla in Lancaster and preventing a nuclear meltdown at Three Mile Island had rekindled his sense of purpose. The shadow world had never left him. Safeguarding the world was what he was born to do. It was what he'd done before he was forced to blow his deep cover in Tehran.

The fire to protect burned within his veins. Cyrus's pulse quickened at the thought of a mission. His only fear was that Layla would never forgive him for returning to the field and once more putting his life at risk. Walking through the minefield of his wife's anger presented a challenge. He would do nothing that would threaten his relationship with the only woman he'd ever loved. She was his foundation.

"Cyrus, I know you've just reunited with your family, but I'm afraid your country needs you. You are the man for this job, and I won't take no for an answer. If you need me to speak to Layla, I will."

Cyrus grinned at the thought of the Ramsad and Layla locking horns. "No, thank you, sir, I'll handle Layla."

"Good. Your work begins at once. The Research Department is creating a new legend for you. The Team has already been notified and is ready to coalesce under your leadership. You will leave for Beirut in three days. I need you and the team there to assist Aryeh. I suggest you put your affairs in order. Tomorrow we begin."

"Yes, sir." Cyrus knew this was a call to serve he could not ignore. *My country needs me. Layla will have to understand.*

CHAPTER 3

It was after midnight by the time Cyrus got home. He threw his keys on the side table beside the door and walked to the kitchen. He hadn't eaten and was starving. His dinner was on the table with a note from Layla:

Wake me when you get home.
Heat the salmon in the microwave.
Salad's in the fridge.
Cerise missed having dinner with you.
I love you, Superman.
Your loving,
Kryptonite.

He chuckled. In Tehran, she'd nicknamed him Superman when he'd rescued her from Evin prison after she'd been kidnapped while on holiday in Dubai with her then college boyfriend. The boyfriend's father paid an extraordinary ransom to have his son released but had left Layla to die. Cyrus, who'd been deep undercover in Iran, had gotten word from Mossad to rescue Layla, a Jewish American whose father Alec was a nuclear physicist and an old friend of Israel's president. It had been love at first sight for Cyrus, although he fought his feelings for months. He thanked God, he finally came to his senses and realized that he couldn't live without Layla. The kryptonite reference was new and befitted her effect on him.

Knowing he'd have to leave in a matter of days, he took the stairs two at a time. First, he tip-toed into Cerise's bedroom, wanting to hold his sweet child in his arms. A sliver of moonlight lit her hair. Her red curls looked like flames splayed across the pillow. He kneeled beside the bed and placed a feather-light kiss on her forehead. To his dismay, her Nile green eyes the exact color of his blinked open. Before she could squeal his name, he placed a finger against her lips. "Shh...Ceri. We don't want to wake *Ima*."

"*Aba*, you missed dinner. Where were you?"

Cerise had become a lot clingier with her parents. Between Layla being gone for a month, and then him moving out for a few weeks because of their marital problems, her world had felt unstable. A wave of guilt washed over him at the thought of leaving her again. "Daddy had to go to the office, *metuka*. I had some things to do, and it took longer than I expected. Forgive me?"

She furrowed her brow, and he nearly laughed aloud at her expression, which was identical to her mother's whenever she was contemplating a decision.

"Oh, Aba, I forgive you." Then, looking toward the door as if to confirm they were alone, she whispered, "But you'd better ask forgiveness from *Ima*. She looked sad you weren't here for dinner. She made your favorite."

He kissed the top of her head. "I'll do that, *metuka*. Thank you for your good advice." He picked up Arnav, her stuffed rabbit that had fallen off the bed. Placing her well-loved toy in her arms, he whispered. "Close your eyes and go back to sleep. I'll see you in the morning, sweetheart."

She closed her eyes and fell asleep so quickly that for a moment, he wondered if he'd just imagined their exchange. He shook his head with wonder. The innocent have no reason to toss and turn. He tiptoed down the stairs to the kitchen. Placing the plate of salmon and rice in the microwave, he hit the rewarm button and watched the carousel turn.

"I asked you to wake me."

He turned. His reaction to Layla never changed. As always, he felt both a carnal burning desire and a spiritual love. Layla was his redemption. Her auburn hair was tousled, and she wore a tee-shirt and booty shorts. He couldn't help his sudden intake of breath or stop the blood rushing through his veins.

"It's late, and I didn't want to deprive you of your beauty sleep. But I can see it doesn't matter because with or without it, you're still the most beautiful woman I've ever seen."

She smiled. "Flattery will get you everywhere. Sit down and let me take care of my Superman."

"I can never refuse you, *eshgham*."

She set the plate on the table and sat next to him. "How did it go, baby?" she caressed his cheek. "Any news on Aryeh?"

"No." He took a bite and hoped it would sustain him through the storm he knew was about to come. "The Ramsad believes he may be a traitor."

Layla's eyes grew wide. "He's wrong. It's not possible. My God, if it wasn't for Aryeh— Cerise and my grandparents might have been murdered in cold blood. We'd have been dead too." She shuddered.

"I know. That's pretty much what I told Noam, but all the evidence points otherwise."

A quirky smile filled her face. "You call him Noam now?"

He shrugged. "He insisted, although I had a hard time doing it."

"So, what are they going to do about Aryeh?"

He took another bite, bracing himself. "The Ramsad wants me to run the operation to find him."

"Good. That means you can find Aryeh and prove he's innocent of whatever it is they're accusing him of doing."

He reached out and took her hand in his. "Layla, it means I'll be running an operation from Beirut. I'll be in the field. It means leaving you and Cerise for a while."

She snatched her hand from his. The color drained from her face. "No! You said your days of being a field agent were over." Tears filled her eyes, and she brushed them away.

Seeing her fall apart tore him inside out. He wrapped his arms around her. "Baby, I don't have a choice. The Ramsad made it clear he won't take no for an answer." He caressed her belly where their unborn child grew.

Layla wove her fingers through his hair. "Can't they find someone else? Why does it have to be you?"

"The Ramsad insists I'm the man."

The anger in her eyes dissipated, replaced by suspicion. She scrutinized him. He averted his gaze, staring down at his food.

"You want this, don't you?" she whispered. "Cerise and I aren't enough, are we? This…" She looked around the kitchen. "This isn't enough. You miss the excitement, the danger, the near-death moments. Tell me the truth."

Raising his eyes, he held her gaze. "Layla, I love you and Cerise more than anything in this world, but this is who I am. It's who I was when you met me. It's who I'll be until the day I die."

She pushed him away and rose from her chair. Tears streamed down her face. He just sat and watched her walk out of the room. The thought of losing her made his heart constrict in his chest. He forced himself to eat. He'd give her some time to reconsider, to cool down. She was a firecracker, and he'd lit her fuse. Right now, he needed to wait until she cooled off.

Layla curled up in bed, hugging her knees, her thoughts in turmoil. Her cheeks burned with anger and frustration. She wanted to claw out Aryeh's eyes. His disappearance had brought on this nightmare.

Taking deep breaths, she calmed her fury. Cyrus was going to Beirut on a mission where he could be killed, and that terrified her. After he'd rescued her from that farm in Pennsylvania where the Hezbollah terrorists had been holding her, she'd developed PTSD. She and Cyrus returned to Israel, estranged and on the verge of a divorce. It was only through counseling and her grandparents' wisdom that they were able to stitch the fabric of their lives back together.

Now, when they'd finally recommitted to each other, Mossad was going to tear him away from her and Cerise again. Was she to stand by and not fight for the man she loved? She dug her nails into her palms until tears welled in her eyes.

She breathed deeply and found her equilibrium. *What am I doing? I'm acting like a child.*

Aryeh risked his life to help Cyrus save her, and this is how she behaved when Aryeh needed Cyrus's help? She needed to think rationally instead of emotionally. She was so afraid of losing him that she'd acted like a spoiled brat. As always, Cyrus was the tower of strength and reason while she was the volatile emotional one.

Despite five years of marriage, Layla still didn't understand everything about Cyrus. This man, this seemingly cold-hearted spy, had blown his cover as a mole to get her out of Iran. His love for her was so deep that he'd risked everything to rescue her from the clutches of a terrorist. Nothing about him had changed. His work defined him. His dedication to protecting the innocent was what made him tick. If she took that away from him, what would he become? She'd be separating him from his soul, his very essence, and the quality that drew her to him in the first place. She would destroy the man she loved.

Her head was spinning. How could she take back the words she'd hurled at him? How could she make this right? As she continued to ruminate, she felt his presence in the bedroom. She was curled up with her back to the door, but she knew his eyes were on her. She pretended to be asleep. *Get ready for bed, Cyrus.*

Her silent wish realized, he walked past the bed. She watched as he disappeared into the bathroom. A few minutes later, she heard the shower running. When she heard the door open, she snapped her eyes shut. Squinting, she saw him emerge from the bathroom in a cloud of steam. The sight of him naked made her heart pound. She never tired of looking at him. Sometimes it amazed her that he was hers. She knew that over the years many women must have made a play for him. She understood why. Cyrus exuded danger and sex appeal. His pale green eyes radiated intelligence and passion. In her heart, she knew he loved no one else but her, but still, her insecurities sometimes got the better of her.

He moved around the room, his muscles rippling like a tiger on the prowl, and the thought of his touch sizzled through her like a volt of electricity along a wire fence.

His sigh when he got in bed was one of frustration. Layla imagined the quagmire his thoughts must be in. She knew she'd twisted him into a knot only she could untie. She scooted back, snuggling against him and heard his breath catch. He didn't wrap himself around her, though, and it annoyed her.

She turned to look at him. His hands were behind his head, and he was staring at the ceiling.

"A penny for your thoughts."

"I'm not sure you'd be pleased to hear what I'm thinking," he said.

"Probably not, but I still want to know."

Silence.

She turned over and rested her head on his arm and her hand on his chest. "You know, I said a lot of things earlier that were thoughtless." She toyed with the hair on his chest. "It's…it's just that I love you so much and I reacted with fear. The thought of losing you…I'm so sorry."

He rolled to his side, facing her, his finger tracing down the curve of her cheek. "I'm sorry too. A lot of what you said is true. I do miss the action, the danger, but it's nothing compared to what you mean to me, *aziz am*. Without you I'm nothing. Soulless. Dead. Do you understand what I'm saying?"

"I do…I know you have to do this. I just want you to come home to me."

He smiled. "Trust me. I will." He wrapped his arms around her and pulled her close. "I think we need to make some memories to keep me warm when I'm lying alone in Beirut missing my muse."

Pleasure swelled in her when she felt his hardness throbbing against her. His lips enfolded hers, his tongue delving deep inside her mouth. All her worries dissolved like a sugar cube in hot tea. Five years together and every time he touched her, it still felt like the first time. She loved his patience. He never rushed when he made love to her. His tongue and lips feasted as if she were ambrosia.

"*Eshgham*." He brought his forehead to hers, his member hard against her pelvis. "Do you have any idea what you do to me? I can't live without you, my love."

She took his face in her hands and kissed him on his forehead and cheeks. "Cyrus, I could never love anyone else."

A deep groan rumbled in his chest. The vibration, like an arrow to her core, charged her desire. She trembled against him.

"I need to feel our bodies as one," she begged. "I love you so much."

"Oh, Layla, your love is everything to me. All I want to do is love you until we both reach the heavens."

She ran her hand over him, feeling him harden even more if that were possible. "Then show me."

He took her with the force of a released dam. She gasped with pleasure, opening to him, giving herself to him. She belonged to him. Their hearts pounded in harmony. She was his symphony, and he, the virtuoso. In an earth-shaking crescendo, they exploded together, their bodies stiffening in the timelessness of love's ultimate union.

Slowly their hearts settled back into an even percussion. Layla adored the weight of his body on hers. "Cyrus?"

"Hmmm…"

"Do you think it's a boy?"

He raised his head and searched her eyes. "I don't know, but it doesn't matter, does it?"

"No, but I want a son."

He smiled, his right brow lifting in an arch. "If it's not, we'll just make another one." He kissed her and nibbled on her lower lip. "I kind of like the process."

She sighed, feeling him harden within her. "Me too." She undulated beneath him, wanting more of him.

"I think we should practice as much as possible," Cyrus whispered in her ear, nibbling on her earlobe.

She closed her eyes, arching into him. "Every great performance deserves an encore."

"I believe the last one deserved a standing ovation."

"Bravo." She giggled as he pulled her in for a repeat command performance.

Once back at the farm's headquarters, Cyrus met Zvi, their resident analyst nerd who had a gift for slicing through data like a shark fin through water. The younger man had the black horn-rimmed glasses going for him, and the unruly dark hair of an absent-minded professor, but he was also built like a bodybuilder.

"Do we know what cover Aryeh is operating under in Beirut?" Cyrus asked.

"He's using one of his many passport identities." Zvi grinned. "He's a German banker named Franz Stark. Aryeh is a master. It's a clean guise. Mossad created a bank in Switzerland with office space, staff, and vaults for private secured banking. Aryeh is an officer of the bank. He enjoys immense deference no matter where he travels."

Yitzhak broke in. "Cyrus, none of us believe for a minute Aryeh is a traitor. If he took the diamonds, it's for a good reason. He's on to something."

"I think you're right, Yitzhak, but the higher-ups have given us a job. We're to find Aryeh and bring him back to Israel. That's what we're going to do."

Yitzhak nodded. "We know the shtick. But we want you to know how we feel."

"Your feelings are duly noted." He looked at his watch. "I'm anxious to assemble the whole team. Let's head back to the command center."

The catering truck was a virtual miracle. Somehow Mossad managed to serve up everyone's favorite foods. Cyrus figured their dossiers were pretty complete. The chef, learning of Cyrus's food preferences, had even made a Persian chicken stew for him. Yitzhak and Ben set up a portable table in the center of the computer center, and everyone pulled up a seat. He joined the others at the table. The team's lunch hour was filled with schoolyard wisecracks and joking.

Ash dug into his burger. "Nira, don't you ever get bored with all those grains and veggies? I swear you're wasting away."

She punched him, nearly knocking him out of his chair. "Does this feel like the punch from someone wasting away?"

Daniel licked his fingers from his brisket sandwich's drippings. "Why don't you two just get it over with and get a room?"

Nira shot him a look that dared him to continue. "You're such a meathead, Daniel. Why the hell would I need an overactive teenager with a gun? We all know Ash gets off on guns, not women."

Ash grinned, taking no offense. "Believe me, baby, guns aren't the only weapon I'm packing." He raised his eyebrows and waggled them like Groucho Marx.

Nira dropped her eyes to his lap. "Looks pretty small to me."

The guys all exploded with laughter, hooting, and whistling.

Ash's comeback was quick. "He's not fully loaded. Watch out when he is, or are you worried you might find something too *hard* to give up?"

Yitzhak was laughing so hard tears ran down his face. "Will you two put a muzzle on it, I'm having trouble digesting my food with all your wisecracks. Besides, Cyrus probably thinks he's inherited a team of depraved teenagers."

Cyrus put up his hands. "Don't drag me into this, Yitz. I'm the only married guy here. My days of sexual conquest are long over, but I'm not so old that I can't remember what it felt like to be always on the prowl."

Ben grinned. "Sorry boss, but we're a horny bunch, I'm afraid."

The team grew silent and stared at Ben. He'd called Cyrus boss, and Cyrus knew he'd crossed some forbidden line. "Oh, come on, guys. Face up to it, Cyrus is our new team leader, and I, for one, don't have a problem with it. Get with the program."

Ben might as well have lit a match to a fuse. Everyone joined in hurling insults at him.

Yitzhak finally raised his hands for quiet, and everyone groaned but settled down. "Cyrus knows how we all feel about Aryeh. No one is probably feeling more out of place than he is. He needs to know whatever our complaints we're still a team, a finely oiled machine. Once he turns the engine over, we'll all work to whatever end he demands."

"I appreciate that, Yitz." Cyrus stood and placed his hands on the table and took a moment to look at each team member. "I want to make it completely clear to all of you, I'm not trying to win your affection or replace Aryeh in your hearts. I'm here to do a job, the one given to me. I know each of you will give me your best because I'm sure as hell not going to take any less." It was time to get down to business. He turned to Zvi. "Tell me, Zvi, does Aryeh have anyone he can trust in Beirut?"

"He does. He has a close relationship with a journalist living in Beirut. Zara Zayani is a reporter working for *Le Figaro* and runs their ad hoc Beirut office. She also happens to be an agent for the DGSE."

Cyrus absorbed this tidbit. "Interesting, French intelligence service. You said *close*, explain."

"They've been through a lot together—terrorist attacks in Paris, Brussels, and Morocco. I'm pretty sure saving each other's life is part of their connection. Those kinds of bonds in the world of espionage generate trust. He would, in all likelihood, enlist her help."

"Okay, so the first thing we'll need to do is set up surveillance on Zara." Cyrus's gaze swept the table for their reaction.

Yitzhak shook his head. "Like I said, finding her won't be a problem, but getting anything out of the lady she doesn't want to be known is a losing proposition. She's good at keeping her cover. As a side-note, she's also in with Hezbollah."

Daniel interjected. "She'd better be good if she's playing with those animals."

Cyrus stroked the stubble on his face. He'd forged a close bond with Cass and David, the FBI agents he'd worked with in America. He understood loyalty. Aryeh would most likely behave in the same manner. Four months ago, when Layla was kidnapped in New York, Cyrus had turned to Aryeh for help. The Kidon leader had met with him but denied his request to become part of the rescue team. In the end, Aryeh had taken out the terrorist that was about to shoot Layla and him. If there is a code of honor among thieves, then the same could be said of spies, even if they were on different teams. "Is Aryeh in a relationship?"

"Nope, no relationship in Israel," Nira answered. "But he's pretty cagey about his personal life."

Cyrus remembered the rambunctious man who'd plowed through lunch with gusto and passion. "Seemed like a guy who enjoys the finer things in life when he's not working."

Ben laughed. "That's Aryeh, for sure. Outside of work, he acts the bon vivant. But when we're involved in an operation, he's a perfectionist. A real stickler, he dots his I's and crosses his T's. He accepts no less from his team."

Cyrus nodded. He hated not being able to share the real nature of their mission, but Noam had made it clear no one was to know, at least for now. Cyrus was walking a tight rope between his promise to Noam and his loyalty to the team. He understood Noam's reasoning—a traitorous mole operating within Mossad put the operation at risk. Aryeh's safety was paramount, but the true reason for his mission, if communicated to the enemy, would put not only his life in danger, but the entire country as well. At least, one part of the equation was spot-on, the team needed to find Aryeh. "Okay, hypothesize with me. What would make a guy who's risked his life time after time for his country suddenly steal seventy-five million in gems and run off to Beirut? Find me the answer to that question, and we'll find the man."

Cyrus looked around the room at each team member. Their faces reflected mixed emotions, but not one of them looked as if they knew the answer. "Remember, our job is to recover the treasure and bring Aryeh home. If we can clear his name, you bet I'm going to do it. My wife and I owe him our lives."

Yitzhak looked at everyone around the table. "We all worked that operation, Cyrus. We know what went down."

"Then you know I want him found and safely brought home. I know you guys keep your family off-limits, but in this case, we need to rule out any possibility of blackmail. Everyone has an Achilles heel. I want a complete dossier on everyone in Aryeh's family by tomorrow morning."

"Cyrus, whatever the top guns are saying, Aryeh is no traitor. Each one of us on the team would stake our careers on his loyalty. Trust me, there's a reason he took the diamonds, and it's a good one."

"I hope you're right, Yitzhak." *The Ramsad has put me in a hell of a position.* Back in Iran, when he was deep undercover for Mossad, he worked alone, not with a team, and therefore his loyalty was only to his superiors. He didn't know Aryeh's team very well, but he knew how loyal they were to Aryeh, and he worried they would be royally pissed at not being told the truth. He sure as hell would. He hoped the old fox at Mossad headquarters would okay his confiding in them once they were safely ensconced in Beirut. With a nuclear threat, the sooner they got to Beirut, the better.

CHAPTER 5

Beirut, Lebanon

Aryeh had perfected the ability to disappear in a crowd, despite his formidable 6'1" frame and two-hundred-pound girth of solid muscle. Killing in close quarters and getting in and out of unfriendly places without being apprehended by the authorities required Ninja talent.

Most of the time, due to the nature of his work, his face bore a scowl, but tonight beneath his blond beard, Aryeh smiled. Known as the Paris of the East, Beirut was a five-thousand-year-old party town, and although his purpose for being in Beirut was critical, he enjoyed a good party.

The driving bass and drumbeat of pulsating music electrified the pale hair on his muscled forearms causing them to stand on end. He was hungry, and the perfume of exotically spiced foods made his stomach grumble. He appreciated Beirut and all it offered. It was the Holy Grail of cosmopolitan assimilation where the oriental and occidental worlds mixed like a perfectly concocted cocktail.

The young and old, the wealthy, and the not so wealthy, tourists and locals, friends and foes, spilled into a cobblestoned Makdessi Street from the bars and restaurants that lined the Hamra district. Neon signs blazed advertising food and drink. Aryeh navigated through the crowd that ebbed and flowed through the streets, his movements as calm and graceful as a *danseur*, a male ballet dancer, until a young man bumped into him and went stumbling backward falling to the ground. In an obvious state of inebriation, the boy groaned and clutched his head, shaking it, his dilated pupils oscillating. Aryeh picked him up as if he was a feather, righting him on his feet. The young man apologized profusely in a slur of Arabic.

Aryeh answered in fluent Arabic. "A bit more caution, my friend. Too much liquor is a recipe for disaster. Tomorrow is another day, and you don't want to end up in a pool of vomit. Do not offend the holy prophet," he reprimanded.

"Yes, *Sayed*." The boy attempted to bow and nearly fell over again. Another boy, presumably his friend, grabbed him by the arms and the pair stumbled down the street laughing.

Aryeh brushed off his sports jacket and walked on. In Beirut, the Qur'an's suggestion from the *Surah Al Maaida* to avoid intoxicants wasn't well observed. It was ten days before Christmas, and celebrations were in high gear. Lights and decorations lit the streets, and Nativity scenes were prominent in the public squares. Aryeh's walk from the hotel had skirted Martyr's Square and the Muhammad al-Amin Mosque, where a gigantic Christmas tree twinkled with lights. Lit in a public ceremony that included a firework display and a Christmas concert, the square was packed with large crowds of Lebanese Christians. However, celebrating Christmas was not on Aryeh's agenda tonight.

The Rabbit Hole Bar and Grill was packed. Aryeh pushed through the door and took in the crowd. A diverse collection of people from all walks of life sat at tightly packed tables. Their voices joined in a din of overlapping conversations. There wasn't a seat at the bar not taken by a patron. With a quick scan around, he spotted a dark-haired woman with burgundy streaks in her hair sitting at the far end of the bar. She was chatting with a swarthy man, but when she saw Aryeh approach, she whispered a few words, and the man stood and relinquished his seat to Aryeh. Her companion nodded his farewell and headed for the door.

Aryeh bent and kissed Zara Zayani on each cheek. Speaking in French, he said. "Who's the suit? I hope I didn't interrupt anything of consequence, Zara."

"No, *mon cher*. I told him I was meeting with a dear friend." She leaned in, displaying her lovely cleavage.

He dropped his eyes in appreciation and then waved the bartender in for a drink.

Zara whispered, "My handlers have concluded I'm too valuable and need protection. Faiz has the good fortune of shadowing me."

"Please bring the lady another drink and bring me a kiwi and gin-infused cocktail, the one with fresh za'atar. A little spice to enliven what I hope will be a delightful evening." He took Zara's hand and kissed it. "Your superiors in France are wise. Your worth is inestimable."

"Perhaps, but it makes me long for the days when I was unrecognizable. A ghost."

"You, a ghost? Purely a figment of your imagination. You have always stood out, and may I add you are as bewitching as ever. I've missed you. How long has it been?"

"Remind me where we last saw each other?" Her eyes glittered with amusement.

"Was it Paris or Rome? No, I remember now, Casablanca. An evening I will never forget. I believe we burned the place down, didn't we?"

"It was an explosive evening in more ways than one." She laughed.

"I've relegated that mission to the dustbin of failures and forgotten wishes. However, I do recall our liaison being hotter than the Sahara in summer."

Her smile warmed him more than the delicious cocktail the waiter set before him. "I wouldn't mind a repeat performance," he murmured under his breath.

She raised her glass and toasted, *"A votre sante!"*

He whispered, *"La'Chaim!"* They touched glasses and sipped their cocktails.

"An encore is a sign of appreciation." She pulled playfully on his beard. "But who knows what the future holds, *mon ami*. Why do I suspect you haven't come to Beirut for the simple pleasures of my bed."

"Zara, I need your help."

She leaned in, her breath warm on his ear. "My company is always favorably disposed to helping our Israeli friends. Would you care to be more specific?"

"I'd rather we discussed this in a more private arena."

"Ah…in my bed, for example."

"In your bed, after I wine and dine you would be more than satisfactory. Later perhaps. For now, I'd rather enjoy my time with you and catch up on your life after Morocco. There is time enough to discuss other issues."

"You have always been a taste I couldn't resist, Aryeh. It's hard to find men of your caliber who give as much as they take."

"I'm pleased to meet your high expectations. Were we different people, it's doubtful I'd ever stray from your bed and the delicious intimacy to be found in your arms. Why search for the elusive when the dream is within reach?"

Her effervescent laughter drew appreciative glances from the men in the room.

"You missed your calling; you should have been a philosopher," she said.

"There is nothing philosophical about the effect you have on the opposite sex, Zara." He stared at her delicious lips. "There's not a man in this room who hasn't fallen under your spell."

Her almond-shaped green eyes held his. "What difference does it make? There is only one man in this room who interests me."

"I praise your good taste and my better fortune." He clinked his glass to hers.

Zara's apartment was on a narrow street off the Rue Gouraud in the Gemmayzeh neighborhood, where charming old French colonial homes intermingled with cafes, restaurants, and galleries. These eclectic establishments gave the area its signature bohemian vibe. The upscale, trendy neighborhood provided the French covert agency's most proven agent with a comfortable base for her collection of Humint intelligence.

Zara opened the door to her apartment, and Aryeh followed her in. Zara's home was a direct reflection of her, a mix of old-world taste and modern comfort. She lit the gas log fireplace and then poured them each a snifter of cognac. Leaving her drink on the bar, she pulled a vinyl phonograph record out of a sleeve and placed it on her antique phonograph. Carefully she lowered the arm of the stylus. The telltale crackle of old vinyl blended with the haunting voice of Billie Holliday. A beautiful sound that played across his mind as smoothly as the cognac.

She raised her snifter to his. "Jazz is the music of spies, Aryeh."

"And why do you think so, Zara?"

"Jazz musicians and spies are both masters of improvisation. We are creative soloists that thrive on nonconformance and originality. We must think outside the box, reinventing ourselves as the rules of engagement change." She wrapped one arm around his neck and pressed against him. They swayed against each other in the firelight.

The woman and the alcohol worked their magic. Her lips tasted of cognac and secret pleasures. He ran his lips down her throat. Her scent of almonds and cinnamon intoxicated him. Her skin, the color of caramelized sugar, smooth and soft, was what he dreamed about when he wasn't planning his next mission. Her allure was irresistible, an indulgence he had never refused.

He knew he was putting Zara in danger by being with her. He was about to become a target of both Hezbollah and Mossad. If she helped him, she would find herself ensnared in a trap with him. What they felt for one another wasn't something they ever spoke about. Their relationship had no chance of becoming more than a few stolen hours given their work. But occasionally, even hidden feelings need to be voiced and acknowledged. "I wondered if you would even answer my message to meet?" he asked.

"After all we've been through together. How could you even entertain such a foolish thought?"

Moments frozen in memory played across his mind. Their escape from a burning Berber camp near Casablanca and nearly dying of exposure in the desert. Bleeding and bruised, climbing from beneath the rubble of a train in Belgium that a terrorist's bomb had derailed. Working together defusing a bomb destined for the Israeli embassy seconds before it would have exploded in a banlieue tenement slum in Paris. He laughed aloud. Their courtship was always set amid death and devastation, yet their bond had only grown over time.

"What's so funny, *mon cher?* I insist you share. It's not fair for you to joke at my expense."

"Most lovers share memories of romantic assignations: a beach, a cabin in the mountains, a cruise in the Caribbean. We share the pleasure of heart-pounding life or death experiences, of bloodbaths and bruises, of ticking bombs, and narrow escapes."

The light went out of her eyes. "It's who we've become, *mon dieu*. It's who they've made us."

"Do you ever think about who you'd be if Jacob hadn't been murdered? If that IED hadn't exploded at Saint-Michel? What if his train had pulled away safely and he lived? Would Zara the spy be living an ordinary life, married with children? I sometimes picture you as that linguistics professor who taught at the Sorbonne."

"When I lost my brother, my life changed forever. All I cared about was revenge. There can never be a normal so long as monsters wage war on the innocent." She sniffled, taking a large sip of cognac. "No use dwelling on what might have been, Aryeh. The woman who taught at the Sorbonne died a long time ago with Jacob. The woman who emerged from the ashes bears no resemblance to her." She studied his face. "You need to focus on the here and now, not on what might have been. Before you is a woman who needs you. Make me forget everything, Aryeh." She leaned in and brushed her lips against his. "You've always been good at making me forget."

Desire traveled through his body, and his hands wrapped around her slender waist. "It's a good thing we're on the same side because there's little I would ever deny you."

The sparkle had returned to her eyes. Zara took his hand and led him to a doorway hung with jeweled beads and tiny bells. "My foolproof alarm system." She ran her fingers through the beads, and a tinkling of bells sounded.

He laughed. "Quite a deterrent."

"My deterrent is loaded and ready on the nightstand. This—" Zara strummed her fingers across the beads and bells. "This is a psychological diversion."

A while later, the temptress had melted beneath him—he finished her with a fury that left them both soaked and breathless. Filling his lungs, he ran his tongue up her neck to her earlobe and nibbled the delicate flesh. She lay beneath him, spread-eagled, and spent with exhaustion. A good hour had passed since they'd removed each other's clothing and begun their dance to ecstasy.

"Hmm, Zara, making love to you is better than a year of therapy."

When she smiled, the love bites on her lips deepened to the color of burgundy wine. "That was delicious, *mon amour*. You've lived up to your name. You are the king of the jungle."

He was tempted to roar in her ear like the king of beasts. Instead, he licked her ear, eliciting a chain of giggles.

"You reduce me to a mere kitty cat," he laughed. "Meow."

"Stop." She tried to slap him away. When he persisted, she slithered from beneath him and flipped him, straddling him on the bed.

"Uncle." He surrendered, raising his fingers in the peace sign. "Make love, not war."

She released him and nestled in the crook of his arm. Drumming her fingers on his chest, she asked, "Seriously. Why are you here, Aryeh?"

"I need your help, Zara?"

"I'm listening, *mon amour.*"

"My nephew Gideon Riese was captured while on patrol on the Israeli Lebanese border by Hezbollah. A month has passed, and all attempts to negotiate his release have failed. I was on assignment when it happened."

"I read about the Iranian Hezbollah plot to blow up the reactor at Three Mile Island. I heard a rumor Mossad was working hand-in-hand with the FBI."

"Rumors travel fast in our business. I was never involved with the FBI, but some were."

She laughed. "Of course, you weren't. Knowing you, you slipped in and out without leaving a fingerprint." She sat up, retrieving their glasses of cognac. They sipped silently for a moment. Her expressive eyes conveyed compassion. "I'm sorry about your nephew."

He stared into the amber liquid. "It's become a nightmare. When I came home, my sister, Gideon's mother, had a nervous breakdown. I have no children. Gideon is the only one to carry the family name. My parents are devastated. My family cannot survive this—I must do something. I need your help."

She swallowed a large sip of the cognac. "In what way can I be of help?"

"There's a mole at Mossad. It's likely he's leaked information to Hezbollah, and they know Gideon is my nephew. My being Mossad puts his life in more danger. They know I won't sit by and do nothing. I can't live with this Zara."

"I'll make inquiries, but what do you have besides yourself that we can barter with?"

"Seventy-five million in diamonds."

Zara's eyes widened. "How? Where did you get them?"

"Mossad."

"You stole diamonds? From Mossad?"

"I'm a dead man walking. Soon I'll be a target of my agency." He hated lying to her, but for his plan to work, Zara needed to buy his story. He was sending her into the lion's den, and her safety depended on it.

"You can't give these murderous thugs seventy-five million in diamonds. Every dollar they get they spend on drugs to fund terrorism, and wars to destabilize the Middle East."

"Do you have a better idea? I'm certainly not going to give them information that will harm my country."

"What is it you want me to do?"

"Put me in touch with Hezbollah. Tell them I've gone rogue, that I've stolen diamonds and I'm willing to pay them a hefty ransom for Gideon."

"You can't do this, Aryeh. It's not who you are."

"Tell me, Zara, what would you have given to save Jacob?"

Her shoulders sank. "Let me think about this. In the meantime, I'll see what I can find out."

"Time is of the essence—I have to move quickly."

"Tomorrow night, I'll message you and meet you at the Rabbit Hole."

"Thank you, Zara. I knew I could count on you."

She pulled on his beard. "You are going to owe me big time for this one, *mon ami.*"

He took the drink from her hand and set it on the nightstand. Then he ran his lips up her neck to her ear. His warm whisper produced a shudder. "Why wait for your payback, why not take a small down payment now?" His fingers traveled the length of her body seeking the heat that emanated from her core. She arched, pressing her body against his touch and moaned. "This is a good start, but don't think it will settle your debt."

"I'm at your service. Take whatever you want. Whenever you want, and by all means, as much as you want."

Aryeh gave a sleepy Zara a quick kiss and whispered, "I'll see you tonight."

Groggily, she mumbled, "Do you want me to make you coffee before you go?"

"No. I'll get it on my walk back to the hotel. I need some air to clear my head. Last night surpassed my expectations."

A tiny smile graced her lips. "Prepare yourself…I'm not done with you yet."

"Now that is reassuring." He slapped her buttocks affectionately. "*Jusqu'à ce soir.*"

Outside Zara's home, he scanned the street, a habit ingrained in him from years of being an operative. Nothing seemed untoward, and he took a moment to inhale the aromas particular to Beirut. The salty scent of the sea and Shisha smoke filled his senses, while the perfume of lemons aroused his hunger.

Aryeh smiled to himself. The night with Zara had satisfied him in every way. He looked forward to spending another evening with the incomparable agent. If anyone could find Gideon, it would be Zara. Her resources ran the gamut of intelligence operatives to terrorist thugs. Her cover as a journalist for Le Figaro was one of the best a spy could have. It had given her access to the PR driven Hezbollah, and she'd even scored an interview with Hezbollah's secretary-general Hassan Nasrallah. If he knew his dear femme fatale, she'd go straight to the top of Hezbollah. The thought of infiltrating the upper echelon of the terrorist organization made the blood surge in his veins.

The morning was still cool, and he'd decided to walk the two-plus miles to his hotel on Chouran Street. After the rush of an exciting evening with Zara, he needed time to gather his thoughts. He knew she'd come through for him and provide him with a contact for Gideon's kidnappers. Seventy-five million in diamonds wasn't something a terrorist organization like Hezbollah could ignore.

It was time he checked in with the Ramsad. He needed to know when his team would arrive in Beirut on their purported mission of apprehending him and returning him to Israel. He knew by now, Cyrus Hassani was in charge of his team. It had been his suggestion to the Ramsad before he left for Beirut that Cyrus becomes the leader of his Kidon unit. Aryeh realized picking a favorite among them might have led to jealousy and disturbed the effectiveness of the whole. It was much better to bring in an outsider.

Aryeh knew well what Cyrus Hassani had accomplished. Cyrus was a legendary spy, yet since he'd returned to Israel, he'd sat at the Iran desk at Mossad working analysis. Cyrus was a man with a target on his head, and with good reason, Mossad had taken him out of the field because the mullahs of Iran considered him a deadly traitor. But four years was long enough to waste the skills of such a prodigious asset. It was time to put him back into play, and what could be more important than stopping North Korea and Iran and their terrorist proxy group Hezbollah from detonating a nuclear bomb in the upper atmosphere? A nuclear detonation capable of unleashing an electromagnetic pulse, killing millions of people. The rogue nations would be free afterward to wreak havoc and terrorize the world at will. The world was on the brink of chaos and only the team, and he could stop it.

Aryeh knew as he walked the streets of an awakening Beirut that the peace and tranquility surrounding him was a deception. The ablutions of everyday existence, the raising of metal grills on storefronts, umbrellas being opened by sleepy waiters in front of restaurants, and the aroma of rich dark espresso brewed fresh every day seemed ordinary in every respect. The reality was that somewhere in the southern suburb of Dahieh, Hezbollah's seat of power, a deadly plot was unfolding that threatened the existence of Israel and the United States.

He'd cut a deal with the Ramsad. He and the team would destroy the ballistic missiles and kill the nuclear physicists and rocket engineers sent from North Korea to oversee the electromagnetic pulse strike, and he'd be given the leeway to negotiate a deal to bring Gideon home. As for the Hezbollah overlords who were overseeing the project, they'd get what they deserved—an early grave.

He smiled, enjoying his morning constitutional. If the plan worked, he would return to Israel having saved the world from the apocalypse and bring his nephew back home to his family.

CHAPTER 6

Mustafa Mughniyeh exited his armored car surrounded by his bodyguards. At thirty years old, he was the youngest member of Hezbollah's Jihad Council. He'd recently assumed Hezbollah's military command after his uncle Mustafa Badreddine's assassination. Badreddine had been murdered under suspicious circumstances near the Damascus airport. The hit most likely carried out by Mossad.

As always, Mustafa hid his face beneath a camouflage baseball cap. Not a single photo existed of him. Nor were there any records or announcements of his birth. His father had planned it that way from his first breath of life. At times he'd wondered whether he'd been created to be a secret weapon. A ghost created with no other purpose than to be an instrument to mete out Allah's justice. Multiple photos of his brother, Jihad, had existed, and now his brother was dead. Whenever Mustafa passed a mirror, it was always a surprise to him. He locked the image in his mind. It was his way of holding on to the years of his life. There would be no photos to recall his youth or the aging of his body. No tangible record of his existence at all.

As was his habit whenever in public, he was careful to avoid any possibility of a camera catching him unawares. Crossing the street, he disappeared inside a newly built concrete building in the Beirut suburb of Dahieh. The southern tip of Beirut was Hezbollah's stronghold and headquarters. The recently rebuilt Dahieh, like a phoenix, had risen from the ashes of the 2006 conflict with Israel.

Mustafa had just returned from Syria, where he'd met with his mentor General Qasem Solatani who was helping Bashar al-Assad in his fight against insurgents. Hezbollah was fighting alongside its sponsor, Iran's Quds force. Mustafa had recently read several articles by a female writer for Le Figaro, who questioned the wisdom of the Lebanese fighting in Syria.

Most Lebanese wanted nothing to do with the Syrian civil war bloodbath and genocide. Mustafa, struck by the journalist's criticism, agreed with her. Wasting his warriors' lives for a corrupt regime turned his stomach. Unfortunately, Hezbollah was dependent on the largess of the Islamic Republic of Iran and its Quds force. Iran's strategic plans to rule the Middle East were in line with controlling Syria. But soon, things would change. Mustafa was working on a plot that would free Hezbollah, throwing off the yoke of Iran and rewarding them with control of their destiny. No more would the mullahs dictate the military strategy to be taken by warriors. His view was simple. Leave the military to the military. Let the mullahs command what pertains to Islamic devotion and practice.

Mustafa and his bodyguards took the elevator to the third floor. He was greeted by Hassan Nasrallah, the Secretary-General of Hezbollah. Nasrallah had been bestowed with the honorific of "Sayyid," which designated he was a direct descendant of the Islamic prophet Muhammad. The burly leader resembled Santa Claus with his broad face, white beard, and jolly demeanor rather than the stalwart, soft-spoken, revered leader, who had fought the Israelis to a standstill in 2006. Hassan enjoyed acclaim throughout the Middle East for leading the first Arab militia to have ever beaten Israel.

"*As-salamu alaykum*, Mustafa."

"*Wa alaikum salam*, Hassan." When Mustafa was in the presence of the old guard, he always felt a stab of pain. By right, his father, Imad, murdered in a car bombing in Damascus, and his uncle Mustafa who'd just recently been assassinated, along with his brother, Jihad, killed in an Israeli convoy strike—should be standing in this room with him. All three had died as martyrs. He lived for the day when he would be their revenge.

He took for granted that he'd been groomed for greatness. It was Allah's will. He lived and breathed the glory of fulfilling the dreams of those who had come before him. The destruction of Israel and bringing the United States to its knees was what he was born to do, and now the moment had arrived. He would be God's instrument.

Mustafa looked around the room. Most of the Jihad Council was present. His eyebrows rose in surprise when he saw that even Talal Hamia, head of Unit 910, Hezbollah's most elite and secretive force was in attendance. In fact, one of the reasons for today's gathering of the Jihad council was to hand over control of Unit 910 to Mustafa. His martyred uncle, Mustafa Badr al-Din, had served as the commander, and the unit bore allegiance to his family. Through the unit, Mustafa would administer attacks on Israel and America in their homeland. Unit 910's purpose was to take the fight to the enemy.

Here among Hezbollah's elite, he was aware of the curious glances he received. He rarely attended the meetings of Hezbollah, preferring to be away from those who curried favor and sought power at these types of gatherings. The slapping on the back and bragging meant nothing to him. His reason for being here entirely different from the others. Later he would attend a secret meeting with Nasrallah and two nuclear scientists and a team of rocket physicists and engineers from North Korea. Tomorrow night the first shipment from North Korea would arrive, and he would take possession of the precious cargo. If he succeeded with his plan, he would change the world forever.

Shortly before the conclusion of the meeting, one of Nasrallah's aides approached him and whispered in his ear. The aide informed him it was Nasrallah's wish to delay the meeting. He suggested Mustafa take his meal now, and they would meet later. It was curious this impromptu change of plans, not at all like the indefatigable man who allowed nothing to dissuade him from the task at hand. Perhaps he didn't want to draw any attention from prying eyes? *Patience, Mustafa. All will be known in good time.*

Zara had dressed modestly in a long jacketed gray suit. Her only adornment was a jade green scarf she favored because it matched her eyes. She wore it loosely over her hair. One of her contacts had made the call to Hezbollah requesting a meeting concerning the kidnapped Israeli soldier, Gideon Riese, and a seventy-five-million-dollar ransom offer.

Zara knew her worth. As a journalist, she managed to walk a narrow line between criticism of Hezbollah's military wing and terrorist activities and praise of their political and social welfare outreach. Hezbollah new that good propaganda was worth its weight in gold. Zara held the goodwill and the ear of the terrorist organization. Nonetheless, she'd drawn their attention, and she knew they often put a tail on her, keeping track of her whereabouts. She'd noticed the two men tailing her and Faiz on their drive to her meeting with the leader of Hezbollah.

She waited, her hands modestly resting in her lap. Hassan Nasrallah entered the room alone. His bodyguards remained outside. Seating himself across from her, he regarded her as he combed his fingers through his beard. "I'm sorry to have kept you waiting, *Anissa* Zayani. Would you care for some tea?"

"No, *Sayyid*, I know how busy you must be with all of these notable visitors."

Nasrallah waved his hand dismissively. "Nothing more than a gathering to celebrate our accomplishments. This gathering of policymakers is to assure our constituents. Now tell me about this offer you've brought."

"I am simply the messenger, *Sayyid*. It came through a third party."

"Yes, yes, of course." He leaned forward, studying her. "Journalists are often used as carrier pigeons."

"As I'm sure you know," she said, "a Mossad agent is the uncle of the Israeli soldier you kidnapped on the Golan Heights in October. The only thing I know about the man who asked me to arrange this meeting is that he stole seventy-five million in diamonds from Mossad, and he is hiding here in Beirut. He wants to offer the diamonds as a ransom for his nephew."

"A Mossad agent willing to betray his country? Interesting."

"I have no idea where his loyalties lie."

Nasrallah again fingered his beard. "And then what? Surely, he doesn't believe he can return to Israel."

She shook her head. "I can't speak for him. I know that his knowledge is worth as much if not more than the stones."

Nasrallah fingered his beard. "Why would I trust this agent? He could be a plant."

"Trust, never. However, it is possible the man could be used and manipulated."

"I will consider what you've told me and deliver my decision to you in a day or two." Nasrallah rose.

"*Sayyid* Nasrallah. What should I tell my contact?"

"Tell him a bargain might be struck between us. You will hear from me."

Zara bowed and left the room. The hallway teemed with bodyguards and officials, most of whom she recognized. She wondered what the real reason for this meeting of Hezbollah's Jihad council could be. It did not appear to be an ordinary gathering to reassure constituents. Hezbollah's highest-ranking officials had come from around the country. Such a consortium of power under one roof was an anomaly.

She dropped her eyes modestly and slowly strolled toward the exit where her car waited. She could sense every head turn her way. She found it easier not to meet the transparent hunger in men's eyes when they gazed at her. It was the reason she bumped into the young man and fell against him. She lifted her eyes. She had no idea who he was, but there could be no mistaking the amusement in his gaze.

"I apologize, *Sayed. Sameheni,*" she murmured.

"And if I don't forgive you? What then?"

Zara stared into his eyes, feigning incomprehension. Annoyance pulsed in the vein at her temple. *The man is audacious.* "I shall have to live with it, as will you." She nodded and walked past him, sensing his gaze following her down the hallway.

Once she'd exited the building, she drew in a breath of relief. She'd managed to navigate her way clear of the unsavory characters in attendance. The man she'd nearly knocked over was her age, and his impolite remark had made an impression on her. She knew every face in Hezbollah's elite, but this man was unknown to her. The crowded hallway filled with only the most trusted meant he held a high status. She recalled the haughty look in the man's eyes, the look of entitlement and confidence he exuded. Her first reaction had been to slap the smug look off his face. Her curiosity awakened, she knew she wouldn't rest until she discovered his identity.

When she opened the door to the car, she could see the reflection of one of the men who'd tailed her earlier. He stopped to look in a storefront window, which was a clumsy dead giveaway. She would have to change her rendezvous with Aryeh.

"Faiz, we're being followed." She smiled. "Let's take them on a joy-ride and give them their money's worth. I believe I haven't had my fill of animals today. Take me to Zazoo." Her writing for *La Figaro* covered politics mostly. Occasionally she wrote freelance articles about other issues. Recently she'd heard about inhumane conditions at the Beirut zoo. She wanted to write an exposé about the plight of animals, hoping that she might improve their living conditions. "I spent my morning with murderers and terrorists, I might as well spend the rest of the day writing about animal cruelty."

The Mercedes slowly pulled away from the curb. Zara looked back and saw the man jump into a car following them. She smiled. *Such idiots.*

Mustafa watched the petite woman exit the building. With just the meeting of eyes, his world had shifted. He'd never met a woman who dared to stand tall in a man's world. He felt compelled to know more about the fascinating foreigner.

A friend of his father interrupted his musings and greeted him heartily. "I am very sorry about the loss of your wife and son, Mustafa. Praise Allah, that your father did not live to see the loss of his firstborn grandson."

Mustafa lowered his eyes in acceptance of his elder's condolences and to hide his guilt. "Thank you for your kind words." How could he tell this man that his marriage had been less than satisfactory? It was only at his father's insistence that he'd married Dasia, the daughter of a high ranking general, sealing the bargain between his father's desire to cement their families standing and the general's insistence that it would prove to be a powerful alliance. But for Mustafa, the arranged marriage was a disaster. He didn't love Dasia, and in truth, she had never loved him. She was obedient but removed. The child had been born from their wedding night union. His military assignments had made it easy for him to avoid going home, and he and Dasia only spoke every few weeks. He suspected that Dasia's ill-advised surprise trip to visit him in Syria was to request a divorce, or maybe it was to reconcile. He would never know. The convoy had been blown up, and Dasia and Ibrahim had perished. At moments such as this, when he was forced to think about his wife and son, he felt guilty that he had never loved them, and now it was too late.

"What you do is of great importance, my son. Allah, may his name be blessed, will provide another wife, and I pray you will have other sons."

"Perhaps one day, I pray." Even as his father's friend spoke to him about his family and his wife, all he could think about was the woman who'd bumped into him.

He shook his head, trying to clear away her image from his mind. How was it possible that she'd dared to dismiss him without ever looking back? He knew nothing of addictions, having always been a man of great discipline, but now he understood why the opium addicts chased after their next high. After just one chance meeting, he was yearning to see her again. He had to find her. He needed to know who she was. He needed to rid himself of this strange attraction based on nothing more than a meeting of eyes.

"Hassan will see you now." He bowed his head to his father's friend and turned to one of Nasrallah's bodyguards. The man led him toward the door where the alluring woman had left only a short while ago. An unfamiliar sensation of jealousy blinded him. *What has she to do with Nasrallah?* His blood coursed angrily in his veins, and a wave of burning anger spread through his nervous system. It seemed impossible to him that the French woman was the reason for his delayed meeting with Nasrallah. When she exited the door, he'd no idea that it was Nasrallah she'd met with. He clenched his fists into tight balls of steel. Inside of him, a storm raged, however on the outside he seemed in a trance. He froze, his feet refusing to move. Unanswered questions holding him in suspension.

The words of his father came to him. *Do not follow the path of others, create your life's destiny. Only by action and careful planning can you achieve your goals.* Mustafa knew that his father had referenced his mission to destroy Israel, but did not this wisdom apply to all facets of his life? Even love and conquering the heart of another required the same recipe to succeed. He reminded himself to adhere to his father's formula of careful planning and action. His father understood what it took to realize the impossible, and so did he.

"Mustafa," the bodyguard asked again. "Sayyid Hassan is ready for you. Please…" his hand indicating the room where Nasrallah waited.

Mustafa, nodded, acknowledging the man. First, he would get Nasrallah to answer the burning question in his mind. Who was the mysterious woman?

"*Abney*, everything is proceeding as planned." Sayyid Hassan Nasrallah stood to greet his young protégé, kissing him on both cheeks. "The shipment from North Korea has safely arrived in Chabahar port and is on its way to Baalbek. It should arrive in three days." Nasrallah patted Mustafa on the back. "Please, come and sit with me, *ragaa*."

After taking their seats, Nasrallah continued. "The North Korean scientists and engineers have arrived and are in a safe house. The factory you requested is finished, situated in a valley difficult to observe from the skies. The perfect foil, a cannabis farm in the Beqaa Valley. It is well guarded and will serve your purpose. Everything you have requested for this operation is yours."

"Thank you, Hassan. What about the enriched uranium for the bombs?"

"Already on-site and in storage. None but a small cadre of my most trusted aides know of this operation. Only the Ayatollah, Qasem, and Bashar know your plan. Our leaders have the utmost confidence that the son of Imad and the nephew of Dhu al-Fiqar will bring glory to Allah and once and for all destroy the enemies of Islam."

Mustafa smiled, recalling his uncle's nickname of honor, *Dhu al-Fiqar*, the magical sword wielded by Ali, the prophet Muhammad's cousin and son-in-law that the Shi'a believed Muhammad named as his successor. "This is the only way we'll succeed. There can be no leaks and no communication once we begin at Baalbek."

"*Shaa alla.*" A knock on the door interrupted. "I have ordered some tea." He directed his words toward the door. "*Taal.*" The door opened, and a woman dressed in a hijab entered carrying a tray. "*Shakira,*" Nasrallah thanked her, and the woman bowed deferentially and left the room.

Mustafa sipped his tea. "*Sayyid* Hassan, I noticed a young woman leaving your office when I arrived. I'm curious as to who she is."

"A journalist. She works for *Le Figaro.*"

"Was she here for an interview or a favor?"

"Neither. The journalist delivered a ransom offer for a captured Israeli soldier."

"Is she to be trusted?"

Nasrallah smiled. "We've long suspected her of being involved with the Israelis. However, there is no proof she is."

"Interesting. If you believe the woman is a spy, why do you allow her access?"

"It is better to keep your enemies close."

Mustafa nodded. "A wise decision." He sipped his tea. "By the way, what did you say her name is?"

"Zara Zayani." Nasrallah grinned. "That one will submit to no man, but Allah blessed her with rare beauty. I pity the poor man foolish enough to try to tame her."

"Yes, too much pride, I would say—but a prize to be certain."

CHAPTER 7

Charles de Gaulle Airport
Paris, France

Yitzhak, with his arms around Nira, stood in line to check in for their flight from Paris to Beirut. They appeared to be lovers who couldn't keep their hands off each other. Each time they moved forward, he whispered in her ear, and she laughed. She looked up at Yitzhak and planted a kiss on his mouth. Around them, people smiled; love was something the French revered. With a nod of approval and a *"Bon voyage,"* from the customs officer, the two swept through security.

They boarded their Air France flight with new identities provided to them by the Mossad's travel department. For the mission, each member of the team had received an authentic passport held by *sayanim*—Jews from around the world who volunteered to supply cover for Mossad agents when Israel called on them.

Yitzhak's French passport profiled him as Andre Chaput, a divorced bicycle-shop owner. Nira had assumed the identity of Anick Fortier, who worked as a sales representative for the art glass firm of Lalique. Andre and Anick were taking a vacation together and left Paris for Beirut on a nine-a.m. direct flight from Charles de Gaulle to Rafic-Hariri. Together they would hastily convert the rented six-bedroom duplex located in Ramlet Al Bayda into a base of operations for the team.

At approximately the same time, Daniel, posing as Alberto Giacometti, a wine salesman, sat at a bar with his trainee Ben, whose passport read Bernardo Orvieto. The two men were drinking a bottle of wine before their flight from Florence to Beirut.

"Boss," Ben spoke loud enough in flawless Italian for those around them to hear. "Tell me about Beirut. Are the women as beautiful as I've heard?"

Daniel sniggered. "You'll see. The town is hopping with action. Just remember, Romeo, this is a business trip, and you're here to learn the wine business. The wine coming out of the Beqaa Valley is improving with every season." He enthusiastically slapped Ben on the back. "*Il mattino ha l'oro in bocca*, the early bird catches the worm."

Over the intercom system, they heard their flight called. Daniel stood and grabbed his attaché case. "Come on, let's get to the gate, and I'll tell you a Beirut love story."

Upon their arrival in Beirut, they would begin surveillance on Zara and start their search for Aryeh. Staying true to their covers, they would also be meeting with restaurant sommeliers and wine merchants.

Ash assumed the identity of Jonathon Cooper, an MIT student who'd grown up in Massachusetts. He flew by way of New York with a U.S. passport and was embarking on a winter break vacation backpacking through the Middle East. He arrived in Beirut on a red-eye and was fast asleep in a hostel not far from the duplex where Nira and Yitzhak were busily transforming the team's operational headquarters.

In a few hours when Ash woke, he'd meet a trusted Lebanese arms dealer at a club. Ash, or Cash, as the team jokingly referred to him, controlled bank accounts in the Cayman Islands. Per Cyrus's instructions, he was stockpiling arms in a warehouse in the Beqaa Valley. Cyrus had instructed Ash to keep this a secret from the team. When Ash had questioned him why Cyrus told him it was better for the integrity of the operation. For the present, he wanted all activity kept to a need to know basis until they were all assembled at the safe house.

Zvi and Cyrus would be the last ones to arrive in Beirut and would be carrying Spanish passports created especially for them. Carlos Alphonse, an entrepreneur, had sold his company to a tech giant and was living the good life in Marbella, Spain. Cyrus, in his newly minted persona of Ricardo Segovia, was Carlos's assistant and bodyguard. They were the only two who would sleep in the safe house. The rest would stay at nearby hotels suitable for their passport holder's incomes and lifestyles. In three days, the safe house would be ready, and Zvi and Cyrus would fly first class on Emirates Airlines from Barcelona to Beirut to take up residency in their luxury duplex overlooking the Mediterranean Sea.

Cyrus opened the door to the Ramsad's office and entered. The blinds, as usual, were drawn closed, and Cyrus entered a darkened room. Noam sat motionless, staring out into the gloom. Cyrus knew Noam Levi rarely left headquarters once a mission went operational. He would eat, sleep, and breathe the minutes, hours, days, and weeks of every detail and move until the mission successfully concluded, or God forbid, failed.

"You leave tonight?" Noam got straight to the point."

"Yes, Zvi and I leave at midnight on a private jet."

The Ramsad nodded. "I've communicated with Aryeh. He believes Nasrallah will take the bait."

"When will we know?"

"Soon. The DGSE agent has delivered the ransom offer, and now we wait for her to hear from Nasrallah."

"And the mole. Any idea who it might be?"

"The mole should be delivering the information we planted that a team of Mossad agents is descending on Beirut to extract the traitor Aryeh and bring the diamonds home. The planted information provides Aryeh the authenticity he needs for Nasrallah to believe his story. As for the mole, we're closing in, but for now, since there is only a handful of people who know the truth, feeding him misinformation is useful."

"Then we're in business."

"Yes, we're in business. Tell me, how has the team taken to you?" The Ramsad folded his hands and leaned forward. Cyrus could understand where he got his moniker; his vulpine expression resembled a fox about to pounce.

"Not badly. Nira is skeptical. She's a hard egg to crack. Her loyalty is to Aryeh, but she's a pro and is responding to my command. Yitzhak is a diplomat, put his cards on the table from the start, and took charge of making the transition as smooth as possible. Daniel's quiet, hard to read. I haven't figured him out, but he seems to be with the program. Ben could charm the devil. He opened up immediately to me, but I suspect beneath his friendly façade, he's a hide, wait, and see kind of guy. I'll have to earn his respect. Ash and I have bonded. He's without a doubt the most well-adjusted killer I've ever met." Cyrus chuckled, "Loves his job. I've taken him into my confidence. He's amassing an arsenal. We should be ready for action immediately."

"What did you tell him?"

"Only that it was possible the mission might expand, and I'd been ordered to prepare for every eventuality."

"Did he question anything?"

"No, he's just thrilled to be back at work and hunting bad guys."

"What about Zvi? He tends to figure things out before they happen. A restless mind."

"Zvi's a genius, totally on board. I don't sense any animosity from him. So, all in all, I think the team is running as smoothly as can be expected given the circumstances."

The Ramsad nodded. "In Beirut, all the soldiers will fall in line. Once you confide the real mission to them, they'll purr like a Ferrari engine. By the way, use caution when surveilling Zara. She has a sixth sense about being tailed. She'll spot you and blow your cover in a minute. Keep a distance. The trust between her and Aryeh goes back for years, a rarity in this business. If I could, I'd recruit her."

"Maybe when this is over, she'll change her mind, and you'll be able to."

"No, I've had her psychologically profiled. She's not a team player. Besides, I think she enjoys the journalist cover. She and Aryeh have cooperated many times. When it works, it's to our benefit."

"What's their relationship? The members of the team think it's romantic." Any insight into Aryeh and Zara would be valuable to know."

"I wouldn't call their relationship romantic. But they do share a passion for the work, and when the two collide a passion for each other."

"From what I've gathered from his file and what the team has told me, Aryeh doesn't seem to have any other relationships that could classify as romantic."

"Long story short, he lost someone, a fellow agent. We nearly lost him after her death. It was a tragic loss. He was in charge, and she was green. Naturally, he blamed himself. There is no recovery from the loss he lives with. He's spent his career making amends for his failure. Who he is, is not what you see."

"Sometimes, it just takes the right woman to change a man."

"What happened between you and Layla was an aberration. Escaping from Iran and saving her life melted your heart. At one point, I thought Zara might do the same for Aryeh. However, the trouble is she's the same as him. Where her heart should be, there is only a petrified stone." Noam shrugged. "Makes for a formidable spy."

Cyrus couldn't help but smile. Over the last few meetings, he and the Ramsad had developed a relaxed repartee together, which dispensed with the formalities of rank. "Does that mean I'm no longer formidable?"

"You? You are an enigma. Now go home to your wife and child and enjoy your last night with your family. Once Zvi has nailed down security, we'll speak. *B'hatslacha*. I'm counting on you."

———◆———

Gilad Abramson sat at the bar at the Pussy Cat Club nursing a whiskey. The strip show hadn't begun yet, and above the din of revelers, the driving bass and beat of techno music made it difficult to think, which Gilad assumed was why he and everyone around him came to the seedy club.

"Sorry I'm late." Shura Al Amin, a Palestinian graduate student at Tel Aviv University, breathed in his ear. She slid into the empty barstool he'd saved for her. She reached under the bar and ran her fingers over his thigh, purposely skimming the bulge in his pants. Her hand, her lips, and tongue brushing his ear aroused him. "Did you bring it?" she whispered. "I'm getting pressure from the bastard."

He nodded, reaching into his pocket. Taking a quick scan around him, he palmed a flash drive and slipped it into her bra, then cupped her breast and tweaked the nipple so hard she gasped. "This is the last one. Tell your handlers I'm done. Tell them I don't care if they post the video on the internet. You and I are finished being blackmailed by them. Do you hear me, Shura?"

She rubbed his hand. "Yes, baby, I'll tell them. I've just been so scared they'd release the tape. My father will kill me. I've told you my family's belief in the tradition of honor killings. It's not just the sex, but the bondage and beating. I…I…"

"I don't give a fuck anymore, Shura. Let it be a lesson to you." He wanted to strangle the asshole who was blackmailing them. When he and Shura had first hooked up six months ago, they'd used an apartment of a friend of Shura's. Gilad had never met anyone like her. She was sexually submissive, loved rough sex and being tied up, and had introduced him to a world he didn't know existed. He'd discovered a type of sex that had proven to be addictive, and the pleasure the beautiful Shura delivered was irresistible to him.

They'd had no idea the apartment they had their assignations in had been wired with cameras and video recording equipment until weeks later when the blackmailing had begun. The videos of violent sex were career ruining for Gilad. But for Shura, they'd mean not only ostracism but possible death for dishonoring her prominent Palestinian family. Instead of going to his superiors, he'd submitted to the blackmail. Using his position as a computer technician and coder for Mossad, he'd delivered classified materials. Now he was a traitor to the country he loved. He'd fallen for the oldest trick in the world.

Even with his world collapsing around him, the scent and the nearness of Shura filled him with desire. "Drink up. I've rented a hotel room. You're going to pay mightily for your stupidity." He drew so close he knew all she could see was the hunger in his eyes. "It's what you want, isn't it, Shura? Pain and pleasure delivered in one bullet."

He couldn't hear her answer above the driving beat of the music, but he could see her pupils dilate and her breath grow shallow. He downed the glass of whiskey, enjoying the slow burn. "Tonight will be one you'll never forget, baby."

Shura stumbled out the door of the hotel room and rammed into a massive chest. Large leather gloved hands steadied her. She shook her inebriated head and focused on the face shrouded in darkness. "I did just what you told me to do. I have the flash drive in my purse, and I drugged him. Here…" She began to search her purse. "Gilad's in the room passed out. Now, let me go, Amir. I don't want to know anything about what you're doing."

The giant wrenched her purse out of her hand. He removed the key to the room and the flash drive. He stuck the drive in his pocket and inserted the key in the door. In a deep voice, he commanded. "I want you, baby. Let me show you how a real man loves a woman. Why should we let this room go to waste?"

Her heart thudded in her chest. Amir was like a god. She'd fantasized about him umpteen times, but he'd never made a move toward her. She imagined he was a master of pain and pleasure. "What about Gilad? He's unconscious on the bed."

"Don't worry about him. I'll make sure he doesn't bother us." He grabbed her hand and rubbed it over the already protruding bulge in his pants.

She gasped. Amir Haddad was a giant in every way.

"Come on, *habibi*, let me give you a ride you'll never forget." His hot breath filled her ear. "You were destined to be my slave." He pressed her into the door, his warm tongue seeking the hollow of her ear. "I've been so jealous of that bastard, touching you, fucking you. You should be mine."

Her breaths grew short, and she felt herself go wet.

He leaned into her and lifted her, wrapping her legs around his waist. His huge cock pulsed against her, and she sucked in her breath.

"Hmm, that's good. Feel how hard I am." He opened the door and carried her into the room, squeezing her ass so hard she whimpered.

Amir set her down on the edge of the bed, and pulled a cell phone, gun, and silencer from his pocket.

Trembling, she asked, "What are you doing?"

He laughed. "It's not for you, baby, relax." He traced the muzzle of the gun across her lips. "I can't wait for you to feel my barrel inside of you, but first, I need to take care of business. I'm afraid your lover has served his purpose."

"But I don't want to see you kill him."

Anger glinted in his eyes. "Why? Are you going to miss his abuse of you? You knew the plan all along. Your instructions were to lure him to the apartment, which you did. You set him up for blackmail. What did you think was going to happen to him once he'd served his purpose?"

"I know, but I can't see someone get shot. I've seen enough killings to last me a lifetime."

"I see. Violent sex is not a problem, but violent death upsets you. Go to the bathroom and prepare yourself for your lover, *habibi*. I want to pretend you're one of those virgins promised to me in heaven."

Taking her purse with her, she took a last look at Gilad and disappeared into the bathroom. She took a shower and reapplied her makeup. After a final swipe of lipstick over her lips, she exited the bathroom.

Gilad was gone. Laying on the carpet was what appeared to be a body wrapped in a blanket. Amir leaned against the headboard, his clothes neatly folded on a chair.

Her stomach did flip-flops when she glanced at the body of the man who moments before had been her living, breathing lover. "Is he dead?"

"Very." He patted the bed. "Come closer."

She perched on the edge of the bed.

Amir pulled her closer. "I said closer." He palmed her breast with one hand, pinching her nipple so hard she moaned. He pinched harder, and she felt a tear inch its way down her cheek. The pain made her bite her lip, and her chest rose and fell with her shortened breaths. "You're hurting me."

"Yes, and you like it, don't you?"

"Yes...ahh...I do."

"I know you do. You liked it with the traitor, but you'll like it even better with me." He nodded toward Gilad's body. "Nothing he did will compare to what I plan to do to you, baby."

Her breath caught in her chest. "What? What are you going to do?"

53

He licked her nipple and sucked until her back bent. "You are such a little thing. There is nothing more demanding of a person's attention than pain. I understand your obsession with it. The pain you will feel when you meet Goliath will be the most sublime pain you've ever known."

"Who's Goliath?"

He took her hand and rubbed it against his cock.

She drew in a breath when she felt his size.

He laughed and pulled her tight against his body. "Don't worry, by the time you meet him, you'll be ready. You'll be begging for him. Just think of him pounding your sweet pussy."

Sitting up, he removed her clothing. He ran his hands over every inch of her. He growled like an animal about to eviscerate its prey and a chill swept through her. Then he dropped between her legs and delicately feathered her clit with his tongue. In her experience, most men didn't know how to please a woman with their lips and tongue, but Amir was unrelenting and skillful. She fisted the sheets, unable to control her writhing body. Doubling down, he stuck his finger in her and stroked her inside while his tongue continued to dart against her clit. Her fingers dug into his scalp, and her hips rose as she came undone, her body spasming with pleasure.

The finger in her became two, circling he opened her. Her lips were parted and open. Hungrily she watched him remove his underwear. He rubbed the tip of Goliath against her lips. Her tongue licked him. "I'll never be able to open my mouth enough to suck you, but I can lick." She rose on her elbow and ran her tongue up and down his length. She watched his face, his pupils dilating, his massive chest heaving as he struggled to catch his breath. Her hand firmly stroked up and down.

Amir's growls vibrated through her. His fists pressed into the bed as he thrust his hips up in a reverse push-up. "Goliath wants you, *habibi*." He pushed her down and lifted her leg, hugging her thigh to his chest.

"Go slow," she pleaded. "You're bigger than any man I've ever been with."

"Slow," he repeated, "go slow." He eased an inch into her, watching as she licked her finger and touched her clitoris. She bit her lip and held her breath. He pushed deeper, making her cry out. "Oh, dear God…I…"

He began to thrust in and out. Clenching his teeth, he snarled. "I want more." He rammed deep inside her, forcing her open. Pain and pleasure filled her in equal measure. He was a piston in a well-oiled engine, driving himself in and out, grunting with each thrust. Her desire was intense, and she exploded, her walls contracting tight around him. His head fell back, and he gritted his teeth. He pulled out of her and flipped her over. He slapped her ass and laughed when she flinched. He spanked her again until she relaxed like a ragdoll. "Do you want more, *habibi?*"

"Yes…yes, don't stop."

Holding tight to her hips, he rammed into her, and she cried out. He gathered a fistful of her hair and drove into her hard and fast. The sound of him slapping against her buttocks and the feel of his massive cock tunneling deeper into her made her collapse into the sheets. She could hardly breathe, but she couldn't get enough. It was the most intense pleasure she'd ever experienced. Amir had the stamina of a horse. She knew the sick part was she wanted it to hurt. She wanted to feel every second of him ravishing her. Hearing his growls sent shivers down her spine. She could even imagine dying with his powerful dick inside of her.

She wanted it to go on forever. Their bodies were drenched with sweat. She reached between her legs and caressed Amir's balls, then she squeezed. His breath caught, and she felt an unimaginable rush at being able to control him. Her moans grew louder, her body undulating against him, "Yes, yes, oh God, you are the best. I love it, don't stop. Keep fucking me, make me come." She clenched, quivering around him, and ground her ass against his groin. "Don't stop," she screamed.

He growled, and his fingers closed around her neck, squeezing as he came with a roar, thrusting, and spurting hot semen into her. His grip on her neck tightened, she couldn't breathe, and she was orgasming. Her body spasmed, clenching, her desire for pain and pleasure finally fulfilled. It was the last thing she felt.

Amir slipped on his gloves and pushed Shura's body over to the edge of the bed. It was a shame he'd had to kill her, but at least she'd died the way she had lived. A final gasp of pleasure and pain. His finger marks on her throat had deepened to a dark shade of purple and blue where the blood had coagulated. He'd intended to kill her with a bullet to the head, and not by strangulation. But in the heat of the moment, a primal urge had come over him.

Shura would have made a lovely concubine, and he would have liked to explore her limits more, but his orders were clear. Once he was in possession of the flash drive, he was to eliminate the mole and the whore. They had become an unacceptable risk. Besides, he had one more task before he could return to Lebanon.

Even so, the sadistic pleasure of sexual orgasm and killing surpassed anything he'd ever felt before. It aroused him more than any experience in his life, and he couldn't help but wonder if he'd ever be given the opportunity again. He knew it was a dangerous addiction, but killing was his life, and this was just a new and exciting way of doing it.

He lifted Gilad's body from the floor and unwrapped it on the bed. The bullet wound was clean. He'd shot Gilad in the temple with the gun and silencer. Composing a scene, he put the gun in Gilad's hand and arranged the bodies, so it looked as if Gilad had strangled Shura and then shot himself. He knew the *Mišteret Yisra'el,* the Israeli police, would collect semen, but separating Gilad's sperm from his own, would be difficult, and the semen would be degraded by the passage of time before the discovery of the bodies. Besides, Amir had no accessible DNA records or data. He'd be long gone before he was identified.

He took a shower, dressed, and admired the vignette he'd created of the two lovers in their final moments. The found bodies of a traitorous Mossad coder and a Palestinian whore would be a thrilling read in the newspapers.

Taking precaution, he took bleach wipes and cleaned every surface in the room. By the time he finished, he was tired and hungry. He left the room, hanging the "do not disturb" sign on the door. A falafel sounded like the perfect reward after a successful night's work.

CHAPTER 8

"Daddy! You're home!" Cerise threw herself into Cyrus's arms.

He picked her up and spun around with her. "How's the love of my life?" It was a standing joke between them, she never tired of correcting him on.

"Daddy, you know Mommy is the love of your life. You can only have one love of your life."

"But, Cerise, I have too much love inside of me, so I'm allowed to have two loves of my life, and I pick you." He tickled her until the sound of her bubbling laughter turned into squeals so loud that Layla came running.

"Cerise, what is going on in here?"

"Daddy's home early. Can we go on the swings, please, please, please?"

Settling Cerise on his hip, he put his arm around Layla and kissed her. "Hi, baby, happy to see me?"

"Of course, I am."

"*Ima*, swings, swings, swings."

"Sweetie, let Daddy relax for a minute, and then we'll see."

Cerise pushed her lower lip out. Cyrus laughed. "I think I've seen that face before on you, Layla."

She placed her hands on her hips and huffed. "Are you suggesting I pout like a four-year-old?"

"No. How could I possibly think such a thing?" He grinned and pulled her in for another kiss. Cerise clapped her hands. Even when there'd been rough seas between them, Cerise had reminded them of how much they loved each other. "I think we should go to the beach, and the swings, and then have an early dinner out."

Cerise clapped her hands again. "Yay!"

He put her down. "Go get your jacket." She skipped from the room.

Layla scrutinized him. "You've been so hush-hush about this mission. When do you leave?"

"Tonight. Midnight. I came home early so we could be together." He put his arms around her and pulled her close. "After the beach and dinner, she'll be exhausted and," he traced his lips up her neck to her ear, "then we'll have some time alone."

Layla placed her hands on both sides of his face. "I know I shouldn't worry, but I'm scared. Maybe it's the pregnancy or my fears since being kidnapped, but the thought of you on assignment terrifies me."

"I know, *eshgham*. I promise you it will be all right. I don't want you to worry, your grandparents and your dad are close by. I've already spoken with Aleck; he'll be keeping a close eye on you two. In fact, he wants you to stay with him while I'm away."

"I'll be fine. Three months pregnant is nothing, and you won't be gone long. This won't be a long assignment, will it?"

"No, I'll be home before you know it."

They walked on the beach, Layla's hand in his. Cyrus kept his eye on Cerise, who ran in and out of the foam of the breaking waves, giggling as she wriggled her toes in the sand. At midnight when he flew from Tel Aviv to Barcelona, he would lock away his worries about leaving his wife and daughter and become the ruthless spy once again. Until then, for a few precious hours, he embraced his role as husband and father, allowing the love he felt for his wife and child to fill him.

"Baby, what do you think about getting a puppy for Cerise?" Layla asked.

He raised his left brow. "Where'd that come from?"

Layla shrugged. "I was about Cerise's age when my parents adopted a puppy. Coco was the love of my life." She poked him in the ribs.

"Hey!"

"Until you, that is."

"Being compared to your beloved canine doesn't seem all that flattering."

"Well, it is. Coco was there for me during the worst time of my life when my mom was dying of cancer. I don't know how I would have gotten through that period without her."

Cyrus pulled her in, kissing her temple. "Does this have anything to do with your fear of losing me?"

"Maybe."

"You're not losing me, Layla."

"I know, but I think it would be good for Cerise. Especially when the baby comes."

He wasn't keen on the idea. He'd never owned a pet and wasn't sure whether he'd be comfortable with the intrusion in his life. "If you think this will help you and Cerise during my absence, I'm all for it. But I don't want you overtaxing yourself. Puppies require a lot of care. What breed were you thinking of?"

"A German shepherd. They're very protective and wonderful with children."

"*Aba, Ima,* look!"

A golden retriever came bounding up and started licking a squealing Cerise. Cyrus looked at Layla. "What the hell? Did you hire the dog to convince me?"

She laughed. "Of course not. But God is known to work in strange ways."

"He certainly is." He ran to Cerise and scooped her up from the onslaught of affection. "Put me down, Daddy. The doggy only wants to love me."

"Are you sure, *metuka*? Do you like being licked all over?"

"Yes, it tickles."

A young man came running up. "Sorry about that. Canan, sit." The dog obediently sat but continued to lick Cerise's toes, within doggy reach.

Cerise squirmed, "Put me down, please, *Aba*."

Cyrus put her down, and she wrapped her arms around Canan's neck.

He held out his hand to the stranger. "Cyrus Hassani. It seems you are a messenger from God. I don't suppose my wife, Layla, and my daughter Cerise hired you to convince me to adopt a pet, did they?"

The young man looked confused. "No. I've never met your wife or daughter before." He shook Cyrus's hand. "Caleb Schneider, nice to meet you. Canan can't resist children."

Layla raised her hand to block the sun from her eyes. "I want to thank you, Caleb, your beautiful dog just closed a deal I was negotiating."

"A deal?"

"Yes, a new addition to our family seems likely."

"Oh, I get it. I don't think you'll regret that decision." He petted Canan on the head. "Well, nice to meet you. Good luck with the new addition to the family. Come on, Canan, let's go." Caleb turned and jogged up the beach, then gave a whistle. Canan gave Cerise a last lick and took off after her master.

Cerise waved after them. "Daddy, I wish we had a dog just like Canan."

Layla wore a smile of victory. Cyrus took both of his girls' hands and began to walk. He knew when to admit defeat. "I think Mommy should take you to the animal shelter while Daddy's away, and you can pick a puppy."

The look on Cerise's face made his heart swell. *Maybe it's a good thing. A puppy will distract them and keep them busy while I'm away.*

"The sea air really knocked her out," Layla said, joining her husband in the kitchen.

"She was nearly asleep when I kissed her goodnight," Cyrus said, handing her a glass of sparkling water and cranberry juice.

"She barely could keep her eyes open at dinner." Layla chuckled, taking a sip of the effervescent drink.

Cyrus rubbed her shoulders. "You look pretty tired too."

"I am." She reached up and caressed his cheek. "But not too tired to love my man."

"Maybe I should give you a massage."

She closed her eyes, enjoying his fingers on her neck and shoulders. "Maybe you should."

He kneaded deeper into her muscles. "You're pretty tense, baby."

What was the point in telling him she was terrified? Why burden him with her fears. Nothing would change by revealing she dreaded the moment when he'd walk out the door, and she wouldn't have any idea where he was, or what dangers he would face.

All-day and night, she'd hidden her true feelings. She didn't want him to carry the weight of her torment. She was afraid it might make him less sharp, less cautious, and more susceptible to the enemy. If anything happened to him, she didn't think she'd be able to go on. It wasn't that she was weak or dependent but losing him would be like tearing her heart from her body.

She dipped her head back and sought his mouth. She kissed him, her fingers twining in his dark hair. She didn't want his questions. She didn't want to lie to him or pretend nothing was wrong. All she wanted was the fiery lover who had captured her heart.

He groaned. "Layla…"

"Make love to me, Cyrus."

He lifted her into his arms, cradling her to his chest. He swiftly strode into their bedroom, his gaze filled with undying love. "I love you more than our first time on the mountain in Varian, *eshgham*."

She buried her face in his neck, inhaling the scent of him. He'd read her mind. Beneath her lips, she could feel his pulse racing, and she felt hers surge, running to catch up.

He lay beside her on the bed. He made to speak, but her finger on his lips silenced him. "I don't want to talk about you leaving. Let me pretend a little while longer this is just an ordinary night. And we're just an ordinary couple loving each other."

She pressed her body against his, loving the feel of his solid muscles against her softness. Their hearts and bodies aligned just as they had the first night they'd made love. She could feel his desire for her fire on all cylinders, and it set her ablaze.

In a ritual that needed no words. They divested each other of clothing, tossing each article aside. Moonlight drenched the bed.

He paused, rising on his elbow. "I want to remember this always. You naked—your skin illuminated by moonbeams. The look of love in your eyes. Nothing in this life compares to it." He flicked his tongue over her nipple, his full lips closing around it, taking it fully into his mouth and suckling. It felt divine, and she arched her back.

Usually, she'd be touching him everywhere, driving him higher. But tonight, all she wanted was to receive. She coveted his lips, his mouth, his arms, and the hardest part of him that was hers alone. He rolled on top of her, and his thickness throbbed against her pelvis. She lifted her head and sighed, taking a breath through parted lips. She wanted to watch him make love to her. Then she'd be able to replay his passion for her in her head over and over again. Something to hold on to while he was away.

He might as well have taken a branding iron to her, his mouth left fiery sensations sizzling, crackling through her. Every inch of her was his, and she couldn't control her moans or the rhythmic movement of her hips as he made his way down her body, and she danced beneath his tongue.

"Baby, you make me feel like a conquering warrior."

"You love that image, don't you? The hero thing turns you on, doesn't it? It's why you love it when I call you Superman. You seek it in life, and you seek it in the bedroom. The first night when you made love to me, you fought your desire trying to be heroic. I think I fell madly in love with you right then and there. It hasn't changed, Cyrus, we're still those two people." Her hand slipped down, caressing his arousal. "Are you still the man who loved me on that lake?" She giggled, knowing what a challenge did to him.

He buried his face between her legs. Her breaths shortened, and her heart pounded. He must have sensed by her quivering when she couldn't take any more. He withdrew, biting and teasing his way up her undulating body until he reached her mouth. Then his tongue sought her kiss in that way that never failed to drive her wild. A sexy smile teased his lips, his eyes blazed.

Every inch of her body trembled with desire for him. This moment reinforced the truth…they existed only for each other, and nothing could tear them apart. It was how she'd felt in that icy cold cabin on a tiny lake in Iran. Afraid they'd be captured and killed—she'd pleaded with him to make love to her because she feared they wouldn't survive, and she couldn't die without knowing what it felt like to be loved by him.

She'd wanted him, the spy, the hero, the man who considered himself incapable of love. Whatever happened, loving him would be worth it. When he'd passionately made love to her that night, he was her first, but she knew immediately no other man would ever take his place. She belonged to him then, just as she belonged to him now.

He touched her gently, and her hips lifted, pressing against his finger pad. His deep baritone teased. "Does my goddess want more?"

"Yes, I want all of you. Nothing more—nothing less."

She cried out when he filled her. He possessed her in the way she loved, slow and steady until she begged him not to stop because she ached to release. On his elbows, he held her gaze. She was at her tipping point, and he knew it. In a heightened state of passion, he thrust, burying himself inside of her. Her legs locked around him, wishing she could keep him there forever.

He collapsed into her; their bodies fused together. His heart banged against her breast, his gasps for breath echoed in her ear, and the warmth of his body cocooned her in safety.

"I will love you *baraye hamishe*," he whispered.

"I love you too. You've never said that before. What does it mean?"

He rolled onto his back, pulling out of her with a sigh. His arms reached out and pulled her close against him, nestling her in the crook of his arm. "It means forever. I will love you forever."

With her head on his chest, she closed her eyes and drifted off to sleep. "*Baraye hamishe,* forever."

CHAPTER 9

Beirut, Lebanon

"Aryeh, it's me."

"*Bonjour, ma chéri.*" He'd been waiting all day for Zara to call and tell him what happened when she delivered his offer to Hezbollah to trade his nephew for the diamonds.

"I've had an interesting day, but I don't think it's a good idea for us to meet."

"Why? What's wrong?"

"Just as you suggested, I had a meeting today and planted the seeds with our friends, and they seemed interested in your proposal. They'll get back to me on it soon. However, there seems to be little trust in this world, and I picked up a tail."

He knew Zara, and it was easy to guess what must have happened next. "Did they have a pleasant day following you?"

The sound of her laughter made him smile. "Yes. We went to the zoo. It was educational for me and boring for them. You would have thoroughly enjoyed yourself, leading two terrorist animals on a wild goose chase. Faiz got wonderful photos of the poor beasts. Now I have everything I need for a freelance article for National Geographic. I'm at my office now, and I'll probably work most of the night finishing it."

"You are a wonder, Zara. Forget meeting in town, but where there's a will, there's a way. Why don't I sneak in the back entrance of your building around midnight? A covert liaison?"

"Miss me that much, do you?"

"You've been in my thoughts all day."

"Liar."

"Most of the day."

"I'll settle for that. Be careful, *a plus tard.*"

"*A bientot.*" He hung up.

The bed was in disarray, wholly covered with clothing. Aryeh began hanging up his clothes and folding and putting away all his personal items. His cell vibrated on the bed again. The Ramsad. He typed in the code that switched the cell to a secure satellite frequency.

"I got your message and passed it on to Cyrus. The team should be operational by tomorrow. Cyrus will message you at the dropbox and arrange a meeting."

"We haven't heard from the goose who laid the golden egg yet, but I'm meeting the *chanteuse* tonight." The Ramsad was used to his riddles, and Aryeh knew he understood that the goose was Hezbollah and the chanteuse was Zara.

"How is the songstress?"

"Divine as ever."

The Ramsad chuckled. "You received the latest Intel from Abe?"

"Yes. The North Koreans arrived, but are squirreled up in a hotel in Beirut."

"Hezbollah is most likely entertaining them with a smorgasbord of harem girls. The clock is running, but my guess is we still have time. The most important thing is Gideon. He must be alive, or we'd have heard," said Noam.

"Let us hope. When it comes to captured Israeli soldiers, Hezbollah's past negotiations haven't usually worked out. Too many times we bring them home in body-bags."

"Trust but verify," said the Ramsad.

What if this supposed interest in the diamonds was only a ploy to get to him and Gideon was dead already? Aryeh suppressed the anger that simmered just below the surface at the possibility. If his dark thoughts proved right, he swore he'd exact vengeance on them. Soon he'd know for sure whether he was bringing home the remains of his nephew or the living, breathing man.

The Ramsad, as usual, read his mind. "Stay positive and focused, Aryeh. Don't let your imagination get ahead of you. I know this is personal, but you must remain detached. Cyrus is your man, use him. There is more to lose here than just Gideon."

"You're right, sir."

"Keep me posted. *Shalom.*"

CHAPTER 10

Zara put the finishing touches on her article about the poor living conditions and neglect of animals at Beirut's zoo. She'd seen enough in life to harden her to man's barbarity to his fellow man. But cruelty to animals incensed her. In a connecting office, Faiz, her photographer and bodyguard, busily edited his digital photos for the exposé she was writing. The article, with its graphic images, was bound to stir things up among animal lovers around the world. Within Zara, a fragile thread remained of the academic idealist she once was.

Animals weren't the only thing on her mind as she typed. Zara had a sixth sense about people. Her curiosity had been ignited when she'd bumped into the young man after she met with Nasrallah. True, he was handsome, and she'd found herself attracted to him. But there was something else, a familiarity, and then, of course, the cockiness he exhibited drew her like a moth to a flame. All of it contributed to her curiosity and kept him resurfacing in her thoughts.

Her phone rang. "There's a gentleman at security named Mustafa Mughniyeh who would like to see you," said the security officer at the main floor desk.

Imad's son? "Please ask him what this is concerning? He doesn't have an appointment." Her thoughts were racing. She didn't know Mustafa, but she was alarmed. She'd heard rumors of him but had never seen him. Why did the son of one of the deadliest terrorists in the world want to speak with her?

"He says it's personal."

"Is he alone?"

"Yes."

67

She blew out a breath. "All right, send him up."

She was astonished when she saw him on the security camera outside of the office door. It was him! The man she'd bumped into at Hezbollah headquarters. She observed him for a second as he stared up into the camera.

She pressed the intercom. "Can I help you with something?"

"Zara, I mean *Alanisa* Zayani, I would like to speak with you?"

"About what?"

"It is personal, and I would rather see your face when I address you."

"I don't know you. Why should I trust you? Did Hassan Nasrallah send you?"

A flashed of anger sparked in his eyes. "I am not an errand boy for Hassan. I am here for myself."

"I'm very busy, and I only have a few minutes to give you." She pressed a button and allowed him entry.

Just inside the entry, he stopped and looked around him. When his eyes locked on her, he waited.

"Would you care for a cup of tea or coffee?"

He gave her a smile that could melt butter. "Tea would be lovely."

She walked to an open doorway, feeling his gaze following her. "Faiz, I have a guest—would you be kind enough to go to the coffee shop and get a coffee for me and tea for my visitor?"

"Sure, Zara." When Faiz followed her to the reception area, he extended his hand to Mustafa. "Faiz Khoury, I'm pleased to meet you."

"Just call me Mustafa, the pleasure is mine." He offered no last name, and Zara could see the tightness in his smile. He was upset at seeing Faiz, a man alone with her.

"Well, I'll be on my way." With a curt nod, Faiz walked out the door.

"Who is he?" Mustafa's displeasure was evident in his tone.

She folded her arms across her chest, signaling her annoyance at his impertinence. "Faiz and I work closely together; he's my photographer. Besides, it's none of your business who he is." She indicated a chair. "Please sit." She took a seat across from him. "Again, I ask you, what is the reason for your coming here?"

"Zara—may I call you Zara?"

"Yes, of course. Please state your purpose, or should I assume you're here to apologize."

"Apologize for what?"

"For your rudeness this morning."

His lip twitched, hinting at a smile. "I'm not in the habit of making apologies when young women plow into me. However, for you, Zara, I'm happy to do so since I'm pleased that you remember me."

"Apology accepted. Now you can be on your way unless there is another reason for your visit." She sat back and crossed her legs.

"There is another reason. I would like to work with you on an article about the situation in Syria. Why Hezbollah is supporting Assad."

Her instinct told her the article wasn't the reason he was here. *Curious*, she thought.

"I've done many articles on Syria. Why would your insights shed any new light on what is already known?" she asked.

"I've just returned from Syria. There is much I can enlighten you about the current situation."

Zara studied his face. "Okay, you've captured my attention. Perhaps we can schedule a lunch, and I'll interview you."

"I won't be in Beirut long, Zara. Would you indulge me and join me for dinner?"

"Tonight?"

"Please, I promise it will be worth your time."

She stared at him. His unexplained visit had nothing to do with an interview. She was sure of it. "I have to finish the article I'm working on, but if you'd like, I'll meet you at Babel Bay at seven."

"Do you not trust me enough to pick you up at your home?"

"Mustafa, if you want to find out where I live, I'm sure you could get one of your flunkies to do it in minutes. I'll take a cab to the restaurant, and you can bring me home. Now, if you don't mind, I have work to do."

His smile was almost genuine. "You are an expert at dismissing me, it seems."

"What would you have me do? Wrap my arms around you and kiss you goodbye?"

He grinned and stood. "What an audacious thought. I am at your service." He strode to the door and opened it. Faiz walked up the hallway with the beverages. Mustafa held the door open for him.

"Leaving so soon?" Faiz asked.

Mustafa thumped Faiz on the back, nearly causing him to drop the drinks. "Sorry for having wasted your time. Enjoy the tea." He looked back at Zara, his gaze taking her in from head to toe. "I'll see you at seven."

She nodded, her lips pressed into a thin line. She was annoyed by Mustafa's disrespect and treatment of Faiz. Tonight she would put him in his place.

Zara turned off her computer. After Mustafa left, she'd spent the rest of the day accessing secure Interpol and other law enforcement sites for any mention of him. She didn't find much. There was plenty of information about his father and uncle. Several reports about his brother, but he was like a ghost. She, of course, had spent much of her espionage career as a ghost as well, so she wasn't surprised, simply intrigued.

The more she considered Mustafa's sudden interest in her, the more she realized running into him might prove to be an unexpected gift. He was of the next generation and probably being groomed to lead. She shook her head in disgust. Imagine raising a child to become a terrorist? The unfortunate trend was occurring over much of the Middle East. What had become of their scientists, their literary giants, their poets? Instead, they were busy creating a generation of experts who specialized in the manufacture of suicide vests and bombs. Her job was to stop them in their tracks before they harmed anyone. If they blew themselves up in the process, *c'est la vie*.

Mustafa presented a perfect target. A man whom she might convince to deliver secrets by ensnaring him in her web. If she could gain his trust, she would be able to penetrate the internal workings of Hezbollah. He fit the profile, but she would have to play him carefully. He was probably trained by the Quds force, a graduate of Terrorism 101, just like his father and uncle. After tonight she would have a handle on what his potential as a source might be.

He'd expended considerable effort in tracking her down, and he'd put himself at significant risk doing so. He was going against what had been ingrained in him since childhood, trust no one, especially women. She wondered how far he would go to satisfy this apparent desire he was experiencing. How much of herself would she have to give to hook him? If he proved to be the mother lode, she'd give it all and seduce him completely. But like torture, she knew slow was better. She needed to make sure the barb was embedded deep. Women didn't factor much in his world. They existed primarily to satisfy the desires of their fathers, husbands, and children. Entrapping a man like Mustafa was a dangerous prospect, but one that might prove to be extremely valuable. In fact, she found the pursuit of him stimulating.

One difficulty presented itself. For the first time in their many years of working together, she dreaded speaking to Aryeh about Mustafa and taking him into her confidence. But not telling him would destroy a relationship built on trust. She was an expert at straddling a fine line, but Aryeh was in a vulnerable position. For the moment, he was a man without a country, which was never a good place for a spy to be.

CHAPTER 11

Zara followed the *maître d'* outside. She'd worn her sexiest dress, an Azzedine Alaïa green banded knit that displayed her every curve. Purposely chosen, Zara wanted Mustafa to know she was nothing like the women he was accustomed to. She was a Western woman, a species of woman she was certain in his insular world he'd never encountered before.

Mustafa jumped to his feet when she arrived, and she was glad she'd worn stilettos. He was tall, and she disliked looking up at a man. When he kissed her, his breath was warm on her cheek, and his lips lingered perhaps a few seconds too long.

He clasped her hand and indicated the seat next to him. "You're the most beautiful woman I've ever seen. You've done me a great honor meeting me."

She smiled demurely. "You've awoken my curiosity. How could I refuse?"

"Still, I'm grateful you were free tonight."

"How could I pass up the chance to dine with the son of Imad. There are not many dynasties founded on terrorism." Zara twisted the knife, relishing the torment she saw in his eyes. She had no intention of mincing words about what she thought of his family. She appreciated the self-control he had over himself at her barb.

"I do not drink, but I've ordered you a bottle of champagne, the best on the menu. You do like champagne?"

"I'm French, of course, I love champagne. But if you aren't sharing it with me, I won't drink. The first of our differences so quickly revealed."

She looked around the room as if everything and anything were of more interest to her than him.

He frowned. "I have never tasted an alcoholic beverage."

"A virgin, how charming." She smiled at him, indulgently. "There's always a first time. I don't believe you'll turn into a pillar of salt or be denied your

73

seventy-two virgins upon ascending to heaven." She gently laid her hand on his thigh and felt the muscles tighten. She was teasing him in every way imaginable, and she was enjoying it. She removed her hand.

The waiter arrived to pour her champagne, but she waved her hand over her flute, indicating no. Mustafa took her hand in his. "Pour us both, *raja*."

She smiled at this swift change. She lifted her glass and waited for him to raise his. Then she twined her arm through his and toasted. "To us, Mustafa, and our budding friendship." He sipped, watching her lips.

"Well," she asked. "What do you think?"

"It's an interesting taste, but I feel nothing."

She ignored his boast. Why did men always equate their tolerance to alcohol as a demonstration of their strength? "So, Mustafa, this is where we begin to learn about each other. I tell you the story of my life, and you share the story of yours. And later, we can discuss this article you propose on Syria."

"I want to know everything about you. Syria will have to wait."

"Everything? I think our conversation might be longer than this meal. If I recall correctly, you said you haven't got much time. Was Syria just a lure to get me here?"

"I'm not planning on learning everything in one night. I'm thinking of a more long-term relationship, and I admit it was a way for me to get to know you better."

She took another sip of champagne, and leaned toward him, closing the gap between them. "You're married, are you not? And you have a son. Why don't we start there?" It was one of the few things she was able to dig up from Interpol.

He gulped the glass of champagne down. She was startled to see a curtain of sadness shadow his eyes. "You want the truth?"

"I only deal in truths. It's my job and my life."

Mustafa motioned for the waiter. Please bring us a sampling of your best mezza and put another bottle of champagne on ice." The waiter topped off their glasses, bowed and scurried away. Mustafa gazed into her eyes. "Where to start?"

"Wherever makes you comfortable. You have my complete attention." She returned his gaze and watched his eyes drift to her lips. "Are you going to talk to me, or kiss me?"

His lips twitched. "I want to kiss you."

She gave him her most seductive smile. "A kiss? I'm afraid our relationship hasn't risen to such a level of intimacy. You did say this was a business affiliation, did you not?" She rested her chin on her hand and fluttered her lashes at him. "Please, begin your story. You have my undivided attention."

He took a deep breath and dragged his gaze from her mouth. "There seems to be a glaring hole in your research on me, Zara. My wife and son were killed last month by the Israelis."

Zara blanched. "I…I…I'm very sorry, Mustafa. I had no idea. Forgive me."

He smiled. "It's not your fault. I have to be honest with you, I was never in love with my wife, and I don't believe she was in love with me. My father arranged the marriage. The loss of my son, of course, is a great sadness to me."

Zara felt pity for him, which was not a good thing. She needed to remain detached. She steered the conversation away. "Why are we here, Mustafa?"

"I never considered love to be of consequence." He averted his gaze as if uneasy with his words. "When I saw you, I felt an instant attraction. It's never happened to me before." His eyes returned to her face, and it was as if he were memorizing every part of it. "Everything in my life has been planned. You are the exception, and I believe there is a reason. What do you think?"

"I see. If you're asking me whether or not I'm attracted to you? I won't lie, I am. But what purpose can this serve?"

The waiter returned and arranged an assortment of small plates before them. Zara tore a piece of pita and scooped up some hummus with tahini dip and garnished it with a pickle. "Open up." Mustafa opened his mouth, and she fed him. A trace remained on her finger, and he watched when she sucked it clean.

"You are playing with me," he said.

She smiled. "Perhaps." Enjoying his bewilderment, she removed an artichoke petal and dipped it in the lemon za'atar dipping sauce and ran her teeth and lips delicately over it, eating the flesh. She patted her lips with her napkin. "Your father and uncle, did they have a major influence on your life?" She filled his plate with a little of everything and then filled her own.

"They shaped who I am. My father and uncle are men of legend. In our world, they are considered to be great men and martyrs of our people." He watched everything she did as if she were under the lens of a microscope.

Frowning, she took a sip of champagne. "I suppose greatness depends on whose side of the fence you're sitting on and what your definition is. Some would call your father and uncle murderers and terrorists."

She ignored the anger darkening his eyes. "You wanted the truth, did you not?" she said calmly.

He said nothing.

"I'm a journalist, Mustafa. I hold a worldview completely different from yours."

"I understand why it's hard for outsiders to understand why we fight."

"You're wrong, I understand perfectly."

"And you disagree. What I do has nothing to do with us."

"I believe in working out differences with civility and diplomacy. Not violently upending the fabric of life. And what do you mean it has nothing to do with us?"

"The destiny between us." There was an unmistakable softening of his gaze, and it drew her.

She studied his face. "And what is this destiny we share?"

"You will understand it soon enough, *habibi*. I felt it the first moment I laid eyes on you."

His endearment was revealing. "You've admitted to knowing nothing of love."

"I said I *knew* nothing of love." His eyes bore into hers. "Tell me about your life."

She shared the truth while omitting specific pertinent facts. It wouldn't do to share her employment by the French intelligence agency, or her Jewish blood. But the most crucial omission was Jacob, her twin brother, who'd been murdered by terrorists during a train bombing in Paris.

Mustafa asked few questions and didn't interrupt her flow of words. She expounded on her childhood in Tangier, and the difficult move to Marseilles. She explained in detail her family's struggles to build a new life. At one point, she grew tearful when she spoke of her parents' disappointment that she'd been stationed in Beirut and lived so far away. It was easy to become emotional when she spoke of how much she missed her family. It was the truth, after all. Zara knew when to show her vulnerability and when to bring down the hammer. She was an expert at wrapping bars of steel around a man's heart, capturing, and ensnaring it until it belonged to her. She wanted to kindle his male instinct to protect. It was essential for her to show vulnerability.

Mustafa took her hand and kissed it; his eyes filled with sympathy. "I too, have known great loss. I've lost too many members of my family and friends to assassination, murder, and battle."

"Don't you ever wonder if it's worth it? I mean living your whole life in a state of war, with a price on your head?"

"One day, we will drive the Israelis into the sea and the Westerners out of our lands, and it will be worth it." He brushed his fingers over her cheek, wiping away the dampness of her tears and took her hand.

Fortunately, you can't read my thoughts, Mustafa. Because I will kill you before that day comes. "Lofty dreams not easily managed, Mustafa. Hezbollah is nothing compared to the power of Israel. I will be an old woman by the time this occurs—if ever."

"It may be sooner than you think. Great things are in the works. Things which will change the world and shift the balance of power."

"What things?"

"I cannot say more."

She eyed him suspiciously. "Aren't you afraid to be seen in a public place like this with me? How will you explain when it's reported back to Nasrallah?"

"Always you bring up Nasrallah. My relationship with him is like a father and son. He would not blame me for entertaining myself with you."

"I'm not your entertainment, nor will I ever be." She pulled her hand from his.

"Zara, a poor choice of words. Forgive me? I have no experience of what to say to you—how to make you understand. I fear to put you in danger, yet I cannot stop myself from wanting to know you better."

"I'm quite capable of taking care of myself, Mustafa. What I'm not sure of is what you want from me?"

"Have I not made it obvious?"

She lifted her glass to her lips, hesitant to answer. Mustafa had been forthcoming and had given her enough information to ensure she wouldn't refuse his advances. "Let us not speak more of this. I wish to enjoy your company. The rest will follow if Allah wills it. Remember Mustafa, you are a man married to a cause and not free to follow your heart."

He laughed. "I would make you my wife now if you'd have me."

"What a ridiculous declaration. We hardly know each other." She gave him a look intended to wither a lesser man.

"One day, you will change your mind, Zara." His eyes drifted to her lips. "May I kiss you?"

"No. Not in public."

The fire in his eyes exposed his desire. "Later, when we're alone?"

"You will take me home, kiss me goodnight, and be on your way. We both have much to think about."

She read the disappointment on his face and looked away. "Ah, here's our dinner."

Mustafa's driver pulled the car to the curb in front of Zara's duplex. She turned to open the door and get out, but Mustafa stayed her. "May I walk you to your door?"

"If you wish."

After opening the car door, he took her hand and walked with her to the bougainvillea trellised entry. She turned to thank him. "Mustafa, I—"

He pulled her into his arms, pressing her against his chest. Slowly, his eyes locked on hers, he dipped his head and engulfed her lips with his. It was surprisingly good, and she responded in kind. He hardened against her, an aching moan escaping from him. "Zara, I don't understand my need for you. It only grows stronger with each passing minute."

She laid her hands on either side of his face. "Don't think too much about it." Her brows lifted, mischievousness in her voice. "Perhaps it will go away if you ignore it."

Laughing as he shared her amusement. "And perhaps the sun will rise in the evening, and the moon will shine at dawn."

"Not impossible. Such places exist." She broke from his arms and opened the door to her apartment. "Goodnight, Mustafa."

"I may have to leave for a day or so, but I will call you and arrange our next meeting."

She shrugged. "As you wish."

She closed the door and leaned against it. She checked her phone. It was nearly midnight. She didn't have much time before Aryeh's arrival.

Aryeh looked up into the security camera and heard the click of the gate release. He was dressed in black. A hood covered his head, making him nearly indiscernible in the shadows. Enough light from the moon helped him navigate his way through the small backyard behind Zara's duplex. The scent of roses and fruit trees thickly scented the air. He slipped through the door, which had been left unlocked and found Zara at the bar pouring two snifters of brandy. She looked more beautiful than he'd ever seen her. The green dress merely an adornment enhancing the curves of her figure.

"I thought you spent the night working. Instead, you look as if you've attended a diplomatic cocktail party."

"I did work, but I had a dinner appointment after. I just got back in time for you."

"Did I ruin it for you?" He couldn't hide the hint of jealousy or curiosity in his voice.

Her brows drew together as she studied him. "Jealousy doesn't suit you, *mon ami*. What's with the ninja outfit?"

He pushed the hoodie back off his head. "Remember, I'm the hunted, and you're under surveillance. I'm not jealous, simply curious."

She handed him his drink. "I had dinner with a Hezbollah ghost, and it was highly revealing."

His head tilted with interest. "Who was it?" She handed him his glass, and he followed her to the sofa.

Aryeh's eyes widened with amazement when she told him her dinner date was Mustafa Mughniyeh. "Well, I'll be damned. The snake born of a long line of snakes has surfaced. Tell me more."

Aryeh was captivated by her story of meeting and dining with the terrorist. One thing was clear the bastard had good taste. He was just one man in a long line of men who'd fallen for Zara.

"He insinuated something, and I haven't been able to get it out of my mind all night," she said.

"What did he say?"

"He was trying to convince me of his greatness and the righteousness of his goal of destroying Israel, and then he said, and I quote, 'It may be sooner than you think. Great things are in the works. Things which will change the world and shift the balance of power.'"

Aryeh stared into his glass of amber liquor and then took a swig relishing the burn down his throat.

"Something is going on with Hezbollah, something they are carefully keeping under wraps," she said. "I sensed it yesterday when I met with Nasrallah. I must pursue whatever this is with Mustafa. My instincts tell me he's the key, the one who can lead me to whatever they're planning. If I can gain his trust, he'll open like a flower petal to a bee."

"Or like a Venus Fly Trap, he'll devour you," Ayreh said. "I don't have to tell you how dangerous this is. This man won't hesitate to kill you if he even gets a scent of your intent."

Her smile sent a rush to his groin. "Of all the men in the world, you know I'm capable of handling a smitten terrorist."

"There is more at stake here than a merciless killer. I haven't been completely honest with you."

"Why doesn't it surprise me you failed to tell me everything?"

"Everything about my nephew is true. However, it's not the only reason I'm here. Noam Levi sent me. I'm working off the grid. We've uncovered Intel that Hezbollah, Iran, and North Korea are planning an electromagnetic pulse attack on Israel and the United States."

Zara's breath whooshed from her. "*Merde*, then it makes sense."

"What makes sense?"

"Mustafa said he'd be away for a few days. He's involved. It's what he referred to when he talked about changing the world forever. It explains why the favorite son, a man never photographed and never seen in public, is suddenly front and center. He's here to make his move in the organization by a daring feat. The defeat of Israel would ensure his princely crown."

"You could be right."

"Then I've been given an important gift. It's up to me to stop this evil plot."

"No. It's up to us. My team has arrived in Beirut. We have to work together, Zara."

"Yes, of course. But now I know what my course is. Maybe I can turn him?"

"Unlikely. What you're going to have to do in the end is kill him and hang Mustafa's head on a fence. Remember, Zara, the only way to kill a snake and send a warning to all the other snakes is to destroy their leaders."

She rolled the glass between her fingertips.

"Let's go to bed, Zara. Tomorrow I meet with Cyrus Hassani, who's leading the team, and I will arrange a strategy meeting between all of us."

"It's been a long day, *mon cheri*. I'll take a raincheck. I don't want to take any chances. Mustafa may have put surveillance on me, and your being here would blow everything."

Aryeh and Zara had no formal relationship, and naturally, they were free to take lovers, but the thought of this terrorist touching her made him want to choke the bastard before he ever got near her. He needed to rein in his emotions and stay focused on the mission. Zara was a professional, and he needed to trust her instincts. "You're probably right. I'll leave the way I came, invisibly." He finished the brandy with one swig and placed his snifter on the coffee table. Then he took Zara's face between his hands. "Be careful, *mon amour*, you are about to play with fire, and I don't want you to get burned." He kissed her on both cheeks and stood.

She smiled. "I trust you to save me if things go awry. Before you go." She stood and walked to a buffet against the wall and opened a drawer. She removed something and returned to him. "These burner phones are programmed only to receive and send calls to each other on an untraceable frequency that routes through an Interpol satellite. From now on, we communicate only with these."

He took it and stuffed it in his pocket. "*Jusqu'à demain.*" He kissed her again and walked out the back door, disappearing into the shadows.

When she'd finished preparing for bed, she poured a glass of wine. She needed to formulate a plan of how to deal with Mustafa. He was vulnerable to her charms for now, but how long would his attraction last? The quicker she got some leverage on him, the better. The excitement of baiting and hooking the enemy filled her with anticipation. She looked forward to his return.

CHAPTER 12

Tel Aviv

To complete the second part of his mission, Amir had befriended a mechanic who worked the late shift for the Dan Bus Company. They agreed to meet up for falafels and beer. By the time they'd finished eating, it was just after 11 p.m. Amir tagged along walking with the mechanic to the bus maintenance facility. They turned down an ally not far from the terminal. It was a shortcut suggested by Amir.

"You didn't have to walk me to work. I'm going to get the wrong idea about you," the bearded Israeli Arab ribbed Amir.

Amir chuckled. "What would I want with your fat ass when I just came from having the fuck of a lifetime? And then, can you believe it, I came inside of her while I strangled her to death?"

The man turned to Amir, who'd fallen a few steps behind. "What? What are you talking about?" His eyes widened with fear, but before he could utter a scream, Amir wrapped a garrote around his neck and pulled it so tight the man's eyes nearly popped out of his head. He struggled, kicking, tugging, and flailing, trying to break Amir's hold. The much larger assassin easily held the man until his body went limp, and his legs collapsed beneath him, his spasming body silenced by death.

Amir quickly swapped clothes with the dead man. The jumper that had been baggy on the dead man was tight on him, but it would have to do. With the blade of his knife, he slit open the mechanic's laminated identification card and glued a photo of himself over the Palestinian's photo and resealed the card's plastic cover with a cigarette lighter. It wasn't perfect, but no one at this hour was going to inspect his credentials too carefully. He lifted the body and dropped it in a dumpster. Brushing himself off, he walked out of the alley toward the maintenance facility. Days before, he'd rented a room in a nearby boarding house. He stopped there and picked up a black lunch box and reported for work.

Amir was not only a deadly assassin, but he was a master bomb maker. He'd worked many times with TATP, a dangerous concoction of concentrated hydrogen peroxide and acetone, and was an expert at working with it. Cooking it up in the kitchen of his rented apartment had presented no problem. He'd painstakingly planned the loading of the bomb onto the number 4 bus.

After Amir's shift was over, he sat in a café on Ben Yehuda Street. For a week, he'd studied the routine of Layla Hassani. Every morning at precisely 8:45 a.m., she drove her daughter to preschool. Every day, like clockwork, she passed the number 4 bus as it made its way along Ben Yehuda Street. Each time he'd seen the little redheaded child in the backseat wave to the people on the bus.

He sipped his espresso and read the newspaper, occasionally fingering the cell phone in his jacket pocket. Glancing up the street, he saw the blue bus come to a stop at a red light. He hadn't expected the stars to align so perfectly and was pleased to see the black Kia pull up alongside the bus. The light changed, and the bus drove forward as did the Kia, but at the last second, just when Amir reached in his pocket and pressed the button, the Kia slammed on its brakes and came to a stop. An aggressive driver in a Mercedes rushed past and nearly clipped the Kia, racing to pass the bus. With a deafening explosion, the bus blew up, and the Mercedes and its driver disappeared in a blaze of fire and smoke. The demolished bus rained pieces of metal all over the road. The black Kia was lucky, it had been blown sideways and rested on two wheels on its side in the oncoming traffic lane. People raced toward the fiery wreckage.

Sirens wailed all around, and police cars and ambulances raced up the street toward the smoldering bus. General Qasem Solatani would be frustrated with the outcome. The general had been specific in his target. The murder of both the traitor's wife and child would serve as payback for the death of the Iranian Quds brothers who'd been killed by Cyrus Hassani in America. Amir cursed and tossed some coins on the table and walked away in the opposite direction. At least he had the flash drive. Amir knew it was likely Layla and Cerise had survived, but there was nothing he could do about it. He needed to get away as quickly as possible. Perhaps he'd take another run at them, but then he considered the likelihood of getting another opportunity and realized this part of his mission was done. A failure.

Amir left Tel Aviv and arrived in Jerusalem, where he taxied to the Allenby / King Hussein bridge crossing. His documents were in perfect order. He traveled under the guise of a Jordanian college professor teaching at Philadelphia University in Amman. His papers showed he'd been visiting relatives in East Jerusalem.

After several hours of waiting in line, and a thorough interrogation by Israeli border control agents, he passed into Jordan and was picked up by his contact, a Palestinian Jordanian. He imagined the bodies of Shura and Gilad had been discovered by now. However, it was of little concern to him once he and his welcoming committee sped away from the border crossing.

He spent the night in Amman. In the morning, after his morning prayers and coffee, the man took him to the Syrian border. He was expected and was met by a Syrian army colonel who delivered a missive of congratulations from al Assad himself. From there, he was provided a protective convoy and safe passage into Lebanon. With his mission accomplished, he arrived for a brief meeting with Hassan Nasrallah. He was looking forward to a few days of vacation by the sea with his wife and son.

Nasrallah kissed his minion on both cheeks. "Well done, Amir. The flash drive proves the Israeli Mossad agent Aryeh has gone rogue, which means we can proceed with our plan. The Mossad team is somewhere in Beirut, expediting their mission to recover the diamonds and capture the traitor Aryeh. Take a couple of days with your family, and then I want you to pick up the agent and bring him to me. Use all security precautions. Make sure the nephew is ready for his big moment. We want the Mossad agent desperate to free him, so rough him up and drug him. I want him too incoherent to relate much of anything except his desire to go home."

Amir nodded his approval. "By the time Aryeh is returned to Beirut and his blindfold removed, he'll have only one thing in mind, freeing his nephew."

"There is something else," said Nasrallah.

"Your wish is my command."

"I'm worried about Mustafa."

"Mustafa? The man lives only for the glory of Hezbollah."

"A change has come over him. Like his uncle, it seems women, or I should say a particular woman has caught his attention. I am concerned it will weaken him."

"Impossible. Who is the siren who could lure a fanatic like Mustafa to the rocks?" Amir jested.

"A journalist. Born in Morocco, her family immigrated to France. I want you to monitor Mustafa and the journalist. I will expect your regular reports on this budding relationship. We must keep Mustafa safe at all costs. The operation must move forward. The people are enamored with the mystery second son of Imad. He is like a movie star to the masses. We must preserve his stature and not allow this woman to tarnish his image. If we need to eliminate her, you will be given the honor."

Amir felt the hunger for the forbidden pleasure rise in his loins. He couldn't get it out of his mind, the imagery of sexual asphyxiation. A vision of Shura played in his mind, the way he'd felt at her exquisite death, his hands around her neck squeezing as he ejaculated inside of her. His heartbeat surged like a train barreling through a mountain tunnel. "Whatever you ask of me, consider it done."

CHAPTER 13

Tel Aviv

Pain.

Why did it hurt so much? A cacophony of harsh, brittle sounds rang in Layla's ears. Her breath came in shallow gasps, and she couldn't see beyond the stream of blood trickling down her face. The smoke made her choke. The world seemed tilted. No, it wasn't the world that was tilted, she was tilted. Everything came back to her in a rush. The explosion had flipped the Kia on its side. Layla couldn't move with her body wedged against the door.

She heard the whimpering of a child. *Oh, dear God, Cerise.* She tried to speak, but her voice came out hoarse and raspy, more like a groan. She tried again, her voice barely above a whisper. "Cerise, talk to mommy. Are you all right?"

"Mommy, I'm bleeding."

Panic seized her. "Don't worry, help is coming." Layla tried to turn her head to look at Cerise, but she couldn't. "Can you see where the blood is coming from, sweetie?"

Cerise didn't answer, and Layla's stomach twisted into a knot.

"I think my head, Mommy. It hurts."

"Help will be here in a minute. I promise we're going to be okay. Don't cry baby, be brave."

Hearing her weeping child was worse than the searing pain pulsing through her body. She tried to see out of the spider-webbed windshield. Her blood pounded against her temples, and her mind spun in circles as she tried to reconstruct what had happened. Did a bomb strike Tel Aviv? All she could remember was being cut off by a crazy driver in a Mercedes and then slamming on the brakes. *Then there was an awful explosion. The bus!*

The ringing in her ears continued, but now she could hear voices and sirens. People were banging on the widows of the car, and the sound of metal scraping metal made her jump. Cerise started crying again, and Layla focused on calming her daughter. She began to sing to Cerise to keep her mind off the first responders who were digging them out.

Rescuers were cutting through the door opposite her. The door tore from its hinges, and fresh air poured into the car. Arms reached for her, and fingers tried to unclick the seat belt, but it wouldn't release. The exploded airbag pressed like a hundred-pound weight against her chest, pinning her. "My child, save her first," she pleaded. *Oh dear, God, please take care of Cerise.*

A male voice answered. "Don't worry. Your child's safe. It looks like she suffered only a few scrapes and bruises. Just breathe, and we'll have you out of here in no time."

She nodded, the sting of tears in her eyes. She needed to breathe, but the pressure of the airbag on her chest felt like a ton of bricks. "Thank you," she mumbled through the waves of nausea and dizziness seizing her.

After several minutes the airbag was disengaged, and the seat belt was cut from her. Strong arms lifted her out of the Kia and gently laid her on a gurney. Her gaze flitted around her. The bus was a blackened hull of mangled metal. Body parts were strewn across the road. Chaos surrounded her as rescue teams searched for any survivors. She closed her eyes and swallowed the bile rising in her throat. *Cerise and I are alive. We're the lucky ones.*

She was in a state of shock and unaware of her own body's trauma. Panic seized her when she felt the warm gush between her legs. Her defense mechanisms set in, her body began to shake uncontrollably, and her screams pierced the air. "My baby. I'm losing my baby." The last thing she remembered was an oxygen mask covering her face, and her muffled screams fading as she slipped into unconsciousness.

Hadassah Hospital

The Prime Minister arrived at Hadassah Hospital after visiting the site of the terrorist attack. In a televised address to the nation, he'd sworn to the families of the dead and injured that there would be a day of judgment. Afterward, he'd gone straight to the hospital.

Enhanced security was everywhere, particularly outside the entrance to the intensive care unit. The hospital looked like a border crossing checkpoint. Soldiers armed with Uzi machine guns guarded every entrance as they eyed and inspected everyone, including the doctors and nurses who shuffled in and out.

The Prime Minister stood with the Ramsad. His gaze fixed on Layla lying in a bed inside the ICU. Shabak, the internal security division responsible for investigating terrorism within the state, believed Cyrus's wife and child were the actual targets of the terrorist bombing. The hospital was now in semi-lock-down, and the prime minister had ordered the nation on high alert. It had been some time since a bus in Israel had been blown up by terrorists. The return to madness put everyone on edge.

Noam Levi interrupted the silence that had settled upon them. He addressed the Prime Minister familiarly with his nickname. "Dodi, I have to bring Cyrus home. I can't shield him from what has happened."

"I agree, but it must be carried out in complete secrecy. Cyrus's visit must be brief, we will need him to return to Beirut as soon as possible. The welfare of the nation rests on the success of his mission. Tell me, how do you plan on managing this?" The prime minister's worried gaze never wavered from Layla.

"Cyrus will fly to Nicosia with Ben for an excursion tonight, and we'll have a private jet waiting to take them to Israel. I've talked to Layla's father and grandparents, and we're all in agreement she and Cerise will be better off in the safe house in Ramat Ha Sharon. So long as Cyrus is in Beirut, they'll remain there, which should placate Cyrus's worries. Layla's grandparents will move into the safe house with them."

"Excellent. Even Aleck should be satisfied with the arrangement." Layla's father and the prime minister had been roommates in college. Since Aleck's move to Israel, the two men had renewed their friendship and developed an even deeper bond.

"She's waking up." They watched Layla's grandmother, Dina, approach the bed and lift a cup of water to Layla's lips. Then the eagle-eyed Holocaust survivor sat on the edge of the bed and took Layla's hand in hers patting it. The two spoke for a few minutes, and then Layla closed her eyes.

Dina joined the two men outside the room. "Layla is devastated at the loss of the pregnancy. She needs Cyrus."

"It will take some doing, but we're bringing him to her. But only for a brief reunion. She needs to understand he must return to the operation," the Prime Minister stressed.

"She is in no shape to understand anything, but we will do what is required. Thank God, Cerise's injury is minor, but Layla's taking the loss of the pregnancy hard."

The Prime Minister nodded. "There will be other children, but I've lived through enough losses to know there is no magic pill to erase the pain of what she's going through."

"We've all lost. To be a survivor means you carry scars deeply embedded that nothing on earth can erase. It pains me to see my granddaughter made to bear those scars."

"Cyrus will bring her comfort," the leader of the nation assured.

"We'll see. Right now, Layla is irrational and blaming Cyrus for not being here."

"She will forgive him. Those two share more than just the love of a man and a woman. They owe their lives to each other. If adversity demands a trial by fire, Cyrus will prevail."

Dina's eyes flashed a distant storm without thunder, reminding the Prime Minister of heat lightning. "Do we know who did this?"

The Ramsad answered. "Security cameras caught footage of who we believe is the murderer sitting in a nearby coffee shop. Facial recognition technology found a match. He's Hezbollah."

He put his arm around the frail old woman's shoulders. "Dina, rest assured justice will prevail." The Prime Minister admired the Holocaust survivor matriarch, whom he considered a woman of high moral integrity and strength.

"God willing." The old woman sighed. "Excuse me, gentlemen, but I want to be with Layla should she need anything." She squared her shoulders and returned to the ICU.

"It breaks my heart to see her having to do deal with more personal tragedy. Dina's had more than her share of tragedy between the Holocaust and losing a daughter," said the Prime Minister.

The Ramsad's forehead lined with worry. "Yes, but she's a soldier and survivor, stronger than all of us." He waited as one of the nurses walked past on her way into the ICU. "Dodi, we've identified the terrorist as one of Nasrallah's henchmen. He could have gotten to Layla and Cerise any number of ways, but he chose to make a statement. The blowing up of the bus was meant to send a deadly message from Hezbollah and Iran—that there is no safe haven for Cyrus and his family."

"What else do we know?" The Prime Minister asked.

"Shortly after the bus explosion, the bodies of the suspected mole and his Palestinian Israeli lover were found in a hotel room dead. Video at the hotel caught footage of the same Hezbollah operative who blew up the bus. Elsewhere in the city, a store clerk discovered the body of an Israeli Arab in a trash bin. The man had worked the night shift at the bus maintenance facility."

"So, all three crimes were perpetrated by the same assassin? Do we have any clue where he is?"

"The likelihood is the monster has already left the country and is on his way back to Lebanon."

"How did he get through border security?"

"False identification papers. We're investigating it now."

"I want the team tasked with eliminating him. He must pay for his crimes."

"I'll notify Cyrus, though I'm sure he would be determined to kill the monster whether we asked or not."

"Tell him after he gets back here. He has enough to contend with." The Prime Minister was worried, nothing must get in the way of eliminating the EMP attack. "In the meantime, let's hope Aryeh makes headway with Hezbollah."

"We should know soon whether Nasrallah has taken the bait."

"Hopefully, he does."

CHAPTER 14

Beirut, Lebanon
Horsh Beirut Park

Cyrus, disguised with colored contacts and beard, followed a path near the deserted tennis courts at Horsh Beirut Park in search of his fellow operative, the man known as the Lion of Judea. Yitzhak had picked up a message from Aryeh that he needed to meet with Cyrus. A steady rain had kept most people away. However, a few braved the heavy showers and strolled with their umbrellas held high through the pine-scented paths. Cyrus strode through a dense stand of pine trees and emerged along a path with a row of benches for people to sit and enjoy the lush greenery.

At first, Cyrus didn't recognize the man sitting on one of the benches. He appeared to be an older gentleman bundled up in an oversized raincoat. Leaning forward, the man rested his hands on a cane. Cyrus walked past the old man, then his instincts kicked in, and he gave the figure a second quick glance. The old man's wink left no doubt confirming who he was.

Cyrus joined him on the bench. "Not a bad disguise. I nearly missed you."

"It's a necessity. It seems I've made Hezbollah's most wanted list. I'm trying to meet them on my terms and not theirs. I've got quite a few things to discuss with you."

"I figured."

"Have you informed the team of what's going on here?"

"I plan on doing it after I talk to the Ramsad."

"I spoke with him, and he okayed it. It's time to bring them up to speed." He changed the subject. "You know about Zara?"

"A little."

"Zara's attracted the attention of Mustafa Mughniyeh, the mysterious son of Imad Mughniyeh."

"That's significant. It seems the cockroaches are beginning to show themselves. Have you told Zara about the nukes and rockets or Hezbollah's planned EMP attack?"

"Yes, I filled her in."

Cyrus studied Aryeh's face. "You're sure she can be trusted?"

"Not only can she be trusted, but she may be our best hope to topple this house of cards. He implicated himself with his own words. Zara thinks Mustafa is involved. Maybe even running the operation."

"What proof do you have?"

"No proof, just innuendo, and instinct." Aryeh tapped his cane on the ground. "It's going to put her in significant danger, but she intends to get as close as possible to him."

"Should we put the team on her?"

"Yeah, put Ben and Daniel on it. I'm going to suggest she meet Mustafa in public places. I'll have to inform her of the tail because she'll pick it up anyway."

"What's the plan?"

"We need to find where they're building the rockets. Zara can make a difference if she gains his trust. If he is involved, she'll persuade him to take her there, or at least close enough for us to figure it out. I'm also waiting to hear from Nasrallah about the diamond exchange for my nephew." They both grew silent as a teenage couple approached. They were giggly and affectionate, obviously looking for a place where they could be alone. The teens ignored the two men and continued up the trail.

"You haven't spoken with the Ramsad?" Aryeh asked.

"Two days ago. Noam wanted to wait until Zvi had everything secured."

Aryeh nodded. "I spoke with him yesterday. It's a bit odd, Noam is usually incessant and hands-on. I've never known him to allow such latitude. There may be something else afoot."

"I'm sure we'll both hear from him soon."

Aryeh reached into his pocket and retrieved a vibrating cell phone. "I'm here."

Cyrus waited patiently. He knew it had to be important. Aryeh wouldn't have taken the call if it wasn't. "Tomorrow night?" Aryeh nodded. "Yes, I know the place. I'll be ready." He stuffed the cell back in his pocket. "That was Zara."

Cyrus's brows lifted.

"Nasrallah wants to meet, which means I've passed the first round of trust. They're taking me to Gideon as an act of good faith."

"It's possible they could be doing it just to lure you in."

"I don't think so. Nasrallah knows the diamonds are hidden safely somewhere here in Beirut. He's not going to do anything that might jeopardize getting his hands on the treasure. Besides, Zara says they're after more than the jewels."

"It's a daring but dangerous risk."

Aryeh smiled. "I live for the risk, my friend. Unlike you, I have no one waiting at home for me."

"True enough. The phone you used with Zara, untraceable, I hope?"

"Totally. The phones link through an Interpol satellite feed, and only to each other. Zara's suggestion."

Cyrus nodded. "Would you consider wearing a tracking device, just in case?"

"Absolutely, not. I wouldn't put a strip search past these bastards."

"New technology. It's foolproof. You'd be the guinea pig or guinea lion as the case may be."

Aryeh laughed at Cyrus's attempt at a joke. "Okay, have someone from the team leave it in the dropbox."

"This technology will allow us to monitor you. I'm putting everyone on high alert until I know you're safe. If anything goes wrong, we'll come for you."

"Sounds good."

"Oh, Yitzhak and Nira checked into the same hotel as the North Korean physicists. They're closely monitoring them. We're working on setting up a wiretap on their rooms."

"We need someone at Mossad headquarters who speaks Korean to translate the tapes once the wiretaps are in."

"I've already seen to it."

"Good." Aryeh stood and leaned heavily on his cane. "I'll check in when I return tonight." Without a goodbye, he turned and shuffled away. When he'd disappeared, Cyrus stood and followed the path in the opposite direction. There was much to do, and he was anxious to get back to the team.

Cyrus returned to the duplex and found Ash lying on the couch in the living room with his shirt off. Cartons of take-out food lay empty on the coffee table. His focus was a big-screen television, where every few seconds, the image switched. He was monitoring the security cameras surrounding the duplex. In preparation for the operation, Nira and Yitzhak had deployed hidden cameras in every room, every window, and entrance. It was Ash's shift to monitor.

Ash was tireless. He'd been working around the clock since his arrival in Lebanon. Busily, he'd procured and stockpiled arms in the barn of a property he'd purchased in the Beqaa valley. Several days of stubble shadowed his cheeks.

Ash's face lit with a smile when he saw Cyrus. "Hey, boss."

"*Chaver*, my friend. Good to see you back. How did it go?"

"I'd say we have enough to take on the entire Lebanese Army and defeat them if that's what you have in mind."

Cyrus chuckled. "I have our sights set on something a bit more manageable." He eyed the considerable amount of real estate on Ash's body covered with tattoos. He'd meant to ask him about it. "You wear a lot of body art. Any significance?"

Ash grinned. "Yeah, every mission since I've been with the team." He pointed above his heart. "Except for this one, the bullseye is for luck."

"Do you have one for saving my daughter?"

He sat up, displaying his back, where a snowcapped Matterhorn held a place of honor. "My tribute to Cerise."

"It's a beauty. What do you think you'll get for this mission?"

"Well, it sure as hell won't be a picture of Aryeh, but a lion might be cool."

"I think you're going to have a slew of choices after my discussion with the team today. Where's everyone?"

"Yitzhak and Nira are babysitting the North Koreans. Zvi's in the technology center upstairs, and Daniel and Ben are trying not to be caught out by Zara."

"I have some news to share, but I want everyone to hear it at once. I'll get Zvi to set up a secure satellite communication with everyone."

A few minutes later, Ash and Cyrus had joined Zvi in the technology center. On the big screen appeared the live image of each member of the team.

Cyrus turned to Zvi. "Everything secure?"

Zvi monitored a laptop. "Yeah, all of their cell phones are routing through our satellite. We're as secure as we'll ever be."

Cyrus revealed the real reason for their mission to Beirut. "Aryeh's not our target."

Daniel pounded Ben on the back, coupled with cheers. Nira wiped her eyes, and Yitzhak grinned, putting his arm around her shoulders. Zvi showed little or no reaction, but Cyrus knew he'd figured it out already. Ash pumped his fist and brought it down to his side, flexing his muscle. "Yes, the lion lives another day!"

Considerable relief filled Cyrus as he waited for their celebration to wind down. They were all talking at once.

A buzz from the satellite phone linked exclusively to Tel Aviv distracted Zvi from the celebration. His gaze grew somber as he listened. "Yes, sir. I'll see to it." He handed Cyrus the phone. "You might want to take this in the other room."

Cyrus took the phone and walked into the adjacent bedroom. "Hassani here."

The Ramsad's tone was compassionate, something Cyrus had never heard from him before. "Cyrus, there's been a bus bombing here in Tel Aviv."

As the Ramsad told him what happened, Cyrus's heart started pounding, and his hands began to shake so badly he nearly dropped the phone. "Fuck!" He sank to his knees. It felt like a sledgehammer had hit him in the chest. He couldn't breathe, could barely eke out the words. "Are they okay?" He closed his eyes, and grabbed the bridge of his nose, fighting to keep it together. Tears streamed down his face. Guilt at not being there for Layla and Cerise overwhelmed him. How many times would he place his family in danger?

He dragged himself to his feet and sat in a chair, his chest heaving as he forced out the words. "How is Layla?" His world was crumbling around him as the pain of what she must be feeling pierced his heart. *I wasn't there...I wasn't there for her. I failed her again.*

"We're doing all we can for her," the Ramsad said. "We're bringing you home for twenty-four hours. Ben will accompany you. I'm sorry it can't be longer, but you must complete this mission."

"We're moving your family to the safe house at Ramat Hasharon. The one Layla lived in with Aleck after you rescued her from Iran. Her grandparents are moving in with her to help with Cerise."

Cyrus pushed aside his guilt for now. He needed to focus. "Who did this? I want to see his face. He has to pay."

"Everything is being transmitted to Zvi. In the meantime, you and Ben will be flying commercial to Cyprus tonight and escorted by the Cyprians to a private jet. It's all arranged. No paperwork, no questions."

"Thank you, sir."

"Cyrus, we think this terrorist was acting under direct orders from Solatani. Neither the mullahs nor the Quds force has forgotten your treason. This depraved act, targeting a mother and her child, smells like revenge."

Hatred surged through Cyrus's veins like molten lava. "I want to go after who did this."

"Temper your fury Cyrus," The Ramsad said. "Focus on Layla and Cerise. Stopping these bastards is all that matters. The right place and the right time will present itself for you to deliver your vengeance."

"I promise you, I will calm down and perform what needs to be done. But I will also have my revenge."

CHAPTER 15

Ramat Hasharon, Israel

At ten p.m., a black SUV with dark tinted windows pulled up to the gates of a two-story Mediterranean villa in a quiet neighborhood in Ramat Hasharon. The driver of the SUV typed in a code on the electronic keypad next to the gate and waited for it to slide open. Cyrus emerged from the back seat carrying an overnight bag. Before he reached the front door, Layla's grandmother opened it.

"It's about time you made your appearance." She turned her cheek up for his kiss.

Dina never minced words. In the beginning, he'd assumed from her pointed looks, cool reception, and feigned indifference that she disapproved of him. But time had taught him it was just her way. Holocaust survivors often skipped the niceties, getting straight to the point. Enough of their time had been stolen from them. When he thought Layla had died in the restaurant bombing in New York, Dina had kicked his ass for losing faith. The old woman had assured him Layla was alive. The old woman's remarkable strength had kept him from falling apart. He valued her advice more than anyone else's.

"Good to see you too, Dina." *The old girl might look frail, but she's tough as nails. A terrorist's bomb isn't going to bring her down.*

"Where's Layla? I need to see her now."

"She's resting. I need to speak with you before you talk to her. Prepare you for her mental state."

He looked up the stairs longing to race up and find her. Hold her. But instead, he followed as Dina shuffled to the kitchen, her bedroom slippers slapping against the bottom of her feet. He made a mental note to buy her a new pair—something frivolous and girlie—when he returned from Beirut.

99

He sat at the kitchen table, and she brought him a steaming cup of tea and a slice of lemon cake. "You're going to need fortification."

"That bad?"

"Not good. Feeling sorry for herself." She shook her head, wiping away a tear. It was a rare display of emotion. "Understandable, of course. She was looking forward to this baby." She sat in the seat next to him.

He hung his head and looked into his teacup. His hand shook as he raised it to his lips. He felt crippled by guilt. "We'll have more."

Dina nodded. "She's not thinking of other children, she's thinking of the one she lost. You're going to have your hands full."

His voice dropped to barely a whisper. "I don't have much time to make this right. I have to go back tomorrow night."

"I know—they told me."

"Is she going to understand?"

"I don't know…probably not."

"What do you suggest I do?"

Dina covered his hand with hers. He glanced down at the blue-veins forming plump ridges on her paper-thin skin. He raised his eyes to her face, the fragility of her petite form in complete contrast to the resilience in her gaze.

"Listen and comfort her. Listen and love her. Above all else, listen and agree with her, then do what you have to do. She loves you, Cyrus, she'll come around. Maybe not tonight. Maybe not tomorrow, but in her heart, she loves only you."

"Thank you, Dina." He lifted her hand and kissed it.

She patted his head. "You're a good man, Cyrus. Don't let my redheaded granddaughter's temper get under your skin."

"I'll try, but she's pretty good at pressing my buttons. I guess that's part of our passionate natures. Tell me, how is Cerise?"

Dina's eyes lit up. "Ah, she is a mini-me, or maybe she's a mini-you. A true thinker, rational, and focused. The child lets nothing obscure her vision." A smile tickled her lips, "or her purpose. Nothing can stifle her will to live."

He could feel his heart swell with pride. "Cerise is something special." He took a last bite of cake and drained his teacup. "Where is Layla?"

"Upstairs, second door on the left. We didn't tell her you were coming. I thought it would be better if she didn't think too much about it."

"I guess I can either expect open arms or a shoe thrown at me."

Dina chuckled. "Keep your head down."

Cyrus took the stairs two at a time and then paused to calm his racing pulse. The bedroom was draped in darkness. He waited for his eyes to adjust. From the bed, Layla called. "I'm fine, Savta. Go to bed."

He cleared his throat. "*Sheereen-am, i*t's me."

Layla turned on her side and rose to her elbow. "Cyrus?"

There was a bandage wrapped around her head. He dropped his bag and rushed to her side and tried to gather her in his arms, but she pushed him away. "Don't touch me."

"I'm so sorry, *eshgham*. I'm so sorry I wasn't here for you."

Like water breaching a levee, the tears poured from her. She covered her face with her hands and sobbed. "It's your fault. The bus—the baby—Cerise. You did this! Always believing you can save the world. Well, guess what? You weren't here to save us."

He went rigid. He knew Layla didn't mean what she said, but she might as well have shoved a knife in his heart. "Layla, please. You know I'd do anything to make it all go away. I wish—" He tried to find the words—the magic elixir capable of healing her broken heart. An apology wasn't enough to make her forgive him, but sorry was all he had to give her. She was right. He'd failed her…He'd promised Dina he'd remain calm and let the words roll off his back, but he couldn't do it. He couldn't listen. He didn't want to lose his temper. He didn't want to return her venom. "I'll be downstairs if you need me."

Layla couldn't stop the tears. She'd tried to be brave for Cerise and her grandparents. She hadn't broken down in front of them. But the loss of her baby held her in its grip, imprisoning her in a cage of pain and self-loathing. But when Cyrus walked through the door the storm of self-pity she'd been brewing inside since the bombing, released in a deluge.

When she was exhausted from the crying, she fell asleep. She didn't know how long she slept. She glanced at the clock and saw it was 2 a.m. She sat up, her eyes searching the room for Cyrus. He sat in a chair hunched over, his head resting in his hands. *How long has he been sitting there?*

"Cyrus?"

His voice was hoarse, barely above a whisper. "Yes, *eshgham*."

"I'm sorry—the things I said were inexcusable."

"No, you're right."

She held out her arms to him. "Please, forgive me. You know how toxic I can be when I lose my temper."

With trembling fingers, he brushed back his hair. "I never lost my temper until I met you. I always kept my cool. You make me feel alive, human. Only you can spark my anger and guilt. I become a trigger on a gun, once pressed I fire."

"Oh, Cyrus. I can't bear the thought of doing that to you."

"You're so deep inside of me, so much a part of me, I'd rather fight with you than agree with anyone else." Before she could respond, he'd gathered her up in his arms.

She slumped against him, shivering. "I've been so scared." She cracked like an eggshell, the pain like a yolk spilling from her. "It was horrible…the bus…the bodies, and Cerise …"

She felt him shudder against her. Looking up wild-eyed, she placed her hands on his stubbled cheeks. "It's more my fault than yours."

He kissed her forehead. "No, my love, how can it be your fault. It's me they wanted to hurt."

"No, you're wrong. It's because of me your cover in Iran was blown, and your life's work ended. It's because of me we had to flee, and you were discovered to be a spy. And it was my fault when I traveled to New York for the art show. I didn't have to go. I know you didn't want me to go, but I was selfish and thinking only of myself. Since the moment we met, I've been trouble for you."

"Don't say that! Never! I wouldn't change any of it. Meeting you was my salvation. You are my heart. My soul. The very air I breathe. You taught me how to live, how to feel again." Cyrus's inner turmoil was written in his eyes. "I wish I could change what happened. I failed you, *esghgam*, and I don't think I'll ever forgive myself."

She pressed herself deeper into his embrace. "Your being here now is all that matters. I'm so glad you're here. I need you…Cerise needs you."

"Cerise will be fine, baby, she's strong like you."

She shook her head. "No, not like me, like you, like Dina. My first thought when I felt the baby…lost the baby. I wanted to die. Then they freed me from the car, and I could see what that monster had done. Like a battlefield strewn with the dead…broken bodies everywhere. So many shattered lives…" She choked, remembering the horror. "I was ashamed. I was alive, and they weren't. It reminded me of Savta, of what she must feel every day of her life as a survivor of the Holocaust. You can't stop asking yourself—why do I get to live?"

He buried his face in her hair. "Never think that again, my love. There's no guilt in living. Don't you know what you mean to me? It kills me to hear you say these things."

"I feel so broken. This baby was special, Cyrus. It was a miracle, our miracle."

"There will be other babies, other miracles. I know this sounds callous, and you know I don't mean it to be. But we can't know what God has in mind. We will have another child, I promise you."

"I know you're right, but it breaks my heart. One minute I had a beautiful life growing inside me and the next minute, only emptiness." She fought back the tears.

"Shhh," his hands soothed her back, gently rubbing the tension from it. When she'd calmed down, he lay her against the pillow. "I'm going to wash up. I'll be right back."

Her hand caressed his cheek. "I'm not going anywhere. Go. You must be exhausted."

Cyrus slept deeply with his arms and legs wrapped around Layla. He'd patiently listened for hours to her, wiping away the tears, helping her navigate the sorrow of losing their child. Exhausted in the early hours of the morning, they'd both fallen asleep cocooned in each other's love.

It was no wonder he didn't hear the tread of small feet and was taken by surprise when Cerise threw herself onto the bed. "Daddy! You're home."

Layla rolled over and grumbled. "Cerise, can't you see we're sleeping. At least don't break my eardrums so early in the morning."

"But *Ima*, Daddy's home and he'll make you better. And you can make another…"

Cyrus grabbed her into his arms before she could complete her sentence, putting his fingers to her lips he whispered, "shhh…"

Cerise nodded. "But, *Aba*…"

He rolled out of bed with her and carried her into the bathroom. Closing the door, he put the toilet seat down and set her on it. "Mommy's tired, baby, she needs to sleep a little longer." He lifted her face inspecting the fine line of stitches from the bombing. "Tell me about your booboo."

"Oh, Daddy, you wouldn't have liked it. There was a loud kaboom, and the car flew in the air, and the bus exploded." She waved her hands, gesticulating the movements of the car. She stuck her lower lip out. "I wasn't brave. I cried a little."

He kneeled in front of her. "Just because you cried doesn't mean you're not brave, *metuka*. Even daddies cry sometimes. It's good to cry. Mommy cried a lot last night, and we both know how brave she is."

"Mommy's been sad. I think we have to get her another baby."

He smiled. Cerise had a way of seeing things in a clear, uncluttered way. She always saw a simple solution to a complex situation. "We will, sweetie, but it has to be at the right time. Mommy has to get better, and she's going to need your help."

"What can I do, Daddy?"

"Here's your job."

"You're giving me a job?"

"Yes, I'm the general, and you're the soldier. Your duty as my aide is to carry out my orders."

She knit her brows. "Okay, what do I do?"

"I'm going to have to leave tonight and finish the job I'm on, so I'm leaving you in charge of Mommy. Your job is to be the best you can be. No waking her up when she's sleeping, and you make sure no one else wakes her up either."

"You mean like *savta* and *saba*?"

"Exactly. You make sure Grandma and Grandpa don't wake her too early. She needs to heal and regain her strength."

"What else, Daddy?"

"I want you to figure out ways to make her laugh."

"You mean like doing somersaults or making funny faces."

"Those are all good. Draw funny pictures, too. But no tickling, that's cheating."

"I like when you tickle me."

He was tempted to tickle her but was afraid it would disturb Layla. "You might hurt Mommy's tummy."

"Why do you have to leave again?"

"Baby, your daddy does a lot of things to help people, and sometimes he has to go far away to do them. But when I come home this time, I promise it's going to be a long time before I go away again."

"You promise."

"Give me your pinkie finger." He entwined his finger with hers. "You promise to be the best girl for Mommy, and I'll promise to come home and not leave for a long time."

"Okay. I promise."

"Now close your eyes." He bent and kissed her finger. "Now, open your eyes and kiss my finger." She did.

"We've made a sacred promise we have to keep. I want you to be like a mouse and tiptoe through the bedroom, and I'll meet you in the kitchen as soon as I get washed up and dressed. Tell Savta that Daddy is starving. You know how much she likes to feed us." He put his fingers to his lips. "Remember, tiptoe."

He opened the door and watched Cerise run on tiptoe out of the room, trailing giggles in her wake. He thought about his promise to her and prayed he'd be able to keep it. He wanted nothing more than to watch her grow from day to day. He didn't want to miss any more birthdays or holidays or even just the quiet times they spent together as a family. He wanted that for her, and he wanted it for all children. If the time came when he'd be called upon again to safeguard his daughter's future and it meant breaking his promise to her, he knew he'd do it. It was a sacred task, and nothing would prevent him from fulfilling it.

Cyrus carried a tray upstairs to Layla. Dina had made her favorite goat cheese omelet, along with pastries, fresh cut fruit, orange juice, and coffee, which she hoped would tempt her granddaughter into eating. Since her release from the hospital, Layla had barely touched any food. Cyrus kneed the door to the bedroom open.

"Good morning, baby. I hope you're hungry, Dina went all out for you."

Layla sat up in bed. "She's worried, I haven't been eating much."

"She's right. You need to eat and get your strength back." He placed the tray table over her legs and sat on the edge of the bed next to her. He leaned in and stole a kiss. "How do you wake up looking like the most beautiful woman in the world? What's your secret?"

"Stop trying to cheer me up."

He picked up the fork and handed it to her. "If you don't start eating by yourself, I'm going to feed you."

Layla took the fork and took a small bite. "It is good."

"I ate enough to feed a small army. Keep eating."

"Did you come home so you could play the mother?"

"I came home because the woman I love needed me."

"How's Beirut?" She took another bite and a sip of juice.

"The mission is moving ahead, but there's still much to be done."

"In other words, you can't tell me anything."

"Not really. National security."

"When do you go back?"

"Tonight."

She lifted the tray and rested it on the bed beside her.

"Baby, you know I'd stay longer if I could. We're lucky they let me come home at all." He picked up the tray and placed it back in front of her. "Come on, Layla, cut me a break. You know how bad I feel about not being here to protect you."

Tears filled her eyes. "I told Savta I blamed you, but I didn't mean it. I've tried to get it through my head. I married a man who serves a higher purpose. I know how important what you do is. But it's not like a doctor who's on-call all the time and gets an emergency at the hospital and has to report. You get a call, and you leave for God knows where, and your life is on the line. Maybe you come home, or maybe you don't."

He needed to control his emotions and that ever-present guilt. Layla was suffering from the after-effects of the bombing and the miscarriage. He had to be patient and let her vent. Cyrus removed the tray from her lap and placed it on the floor. He lay beside her and pulled her into his arms, holding her close. "I know this is hard for you, but I also know the woman I married. Beneath all of this fragility is the strongest woman I've ever known. Layla, we are not going to let this tear us apart. Ever. You are my breath—without you, I'm nothing. I will never give up on us, and I beg you not to give up on us."

It was an emotional plea, and her eyes blinked back tears. Cyrus leaned in and touched his lips to hers in a gentle kiss that soon turned passionate. When they broke apart, they were both breathing heavily. "I love you so much, Layla. Every day I thank God I found you."

Her smile was radiant. "Superman would be pretty hard to replace."

He chuckled. "You better believe it. Now would you do Superman a small favor and eat your breakfast. It's a beautiful day, and I'd like you to get dressed. Then I'll sweep you off your feet and carry you downstairs to a nice lounge chair by the pool, and you and I can relax until it's time for me to go. Cerise would love to go swimming. She'd also like to see her mommy return to herself. She's worried about you."

"You're right, poor baby, she went through so much in the last few days. Did she say anything?"

"She said we need to get you another baby so you can be happy again."

"I'm sure you agreed wholeheartedly."

"I told her you needed to heal first."

"My sweet girl, she needs a little normalcy, we all do. What would I do without you?"

"Those survivor genes are pretty strong. My guess is you'd stubbornly plow forward and make the world conform to your wishes. You certainly have a way of making me conform to them." He laughed.

Layla jabbed her finger in his rib. "You make me sound like some femme fatale or a spoiled brat who insists on getting her way."

"Well… You've managed to wrap me around your little finger. I imagine you could do that to any man you chose." He picked up the tray and placed it in front of her again. "Now, don't make me look like a failure to Dina. Eat."

Layla gave him a smirky grin. "Maybe I shouldn't eat and make you deal with the iron lady."

"Even you aren't that cruel." He kissed her again. "If you don't eat, I'm going to take you over my knee."

"Promises, promises."

While Layla and Cerise took a nap after lunch, Cyrus watched television with Dina and Morris in the living room. The programming was interrupted by a news alert. The pictures coming out of Syria were alarming. Images of men, women, and children, spasming and frothing at the mouth from the deadly use of chemical weapons. Assad had again disregarded the Geneva Protocol banning the use of chemical or biological weapons. The man was a monster.

Cyrus was on a mission to stop the use of EMP, but what was to stop Hezbollah, or Iran, or some other bad actor in the Middle East from getting their hands on and using chemical weapons against Israel? His phone vibrated in his pocket. He walked outside to take the call.

"Have you seen the news coming out of Syria?" It was the Ramsad.

"Horrifying. What do you think about it?"

"I think we have to make sure it doesn't happen again," Noam said grimly.

"I'm sure there will be an appropriate response. I think this is something the world can agree on."

"We will see. How's Layla and Cerise?"

"She's a wreck, but I'm getting through to her. Cerise is a miracle. The child takes what's thrown at her and bounces back. I guess all kids are like that."

"Not true. It's her nature. I call it the survivor gene."

"Yeah, she's got them in spades."

"What time is your flight tonight?"

"Midnight. It's hard to leave, but this attack in Syria only reinforces my commitment to stop these killers."

"Exactly. It's time to teach them a lesson they will never forget."

CHAPTER 16

Beirut, Lebanon

Aryeh turned the do not disturb sign facing out and closed the door to his room. He'd attached door sensors to the door; no one could search his room without his knowledge. If the door opened, a minuscule hidden camera would be tripped, and film whoever entered the room.

Earlier, he'd received a text from Zara. *I've heard from our friends. Take a taxi to the Starbucks at Fursan El Haykal Street and wait inside. They will text me when they arrive. A gray Mercedes will pull up. You'll have two minutes to exit. No weapons. Expect to be searched. I have no idea where they are taking you. Good luck, mon ami!*

Before leaving the hotel, Aryeh had spoken with Cyrus, who'd just returned from Tel Aviv. Aryeh was not entirely on his own. The team would be on standby, ready to move if necessary. He was wearing new tracking technology. What looked to be a mole on his ass was a tracking device sending signals back to Zvi in the technology center of the Mossad safe house. If anything went wrong, the team would have a general idea of his whereabouts. Not much in the way of protection, but it provided him with a modicum of confidence.

The whole team had joked and put in their two cents about where to put the mole. Nira had come up with the winning location. "No one is going to be checking your ass too carefully. If they do, you've got bigger things to worry about." That was enough to set off a string of crude jokes all at the expense of their former leader, who took them all in stride. The team was operating like a well-oiled engine since they'd learned Aryeh wasn't their target.

After learning about Layla being the target of the deadly bus attack in Israel, they'd rallied around Cyrus. He was now one of them, and whatever trepidation had existed before was no longer an issue. Aryeh also made it clear he'd thrown his full support behind Cyrus.

A cold breeze blew through Beirut that night as Aryeh drank a steamy black cup of coffee, his gaze switching from the parking lot to his cell phone. He'd spied a couple of Mercedes cruising the street in front of the Starbucks, but none of them had been the one. He was anxious to see his nephew and his condition. He also wondered who he would be meeting with from Hezbollah. It seemed unlikely it would be Nasrallah. However, the puppeteer would most certainly be watching. His phone dinged, indicating an incoming text. Zara's text read, *Hi, two minutes. Good luck.*

He drained his coffee and walked out into the night.

Two men jumped out of a gray Mercedes and quickly frisked him. They took his cell phone and indicated he get in the car. He slid into the backseat, and the two men bookended him on either side. Both men were right out of central casting, bearded and brawny, with bulging muscles that strained against their jackets. The guy who took his cell phone opened it and pulled out the SIM card before tossing the phone out the window. He pocketed the SIM card. Before the car had left the parking lot, a cloth sack came down over Aryeh's head.

He leaned his head back against the seat and shut his eyes, letting his mind drift. He expected this to be a long drive. There was no way they were holding Gideon anywhere near the city. He wasn't afraid, just anxious to get to Gideon. In the heat of an operation or a fight, adrenaline kicked in, and the body and mind ran off training and experience. This slow dance was excruciating. He needed to see his nephew alive.

Three hours later, they arrived. The foot-soldiers jumped out of the car and yanked him out. Their meaty hands encircled his arms and propelled him forward. A door squeaked open, and they escorted Aryeh inside. They descended a stairwell. Their footsteps echoed hollowly on the stairs. They passed through a locked door that automatically clicked open and strode down a passageway. Another door creaked open, and they removed the sack. He blinked rapidly, the fluorescent light blinding him. He was told to strip, and one of the bookends inspected him thoroughly. The transmitter disguised as a mole on his ass garnered no attention, and Aryeh breathed a silent sigh of relief. After searching his clothing, they told him to dress. Producing a chair, they told him to sit. Finished with him, the two men left the room.

Aryeh looked around. No windows. Just a desk and two chairs, one of which he occupied. Gray-black walls of concrete surrounded him, and the same concrete was duplicated on the floor. Above the desk, a fluorescent fixture flickered and buzzed, the way they do when the bulb is about to die. Nothing distinguished the room from any other prison cell he'd ever seen. Silence engulfed him, no sound emanated through the walls, which probably meant they were several feet thick.

After a few minutes, the door creaked open. A large muscular man entered, dressed in the para-military camouflage uniform of a Hezbollah officer. Seating himself across from Aryeh, the two men studied each other. On the desk, he laid a file, which he opened.

He spoke in Arabic. "We understand you're interested in a combatant prisoner, a soldier detained in Syrian territory."

"Gideon Reise, my nephew, was on border patrol on the Golan Heights, which is not Syrian territory. If you study your history, you'll find the British Empire mandated it to Israel. It would serve you well to remember, Lebanon, Syria, and Israel were all created from the mandate. So, I differ from you in my interpretation of where Gideon was illegally seized."

The man smiled thinly, but his eyes held contempt. "A man who is a traitor to his country is not in a position to defend his country's borders, or its right to exist."

"I am only stating the facts. My traitorous actions are a last attempt to protect my family. Even you must acknowledge the justifiability of putting family first."

"We think differently. My work is Allah's work and takes preference over my family. But we are not here to speak of our beliefs. We are here to consider your offer."

"May I know who I am addressing?"

"You may address me as Amir, and I will address you as Aryeh. Tell me, Aryeh, what is it you would ask of us?"

"I want my nephew, Gideon Riese, to be exchanged for seventy-five-million in diamonds. Diamonds, which I have hidden in Beirut."

"And if we should agree, what then? You can't return to Palestine."

"I'm a spy. I'll disappear."

"We have something else in mind."

"I'm listening."

"For years, the party of God has been infiltrated by Israeli agents. With their assistance, there have been assassinations and missions compromised.

It is time for us to counter this espionage. It is our belief you will make a perfect deep-cover agent."

"I stole diamonds from Mossad, which you're going to take possession of if we make a deal. The only secrets I'll be privy to are those whispered by other inmates in prison."

"You're going to return the diamonds and bring home your nephew and two other prisoners. You will return a hero."

Aryeh's eyes narrowed. "Why would you trust me to fulfill the deal?"

"First, everything that's transpired in this room has been recorded and can be delivered to Israel in an instant. Secondly, we know about your relationship with Zara Zayani. We've suspected her for some time as being an agent. She will remain free at your dispensation, but if you fail us, she will be taken into custody and tried as a spy. Prison for a woman like her would be painful in many ways. So painful she might wish for death."

"Surely you realize I might tip her off and she could flee Lebanon for France."

"She won't flee."

"Why not?"

"Her partner photographer Faiz Khouri was picked up this evening. I'm afraid he is to remain in our custody. I don't believe she wishes to be the cause of his death. I understand he has a family in Marseilles. She has a choice. Keep him safe by cooperating with us and continuing in her persona as a journalist for *Le Figaro* or sign his death warrant. Zara's situation is similar to your own. She, too, will work for us."

"I need some time to consider this."

"Of course. Perhaps you'd like to see your nephew. It might help in your deliberations. Afterward, you'll be driven to Beirut, where you'll be set free. We will be in touch with you. I trust you will make the right decision."

Aryeh followed a prison guard down a dark hallway with flickering motion detector lights. It was dark and dank and elicited an eerie otherworldliness. The guard unlocked a steel door. Opening it, he motioned for Aryeh to enter. Once inside, the door was locked behind him. The room was cold and smelled of piss and shit. A single light bulb lit the darkness. A cot rested against a wall, and on it, a figure huddled under a thin blanket.

"Gideon?"

The prone figure on the cot tried to speak, but a coughing spasm overtook him. The broken man shook uncontrollably.

Aryeh perched on the edge of the cot and raised Gideon up to a sitting position and studied his face. Red rimmed, dilated eyes stared back at him. His face covered with bruises and dried blood was unrecognizable. Aryeh could only imagine the beatings he'd endured. Gideon's once muscled body had withered to skin and bones. But he was alive, and Aryeh focused on the positive.

"*Dodd* Aryeh?" Gideon's voice was hoarse and sickly. His body trembled, and his face was flushed. Aryeh felt his forehead, and his palm burned with heat.

"Yes, I'm here Gideon. I'm going to get you out of this hellhole, I swear it."

Gideon's shoulders shook, and he broke into tears. "I never thought I'd ever see any of you again. I've done my best to believe, but…" He broke into sobs, his words garbled and incoherent. Drugged. He swayed, and Aryeh helped him to lie back down.

"Listen to me, Gideon. Arrangements will be made soon for you to be released, but it's going to take a while longer. You need to be brave."

"Oh, God, you're leaving me here!" He gagged. "I need to throw up."

Aryeh stood and grabbed the only thing in the room, a bucket filled with refuse. He held Gideon's shoulders as the younger man puked into the bucket. When he finished, Aryeh used the filthy blanket on the bed to wipe his face. "I don't want to leave you, son, but I promise you it won't be long before you are free. Okay?"

Gideon nodded. "All I want is to go home, Uncle."

"Have they been drugging you and beating you daily?"

"In the beginning, they beat me, but when they realized I had nothing to tell them, the beatings stopped. Today was the first time they drugged me and beat me again." A wry laugh escaped his lips. "Not a good thing to be punched when your head is already spinning."

Aryeh smiled and stroked Gideon's head affectionately. "I see you've kept your sense of humor. It is important for your sanity. Why isn't there any water in this room?" He stood and banged on the door. When the guard returned, he ordered him in Arabic to fetch some water. Thankfully, the guard returned a minute later with a bottle of water. Aryeh thanked him and returned to Gideon. He twisted off the top and raised Gideon's head, helping him to drink. When he finished, Gideon managed a smile. "I'm ashamed to have you see me like this."

"I promise you'll recover and heal. You'll regain your strength, and this will become just a distant nightmare."

"I'll never forget this, Uncle. But I've learned how precious life is and will never take it for granted again."

Aryeh nodded. Agreeing and offering support was the only thing he could do for the moment. Getting his nephew out of Beirut and home to Israel was what mattered. "Listen, Gideon, the sooner I get out of here, the sooner you'll be free. I promise I will not let you down." He stood and walked to the door and banged. It opened. He turned back to his nephew and said, "*Lahitraot.*"

Gideon's eyes brimmed with hope. The word's meaning struck deep—goodbye, for now, see you again soon.

Aryeh was led back to the room where he'd met with Amir. The officer sat where he'd left him. "I hope your reunion was satisfactory."

It was all Aryeh could do not to explode and grab the man by the throat and strangle him. "If you want my cooperation, I suggest you tend to my nephew. He needs to see a doctor. He has a fever and a violent cough. I want him made comfortable in a clean room with a comfortable bed and fed broth and tea. I want him released alive—not dead."

"Have you come to a decision?"

"Yes. I agree to your terms. Now explain to me what I tell Mossad as to how I arranged the miraculous release of Israeli prisoners?"

"You are holding seventeen Hezbollah operatives in your prisons. We will exchange your three for seventeen of ours."

"Fine. As soon as I return to Beirut, I will make the arrangements with the government. It shouldn't be too hard to convince them."

"Oh, by the way, until you do, I'd be careful. Your government sent a team to extradite you to Israel. It seems your theft of the diamonds does not sit well with them. It's a pity we can't relieve you of them."

"Thanks for the tip-off, I'll keep my head down until Mossad calls them off."

Amir smiled cynically. "*Lahitraot.*"

The use of Aryeh's parting word to Gideon indicated his conversation with Gideon had been wiretapped. "I'll do my part. You make sure you take care of yours."

Amir shouted, and the men who'd transported him returned. A sack again covered his head, and he was led from the room.

They left him at the Starbucks where they'd picked him up. He took a taxi back to his hotel room.

Aryeh's room was intact, no breach, no entry, or disturbance.

It was 2 a.m., but the ever-alert Ramsad picked up on the first ring. Aryeh gave him a concise report. The Ramsad listened without interruption. When Aryeh finished, the Ramsad spoke.

"We need to coordinate this with Cyrus and the team. We need to find out where they're assembling the missiles. Zara may hold the key."

"I'll speak with her today. See if she's heard from Mustafa." He was worried about Zara—her cover now blown put her life in grave danger.

"My gut instinct is Mustafa is involved with the EMP plot. He may even be the big *macher* directing the EMP operation. I'll speak to the prime minister about the prisoner exchange. Oh, did I mention we found the mole."

"Bingo. Great news. Who is he?"

"He's dead. The murderer tried to make it look like the young man murdered his Palestinian girlfriend and then turned the gun on himself. Forensics didn't buy it for a minute. We suspect blackmail. It's a tragedy. The boy held promise. We're not releasing any information on it. We'll notify the parents about his death, but not the circumstances. It will serve no one."

"I need to huddle with Cyrus and the team. We need to coordinate, and he needs to know Nasrallah is on to him."

"Careful." The Ramsad always told him to be careful even though he knew Aryeh was an expert at spotting a tail and losing it. He also knew Aryeh never took chances when it came to discovery.

"Yes, *Aba*."

The Ramsad chuckled. "You are a pain in my *tuchus*. Remember, you mustn't be seen with anyone from the team."

"No need to worry, fearless leader. Cyrus and I will figure something out. Between the two of us, we could probably thread the eye of a needle blindfolded."

CHAPTER 17

Baalbek, Lebanon
Cannabis Farm

Mustafa had stopped communicating with Nasrallah when he arrived at the cannabis farm, where the building of the missile was taking place. The use of cell phones was forbidden. It was crucial for the security of the operation. The two-story building had at one time been a greenhouse, but in recent months the innocuous building had been remodeled by Hezbollah and reconstructed into an assembly plant and rocket launch facility. From the outside, it remained ordinary, but inside it was state-of-the-art.

Mustafa observed activities below from a second-story catwalk bordering the circumference of the building. From the ground, space was open to the ceiling. Physicists, engineers, and others worked below. Everything was proceeding as planned, but Mustafa was still bothered. Not about the staging for the EMP delivery system, or the danger of loading the nuclear payload. He was upset over his conversation with Nasrallah. The secretary-general had informed him he suspected Zara was a spy. Mustafa had already intuited the possibility and wasn't surprised by it. After all, a journalist meeting with the supreme leader was unusual. What was strange was his reaction. He found the knowledge had only intensified his attraction to her.

It set the stage and provided a landscape of intrigue and desire. A cat and mouse game with sexual overtones. Zara had become a prize for him to win, a challenge he couldn't resist. He was compelled by the mystery surrounding her, it made him want to see how close to the fire he could get without getting burned, but the missile assembly operation would require extra precautions. He would never allow a woman to take down his operation or interfere with his plan.

An extra layer of security would be necessary. More boots on the ground to protect a mission nearing completion. One layer of subterfuge employed seemed to be working. The nuclear physicists and engineers held at the hotel in Beirut were merely actors. The real scientists and experts had been flown in by private jet to a small airfield, and immediately transported to the cannabis farm and put to work upon arrival. Staying one step ahead of any possible surveillance or breach in security by Mossad or the CIA was crucial to the outcome.

In the meantime, there was nothing for him to accomplish at the cannabis farm. He was anxious to see Zara again. He knew he was becoming obsessive about her, but Mustafa believed he held the winning cards to control her.

Beirut, Lebanon

Cyrus sat in the computer center at the safe house with Zvi and Ash watching a live newsfeed coming out of Israel. The United States, France, and Britain were carrying out bombing raids in Syria in response to the dictatorship's use of chemical weapons on women and children. A scientific research facility in Damascus, a chemical weapons storage facility west of Homs and another command post near Homs were targeted and destroyed. There were unconfirmed reports of auxiliary targets hitting a military base near Dimas, an army depot in Qalamoun, and a fortification near Kiswah where Iran was believed to be building a base. In the prior weeks, Israel had carried out airstrikes, hitting a Syrian airbase being used by Iran to launch drone strikes against Israel.

Ash whistled. "Look at the fireworks. The mullahs aren't going to be so happy about the Western devils spoiling their fun in Syria. Solatani is going to sprout a lot more gray hair, don't you think?"

Cyrus wasn't as thrilled as the team's sniper. "It's going to put a lot more pressure on Hezbollah to retaliate. Sure enough, a minute later, Hassan Nasrallah released a braggadocio statement, "The forces of the resistance today have the ability, the power, and the missiles to hit any target in Israel." It was a threat resounding with clarity in both Tel Aviv and the Beirut safe house. Cyrus knew there was only one acceptable outcome, the destruction of Hezbollah's nascent nuclear threat. Nothing less than complete eradication, regardless of the cost or loss of life on either side, would be satisfactory.

"Jeez, I'd love to get that monster in my riflescope sights," mumbled Ash under his breath.

"What we need is to find where they're building those damned rockets before it's too late." Cyrus's hand scrubbed his bearded cheek. He was feeling impotent and frustrated by the lack of progress with the mission. Inactivity had his thoughts straying to Layla, and he couldn't afford to be distracted by his worry for her.

"At least the North Koreans haven't moved from the hotel, so there can't be too much going on yet," Ash added.

Cyrus looked at Ash as if he was a savant. *Of course, they hoodwinked us.* "Shit!"

"What? Did I say something wrong?" Ash asked, seeing the change come over Cyrus's face.

"No. You said something right." He swiveled his chair to Zvi. "Tell Nira and Yitz to forget the Koreans and report back here."

Zvi's brow wrinkled. "Why? What's up?"

"Those Koreans are planted. They're being staged to throw off any surveillance. I need to talk to Aryeh, face to face. What do you suggest, Zvi?"

"We use the dropbox and arrange a meeting somewhere inconspicuous but in the open."

"What like a Turkish steam bath?"

"Might work." Zvi grinned. "Kind of like a James Bond novel."

"Do it." His thoughts strayed to Layla again. "By the way, has headquarters sent you any photos of the bastard who blew up the bus?"

Zvi cocked his head. "What are you psychic. I'm just uploading a complete dossier now."

Cyrus pulled up a chair beside Zvi. "Load them up. I want to see them."

Zvi hit some keys, and a series of photos cropped from video footage appeared on the screen. Next to the images scrolled all pertinent information known about the terrorist. Cyrus studied the photos, committing the man's face to memory. "No matter what, I'm not leaving Lebanon without killing this animal."

Ash leaned over his shoulder. "Please, boss, let me be the instrument of your revenge?"

"Believe me, Ash, it would be my pleasure. I don't care who gets him so long as he's dead."

"Do you want me to print everything for you?" Zvi asked.

"No, just make sure I can get into it with my phone. I want Aryeh to see him. As for me, I won't forget his face until he's dead."

CHAPTER 18

Beirut, Lebanon

Zara paused in the middle of the square. She was dressed in a tailored mint green pantsuit and matching pashmina with wedged sandals. Dark sunglasses and a hat completed the look. It was warm, and she removed the pashmina, slipping it into her handbag. Her sharp eyes scanned her surroundings—she'd spotted a tail a few blocks back when she'd stopped at a shop window.

Mustafa had texted Zara the night before and wanted to meet her for lunch. She'd feigned an overwhelming amount of work but finally acquiesced. She'd agreed to meet him at Martyr's Square in front of the Al-Amin mosque. She'd chosen to walk to Café Em Nazih, a garden restaurant known for its lovely setting and privacy.

Adjusting her hat, she checked to see if the tail was still there. Nothing caught her eye, but she was in a large public square with a hundred or more people milling around. It would be easy to keep a distance and still keep her in view. She sighed. It didn't matter whether she was being followed. There was nothing secretive about meeting Mustafa in broad daylight.

She scanned the square again for Mustafa when someone came up behind her and whispered in her ear. "Looking for someone?"

She whirled. "Mustafa!" His beard was gone, and his dark wavy hair was neatly trimmed. Wearing a sleek dark gray suit and blue tie, he looked like a prosperous businessman or a *GQ Magazine* cover model. She couldn't see his eyes behind his mirrored sunglasses, but he grinned at her, his teeth blindingly white in the sunshine.

He continued to grin, enjoying her startled gaze.

"You look different...I..." Was it possible she was at a loss for words? *He was much better looking than she'd remembered.*

"It's my disguise. Westerner. What do you think?"

"I wouldn't have recognized you."

He frowned. "Are you saying you're not too keen on the way I normally look."

"No. It doesn't matter to me one way or the other. But yes, I'll grant you it's a good disguise."

His smile widened. "I love it when you do that."

"Do what?"

"Hide from the chemistry between us. Pretend you feel nothing."

"I don't deny it, Mustafa. I'm just putting it in a proper perspective." She looked around the square. "Are you taking me to lunch or not?"

"I most certainly am." He opened his arm with a flourish, indicating she lead the way. It was a fifteen-minute walk to the restaurant, and the weather was delightful. They strolled along George Haddad Street, their light conversation encompassing the beauty of the day and the bustle of activity around them.

Everything seemed carefree and airy until they came to an intersection at Youssef Hani Road. Mustafa's phone rang in his pocket, and he reached for it, pausing mid-step. Zara looked back at him and stepped off the curb. A screech of tires and the roar of an engine drowned out every other sound. She turned toward the sound and froze. A car was barreling toward her as if fired from the muzzle of a gun. In the blink of an eye, her life flickering before her like an old black and white filmstrip. She was going to die just as she'd lived. Alone. With no great love of her life to mourn her passing. There would be nothing to recall. Every minute of her existence was in a file some office clerk would bury in a drawer, barely glancing at the description: Zara Zayani, TOP-SECRET.

She closed her eyes and said a silent prayer. Strong arms grabbed her, and she fell backward to the ground. She heard a groan and the sound of the vehicle racing past at such a speed, she felt a whoosh of air when it passed.

She felt her lungs fill with oxygen and opened her eyes to the blue sky above.

"Shit! What the hell just happened?"

She was lying on top of Mustafa, who was cursing. "I-I'm not sure. That car almost ran me down." She rolled to the side and placed her hand on his chest. "Are you okay?"

He clutched his side and grimaced. "I think I'm just bruised and had the wind knocked out of me." He raised his head and squinted in the direction of where the car had headed. He'd lost his sunglasses, and the squinting produced fine lines around his eyes. "That was a premeditated hit."

She nodded.

He reached back and touched the back of his head, wincing. When his fingers came away, they were smeared with blood.

"You're bleeding, Mustafa. You need medical attention."

"I'll be fine. What I need is to get my bearings and clear my head." His eyes looked dilated, and he shook his head, confirming her diagnosis.

"Forget about the restaurant. Let's grab a taxi and go to my place, and I'll take care of that cut." She opened her purse and grabbed some tissue and handed them to him.

He sat up and pressed the tissues to the back of his head. "Okay. I've lost my appetite anyway."

Zara cleaned the gash on Mustafa's scalp and then applied antiseptic. Gently she adhered a band-aid to his cut. He'd sat quietly on the toilet seat cover while she ministered to him. She raised his chin and met his gaze. "You and I may see the world differently, but you saved my life. Thank you."

He rose towering over her and grinned. He took her hands in his, kissing one palm and then the other. She didn't pull away. It was endearing the way he showed his affection. "You're welcome."

She was glad he didn't say more. She wanted to pretend for a little while longer, that he wasn't who he was, and she wasn't who she was. She wanted to hate him, but he'd saved her life.

She was very aware of how intimate their current situation was, and from the way he was gazing at her, so did he.

"Maybe we should eat something," she suggested with a quirk of her lips. "Would you like some lunch now? I can whip something up."

"I'd like that."

He was behaving like a gentleman, and she found it disconcerting. It would be better for her if he displayed coldness, aggression, selfishness.

He followed her to the kitchen, where she opened a bottle of red wine and filled two glasses. She handed one to him, but he refused. "You know I don't drink. The other night was an exception."

"I'm not taking no for an answer. You need to relax, and a little wine will suppress the pain. Besides, I need a glass, and I don't want to drink alone."

He took the wineglass from her and took a sip. "It's good."

"It's French. Of course, it's good."

He leaned against the counter, watching her layer a baguette with sliced figs, cheese, and escarole. She whisked some vinaigrette in a bowl and poured it on top and cut it in half, placing each half on a plate. She paired the sandwich with tabbouleh salad and set the dishes on the table.

Mustafa sat beside her and took her hand and pressed his lips to her fingers. "Thank you."

She didn't pull away, and they gazed into one another's eyes for several seconds. "You saved my life. A baguette couldn't possibly equal that."

"Watching you make it for me did."

"Don't be silly, I made it as much for me, *mon ami*. It seems near-death experiences make me hungry." She took a bite and smiled with satisfaction. "Would you care to enlighten me as to who called you at the exact moment that I stepped off the curb? I think we can agree, it's rather suspicious."

His eyes darkened. "I don't know, but I intend to find out. I can't believe how close I came to losing you."

She chuckled and shook her head. "I think you would have survived losing me just fine. But someone is clearly not happy with our friendship. They probably believe I'm a threat to you. Which makes me a threat to them."

"You may be right. But God has put you in my path for a reason." The low rumble of his voice was like a caress. "I do not believe in chance. When we bumped into each other at Hezbollah's headquarters, I was driven to know more about you. I admit what I felt was a physical attraction, but it's grown into something else since then. It's as if Allah placed you in my path for a reason. Perhaps he chose you for me."

She felt the color rise to her cheeks and looked away. "You don't know what you want or what Allah's plan is. You've never met another woman like me. You've told me you've never known passion or been in love. You're like a child who wasn't invited to the party. You just feel like you missed something. I could have been any woman."

He waved her words away. "I'm surprised at you, Zara. Someone as intelligent as you should be able to see this is about us and no one else. No other woman has ever had this effect on me."

"We are unsuitable Mustafa. We live in different worlds."

"What does it matter who we've been or what we are? The only thing we should care about is what we'll be together. I know you think it's impossible, but when we met, everything changed. It felt like magic. I knew we were meant for each other. Without knowing it, I've been waiting my whole life for you."

"You're right about that, I don't believe you. What is it you want from me? Am I the forbidden fruit you can't resist?"

"I could out-and-out deny it, but the truth is I don't know. Perhaps it's part of what I'm feeling, but I know what I feel whenever we're together." Mustafa shook his head and smiled. "Even arguing with you makes me feel alive. We can't always choose who we love, Zara."

He was right. Zara felt her own heart staging a rebellion. She was attracted to him, and no matter how she tried, she couldn't shove it under the rug. "You'd be better off looking elsewhere for love. I can only bring you trouble. You shouldn't be blind to the truth."

"I have never run from trouble, and I don't intend to do it now. I'm not afraid of the truth even if it reveals I've been wrong."

"What happened today is a warning to both of us." She took a deep drink, avoiding the directness of his gaze. She felt guilt at the change in the direction of her feelings. Mustafa was her mark, yet she was succumbing to an overpowering attraction to him. If she went by the manual, she should recuse herself from her investigation of him. Emotional involvement was strictly verboten. She needed to keep her promise to her murdered twin brother Jacob in mind. She needed to stay focused. Her life's purpose was to stop terrorists from killing and destroying innocent lives. The terrorist who had worn a suicide vest and blew himself up wasn't much different than the man courting her. By stopping Mustafa from launching an EMP attack, she was staying true to her promise…but sometimes, he said things that gave her pause. Words that made her rethink her life and actions. Had she reached the fork in the road and taken the wrong path? Had she gone right when she should have gone left? Was the direction of her life, leading to a dead-end?

"You should go." She stood and cleared the dishes from the table and deposited them in the sink. With her back to Mustafa, she regained her determination to resist her attraction to him. Washing the dishes gave her a moment to regain control. She scrubbed the plates much harder than necessary.

When his strong hands encircled her waist, she sucked in her breath. He pressed his body against her, and she could feel him trembling. The warmth of his breath filled her ear, "Don't fight what we're both feeling, *habibi*. Don't send me away. There is an old saying that when you save a life, that life belongs to you forever. It becomes your responsibility. You belong to me."

He turned her around, and before she could protest, his lips pressed on hers. The passion of his kiss invaded her senses, and all her protestations dissolved in an instant. Her wet hands rested on his back, and she returned his kiss. Pushing her against the sink, she felt the tautness of his muscles and the power of his desire. She knew if she didn't push him away now, she'd never push him away. *Dammit*. She was falling down the rabbit hole.

They broke apart gasping. Confusion and fire burned in Mustafa's gaze like twin emotions. No matter what they'd said before, she didn't expect such an intense reaction to a kiss, and judging from his face, neither had he. Then without a word, he picked her up in his arms and kissed her breathless again. "Which way to your bed?"

"Through the living room." She hardly recognized the desire in her voice. She was failing miserably at resisting him. At this moment, she wanted him, and she couldn't think beyond her passion.

He strode toward the back of the house, through the beads and tinkling bells that chimed as they passed through. He laid her on the silken coverlet. Stepping back, he undressed before her, his eyes never leaving hers until he stood naked. He was hard, and his shaft rose solidly from his groin. Everything about him turned her on, but it was the softness in his eyes that touched something that existed only in her dreams. In her life, there was no space for companionship or love, but somehow Mustafa, of all the men in the world, made her question her decision.

She sensed he felt the same by the rise and fall of his chest, the way his breath came unevenly. His excitement infected her. She wondered if he could hear her own heart thumping in her chest like a kettle drum. He approached hesitantly as if he were afraid that any minute, she might change her mind and order him away.

He lay beside her, not quite touching her. He confessed, "I'm a novice at this. My wife was the only woman I ever…I was never able to please her. Truth is, neither of us felt any desire for each other. I tried to convince myself it wasn't important, but now I know it is more important than anything." He cupped her face and gently kissed her. Delving into her, he explored her mouth. "Do you understand how sensual your kiss is to me? When we kiss, a whole new world opens to me, a world I've never known. It's a longing—achingly sweet—a yearning to know more."

"Why didn't you seek your pleasure sooner, from other women?"

"I listened to others speak of their conquests, but the sordidness of their boasts was unappealing to me. I wasn't looking for sexual release. When I saw you, I could no longer ignore what was missing in my life."

"*Coup de foudre.*"

"What does it mean?"

"Love at first sight."

He kissed her and pulled her close. "Yes, I think you're right." He took his time exploring her neck and ears. She couldn't help but be charmed by the way he patiently waited for her encouragement. She placed her palm against his heart and could feel his accelerated heartbeat. She ran her hands over his arms and his chest. His body was chiseled, the muscles tightened beneath the delicacy of her touch. *He's probably lived in training camps much of his life.* The pleasure in his eyes was spellbinding, but she remained detached enough to realize his passion for her might enable her to control him. "Don't you want to take my clothes off, *mon amour?*"

He smiled. "More than anything, *habibi*. Please don't think this foolish, but I've never undressed a woman before."

"Don't you think it's time you learned?" She laughed. "You didn't have any trouble removing your own clothing."

"That I know how to do." His laughter came from the deepest part of him, and it traveled through her and settled in her heart.

Her suit jacket was already off, but she still had on a sheer white silk blouse and pants. "Here, give me your hand." She placed it over her breast, holding his gaze. "Do you want to kiss my breasts?" He closed his eyes and inhaled deeply.

She sat up and unbuttoned her blouse and shrugged it off. Mustafa's gaze fixed on her lacy white bra. She slipped her pants off, leaving on her matching lace underwear. It was like leading a horse to water. His eyes burned with fire, but he didn't move. She cupped his face and drew it to her breast. His tongue brushed her nipple, protruding through the lace. "Do you like seeing a woman in pretty lingerie?"

"Very much." He slipped her bra straps off her shoulders and pulled the bra down to her waist, freeing her breasts.

His breath caught. "Your breasts are beautiful. The loveliest I've ever seen."

"You haven't seen too many from what I've gathered."

"I don't need to." He suckled her nipples, his tongue swirling. She arched into his mouth, a deep moan resonating from the deepest part of her. "Keep going," she whispered, raking her fingers through his hair. He squeezed her breasts together, his mouth sucking each nipple, his tongue grazing from one to the other. Not letting go, he kissed his way down her stomach. When he reached her lace panties, he buried his tongue and nose in her, inhaling her scent. "Oh...your body is Heaven on Earth." He pinched her nipples and pulled her panties down and ran his tongue up and down her slit. And then he was sucking her as if she were a piece of candy. She couldn't keep the moan from escaping, and her hips rose for more.

He murmured, looking up to see her response. "I love kissing you here." His fingers slid up and down her opening. "It's like kissing the petals of a flower. Tell me what to do to give you more pleasure." He stuck his finger inside of her, opening her, and flicked his tongue over her clit.

She could barely speak. "You're doing fine. Don't stop. Go with your desire."

"I desire to fill you with this." He stroked his cock. "I want you so much, I ache. It's painful this need for you. You do want me, don't you?"

She playfully slapped him on the shoulder. "Of course, you silly man. You need to take control before I change my mind."

She watched the fire ignite in his eyes and teased. "Or don't you like being in control?" She reached down and stroked him. He closed his eyes and sucked in his breath. Teasing him aroused her. She let go of his cock, knowing he couldn't take much more. "Make love to me. Let me feel your desire." She turned to her side and pushed her ass against his hardness.

"Mm...I've never done it like this."

"You're going to love it." She reached back and ran her hand over him, pulling him toward her. She stroked and rubbed his thickness against her wetness. He grabbed her waist and thrust into her with a growl. He finally understood what she wanted as he reached over her hip and delved his fingers into her moist center. He stroked her with each thrust. "Oh...*mon amour*..." She sighed. He was strong and hard, and her pleasure mounted with each penetration.

"Zara...*habibi*..." His moans echoed in her ear like the hot Sirocco wind across the Sahara Desert, "...you're mine, my love. I love you." He pounded against her, his breath ragged with his exertion.

When she exploded, it was as if the stars fell from the heavens and rained down around them, burning everything in their wake. He followed her like the tail of a comet, his lips pressed to her neck, growling her name in orgasm. If anything, he held her tighter and closer than any man had ever done before. As if by the press of his body against her, they could merge into one forever.

She wanted to resist him, tried to stop herself from liking him more than she should, but a battle raged within her. Why him? Of all the men she'd ever known, why did he draw such a buoyant feeling from her? Half-dozing in his arms, she realized none of her lovers had ever said they loved her, but Mustafa had, and for some reason, she believed him…

Could she change him? For a heartbeat, Zara entertained the notion. Could she bring him to her side?

Don't be a fool. He's groomed for only one purpose, to kill.

It was impossible. She had to regain control. This. This was all just a fantasy. *Remember! Think about all the innocents his kind have terrorized…* She must remain strong. Detached. Or all would be lost…

He was kissing her neck and collarbone. "All I want is to begin again, to love you every way imaginable, Zara. Can you understand that you've altered my world forever?"

I wish I could believe you. "Have I? Don't make promises in the heat of passion. You will never keep them."

He pulled out of her and rolled her over to face him. Strong arms encircled her, forcing her to look into his eyes. "You're wrong, Zara. Yes, this is a passion I'm not willing to let go of. Yes, I'm willing to risk everything I've ever believed in for you. Yes, I'll do anything to keep you safe. Yes, I've had you, and yes, I still want you. If anything, much more than before."

"Why?"

"Must we go through this again? I accept what God gives me in this life. I do not fight what comes naturally. What I feel for you is like breathing. It is a natural part of me. I have no reason to question why."

She sighed. "I'm willing to give you time to prove what you're claiming, and I'm willing to admit I want to believe you." *This has nothing to do with my feelings. I need to remain cold. Detached. Determined. I must find out where the missiles are.*

But no matter how she told herself to say in control, a tiny flower of hope unfurled in the most secret of places—her heart. She cupped his face. "When do you leave Beirut again?"

"I'm not sure. There are a few more things I need to take care of here." He kissed the tip of her nose. "I'm going to leave soon, but I'd like to see you for dinner. Since we missed lunch, I owe you a meal."

"You owe me nothing, Mustafa. I need to get to the office to finish up some work, but I could meet you for a late supper."

"Perfect. Everything about you is perfect."

She laughed and rolled on top of him. "But first…"

CHAPTER 19

Beirut, Lebanon

After Mustafa left, Zara went to the office she shared with her photographer. She'd tried to reach Faiz all afternoon with no success. He hadn't checked in with her, which was unusual. Faiz was unfailingly punctual. She couldn't imagine what could be holding him up. The man was meticulous about his work, whether it was his photography or his protection of her. Since she'd become entangled with Mustafa, she'd insisted Faiz keep a low profile. She didn't want to arouse Mustafa's suspicion about her relationship with him.

The satellite phone, the one linked to Aryeh alone, vibrated on her desk.

She blew out a breath of relief. Apart from everything going on with Mustafa, she'd been crazed with worry for Aryeh. "You certainly have taken your sweet time, *mon cheri*, in making contact. I've been worried about you. Not so much your safety as you hold the diamonds, and they'll do anything to get those."

"He knows."

"Who knows?" she asked, a chill skittered up her spine.

"Your cover is blown. Nasrallah, the whole fucking organization, knows you're a French agent."

"That's impossible."

"Do you know where Faiz is?" Aryeh asked.

"Tell me what you know, goddammit?"

"Faiz was picked-up. Hezbollah is holding him. They're going to make a deal with you, just like the one they made with me."

Bile rose in her throat. The thought of Faiz held captive by those monsters made her sick to her stomach. "You know I'll do whatever it takes to keep Faiz and Gideon safe. But what kind of deal are we talking about?"

"Listen carefully, Zara, you're going to agree to everything just like I did. Faiz's life depends on it, as does Gideon's. You'll be agreeing to work for

Hezbollah as a mole. Of course, this is only temporary. Once we destroy the missiles, it will all be over. Our message will ring loud and clear and put the fear of God in these animals. You'll be able to return to France. Regardless, your work in Lebanon is finished."

"*Merde*! Does Mustafa know?"

"I don't know if Mustafa knows. My guess is he knows they suspect you of being an agent."

"They tried to kill me today. Mustafa saved my life."

"Fuck! That makes sense. They're worried you might interfere in the operation, which means Mustafa is up to his ears. It's only going to get more dangerous for you. I hate to say it, but maybe you shouldn't continue to see him."

"Not a possibility. He's caught in my web. He's mine."

"Zara, you can't trust him. He's playing you."

"No, Aryeh. There are things beyond being an agent, things I know as a woman. He's hooked, and he won't harm me."

"Zara, do you hear yourself? Have you lost your mind?"

"He has this exaggerated belief that because he saved my life today, he's now responsible for it. I'll feed into his trust and bring out his male instinct to protect. It's the only way we're going to find out where they're building the rockets."

"I'm warning you he can't be trusted. He's a terrorist. Right now, his cock is muddling his mind, but he will sober up, and you'll be the first thing he sacrifices."

"Stop acting like a jealous lover and start acting like the spy who should be focused on protecting his homeland and the world. I can handle Mustafa."

She waited. She knew Aryeh was analyzing and mining the possibilities, the pros and cons of her relationship with Mustafa. "You're right, Zara. I'm not thinking straight. You're a pro, and if he believes your life is in danger, he'll keep you close. You're our best chance of figuring out where the hell they're building these weapons of mass destruction."

"Now you're thinking like the king of the jungle."

"I'll talk to Cyrus. There's some new tracking technology our scientists have developed. I used it when I went to see Gideon."

"Fine. I'm open to tracking technology if it's safe. I'm meeting Mustafa for dinner. When do you think I'll hear from Nasrallah?"

"Soon, I imagine. But I'm worried about another possible assassination attempt on you."

"I have a feeling Mustafa is ensuring my safety even as we speak."

"Be careful, Zara. He's a wolf in sheep's clothing."

It angered her, Aryeh was allowing his personal feelings to intervene. *But then again, you're the one fighting an insane attraction to a terrorist.* "I'm not Little Red Riding Hood, Aryeh. I'm highly experienced at unmasking men with razor-sharp teeth. *À demain, mon ami.*"

Hamra, Beirut

Clouds of steam enveloped Cyrus when he opened the door at the *Al bakawat,* a Turkish steam bath. He was sure Zvi was at this minute laughing his head off with Ash back at the safe house, the two of them trying to picture the covert meeting between Aryeh and himself, naked except for towels.

Zvi had taken Cyrus's jest of meeting Aryeh in a steam room and made it happen. The team nerd had torn a page out of Ian Fleming's famous spy novels and arranged for Aryeh and him to meet in the most public of non-public places. Wearing nothing but a towel and rubber slippers, Cyrus didn't feel like the master spy, *007,* what he felt was naked, unarmed, and vulnerable. He swore he would read the riot act to Zvi when he got back to the safe house.

It was the dinner hour, and fortunately, the baths weren't busy. Cyrus wore his disguise of brown contact lenses and a beard, which he hoped would stay glued to his face, given the heat and moisture. He carried his cell phone. If the billowing clouds of liquid heat or the sweat pouring down his body didn't cause his phone to malfunction, or his beard to take flight, it would be a miracle.

Squinting through clouds of steam, Cyrus saw one man sitting on a white-tiled step. The man was bent forward with a towel draped over his head, his elbows resting on his knees. Cyrus could just make out the man's thick, muscular calves, triggering a memory of a man with spiked blond hair, Bermuda shorts, and a Hawaiian shirt. He'd met Aryeh for lunch at Edna, a Persian restaurant in Ramat Hasharon. It was hard to believe only five months ago he'd faced the worst period of his life. He'd been devastated, believing Layla had been killed when a restaurant had been blown up in Manhattan. He'd wanted to join Aryeh's team and take vengeance against the terrorists. Aryeh had refused him then. But now their relationship had come full circle, and Cyrus was leading the same team. He sat next to Aryeh on the step. "I'm going to kill Zvi if my cell phone melts."

Aryeh removed the towel from his head and grinned. "Relax. How often do you get to shed a few pounds without busting your balls?"

"I'll keep my pounds, thank you." He squinted through the steam, thinking about the positives of meeting in what felt like Hell's kitchen. No one could keep video cameras or recording devices in working order under these conditions. "I've pulled Nira and Yitz off the North Korean scientists at the hotel. I believe Hezbollah has staged a diversion to throw us off. We've wired their rooms and phones. We can continue to monitor them, but I think we're being played."

"Makes sense. Have you spoken with the Ramsad?"

"Yes, I've heard the terms for your nephew's release. It's good to know I'm speaking with a newly conscripted mole working for Hezbollah. What about Zara? Any progress?"

"They tried to kill her. Nearly ran her down on the street. I'm worried about her, but there's nothing to be done. She's our best hope to finding out where they're building the rockets. She claims Mustafa has fallen head over heels for her."

"Classic honeypot trap. Older than time itself. A man in heat is an easy mark."

Aryeh wiped the rivulets of sweat running down his face. "Believe me, two can play that game. I'm not buying she's holding all the cards. I have no intention of letting her become the sacrificial lamb."

"You care about her that much?"

"Let's just say we share bonds that I'd rather not discuss."

Cyrus nodded. "Reading you loud and clear." He wiped off his cell phone screen, tapped a series of codes, and handed the phone to Aryeh. "Does this face ring any bells?"

"He's the bastard I negotiated Gideon's release with, and he anointed me as a mole for Hezbollah. He's a cold prick. A classic sociopath."

"He blew up the bus in Tel Aviv that nearly killed Layla and Cerise. He killed fifty innocents. I'd put him in the serial-killer-sick-mother-fucker category. The forensics team believes he asphyxiated the honeypot he was handling during sex with her. He shot her boyfriend, the Mossad mole, and tried to make it look like a murder-suicide. Take a look at the photo of Nasrallah with him in the background."

"He calls himself a general. What do you think, bodyguard, advisor, or assassin?" Aryeh hissed.

"I'd say all three."

"Doesn't surprise me. I take it you want this bastard dead?"

Cyrus frowned at the face on the phone. "I won't leave here until he's dead."

Aryeh smiled. "I'll bet our beloved angel of death, Ash, asked to be the deliverer of the sword of justice."

"He did. I'd like to do it myself, but I'll take dead anyway I can get it. So, what do you want to do with Zara?"

"She's seeing Mustafa tonight. I'll touch base with her tomorrow."

"What's wrong with tonight?"

The only sign of Aryeh's displeasure was the force with which he threw his towel to the floor. He grabbed a fresh one from the pile near the door. "Tonight, she'll be indisposed."

"Okay." Cyrus rubbed a towel over his face. "Let's see how that goes. What do you think about using the mole tracking system on her?"

"I mentioned it to her, and she's open. I'm just worried the bastard has memorized every inch of her body by now. I'm sure he'd notice."

"We could embed it in her scalp. Hide it under her hair. I doubt he's studied every inch of her head."

Aryeh's scowl deepened. "It might work. I'll explain it to her."

"It would go a long way in keeping her safe."

Aryeh drew his brows together. "I don't know why I'm so worried. Zara's a seasoned spy, but my gut tells me something is wrong with her. I can't put my finger on it. If I didn't know better, I'd swear she's got a thing for this bastard."

"I know it's not my place, but maybe you care for her more than you let on. Maybe you're a tad jealous." Cyrus wasn't about to start digging too deep into Aryeh's displeasure about Zara and the terrorist's entanglement. Suffice it to say, the steam surrounding them wasn't the only hot vapor circulating in the confined space.

"Maybe, you're right. But my instincts point to trouble ahead."

"Just don't let it cloud your thoughts or your actions. There is trouble ahead, the destruction of Hezbollah's missiles.

CHAPTER 20

Beirut suburb of Dahiya, Lebanon

Mustafa pulled up to the apartment building in Dahiya, the predominantly Hezbollah controlled neighborhood in Beirut in a Mercedes with black-tinted windows. He jumped out of the car, followed by two trusted bodyguards.

"Wait for me here," he told his men.

The buzzer sounded, and he entered through the electronic doors. After leaving Zara, he'd called and requested a meeting with the secretary-general.

He walked into a traditionally appointed living room with thick Persian rugs and a plush overstuffed red sofa. On the coffee table was an elaborately etched silver Persian tea service, with matching silver tea glass holders. A gift from the Ayatollah, he was sure. Steam rose from the cups, infusing the room with the fragrance of Jasmine.

Sheikh Hassan Nasrallah rose from the sofa, his aba or black robe covered him from head to toe. On his head, he wore a black turban, a symbol of his power and holy calling. Like the Ayatollahs of Iran, the secretary-general used every opportunity to reinforce his claim of being a direct descendant of Muhammed.

"Sayyid," Mustafa kissed the cleric on both cheeks.

Nasrallah's eyes glinted. "*Akhi*, there is no need for such formality between us. Have you brought me news from the cannabis farm?"

"Everything is proceeding as planned. There was a delay when a part came in damaged, but its replacement is coming from Tehran."

"Good, I'm pleased to hear it. At last, we will have a missile capable of carrying a small nuclear warhead. I've spoken with Tehran. With the Iran deal falling apart, the Ayatollah has no compunction about striking the Americans at the same time as we strike Israel." The general secretary leaned forward, bursting with enthusiasm. "The mullahs played the world into believing they'd ceased uranium production. What they did was shift their development of ICBMs to underground military bases."

Nasrallah looked upward. "It's a pity General Moghaddam didn't live to see his dream realized. May Allah bless his soul. He died a hero's death in the service of his people. Of all things, an explosion at a missile facility he secretly built."

A few seconds passed in silent memorial to the fallen hero. "The Ayatollah has indicated Iran is prepared to join us in a coordinated EMP attack against the two devils. Together we could completely disarm them and leave them powerless."

"Allah be praised. Will this mean a delay in our timetable?" Mustafa asked.

"Maybe a few days, no more. The Iranians have been ready for some time now. They never complied with the agreement. For them, it was business as usual. But what a windfall for us when the Americans delivered a planeload of money. It has financed our activities for years to come."

Mustafa blew on his tea. "Hassan, a strange thing occurred today."

"And what might that be, my son?"

Mustafa studied Nasrallah's face. "I was to have lunch today with Zara Zayani, but something happened."

"I've warned you she is trouble, Mustafa." Nasrallah avoided meeting Mustafa's gaze as he raised his teacup to his lips.

"You did warn me, and I took your warning to heart. However, the trouble did not come from Zara. An assassination attempt nearly ended her life. Had Allah not intervened, I too would have died."

"That is unfortunate." Nasrallah met his gaze. "Perhaps you should heed the warning. Sometimes it is dangerous to tempt fate. I will investigate it. Perhaps you have enemies unaccounted for among the people. You must take greater care, my son."

"I'm capable of enjoying Zara's company while also keeping her ignorant of what we've planned. In fact, if anything, I can throw her off the scent of what we are planning. What better way to prevent a too curious journalist from learning too much?"

"She's not only a journalist, Mustafa. She's a spy, an agent for the DGSE. You're playing with fire."

"A spy?"

"Yes. We've suspected for some time Zara was a French agent. Even though she has written favorably about the organization and we've found her to be useful, that usefulness could be coming to an end."

Mustafa showed no reaction to Nasrallah's revelation. "Perhaps my relationship with her becomes more valuable now."

Nasrallah waved his hand dismissively. "Ridiculous."

"Who better to manage her than me? If she's proven valuable in the past, who's to say she won't be even more valuable in the future? We'll need a way to explain our attack on Israel to the rest of the western world. Not that they've ever cared much as to the fate of the Jews."

Nasrallah stroked his beard. "You pose an interesting proposition. You should know that we've managed to recruit a Mossad agent. Someone who's been a thorn in our foot for some time. Zara brought him to our attention, which means they share close ties. She could be working with him, who knows?"

Nasrallah's emphasis was clear. He was insinuating that Zara and the Mossad agent might share a sexual relationship. Mustafa refused to be drawn into Nasrallah's trap.

Nasrallah continued. "Turning this Mossad agent will provide immeasurable access to Israel's secrets. Of course, that presumes Israel continues to exist. We took her photographer, also an agent, into custody. We'll use him to recruit her and keep her in line."

"Allah be praised. A perfect situation and a great credit to you. Then my relationship with her can be useful to us. I can be the guarantee that she doesn't double-cross us."

"Perhaps you're right, but I warn you she can't be trusted."

"I trust only in Allah."

The two men sat in silence for a moment. The door to the apartment swung open, and Amir, dressed in military fatigues, entered. Mustafa eyed Amir warily. Amir had proven himself to be a man who would do anything to retain his dominant position, and Mustafa didn't trust him. A whispered rumor had circulated that Amir Haddad, who'd overseen his uncle's security in Damascus, had intentionally slipped up, allowing the Israelis to assassinate his uncle. Mustafa felt certain Amir would do whatever it took to further his own agenda, including eliminating anyone who got in his way.

"*As-salamu alaykum*," Amir greeted both Nasrallah and Mustafa. "To what do we owe this honor, Mustafa? I understood you were preparing for the apocalypse in the Beqaa Valley."

Mustafa smiled. "Things are proceeding to plan, but I am not needed there yet. I had things to attend to here in Beirut."

"Yes, I imagine you do."

Mustafa turned to Nasrallah. "You will consider all we have spoken about?"

Nasrallah smiled. "All will be taken into consideration."

Mustafa rose. "Then I will take my leave. There are security issues I must address."

"Let me know if I can be of any help." Amir stood, towering over Mustafa, and offered his hand.

Reluctantly, Mustafa shook Amir's proffered hand. "Yes, you will be foremost on my mind should I need assistance in the days ahead."

Mustafa sat in the back seat of his Mercedes, staring out the window. His head was spinning. His reassurances from Nasrallah were non-existent, and Amir's arrival at the apartment and incendiary remarks only furthered his discomfort. It was impossible to ignore the truth, Zara was in grave danger. Protecting her would bring him in direct opposition to his commander's wishes. But his feelings for her made it impossible for him not to protect her. He needed to find a way to fulfill his promise to his father to disarm and destroy Israel and keep Zara safe from the monster, Amir. He'd heard about Amir. The man was a misogynist and a sadist. There was ugliness in his eyes, and Mustafa didn't put anything past him. The thought of him anywhere near Zara sent chills down Mustafa's spine.

He left the car about a block from Zara's office.

Zara buzzed him in and stood with her hands on her hips. "What are you doing here? I thought we weren't going to meet until this evening. I told you I had work to do."

"I'm sorry, but our plans need to change." He embraced her and held her gaze. "Zara, you are in danger, and I want to keep you safe."

She pulled away, putting some distance between them. "What are you—"

"I met with Nasrallah, and what he said, I believe, threatens you. I want to take you to a place where you'll be safe. It's a vineyard in the Beqaa Valley, not far from where my mission is unfolding. It belonged to my uncle. Only those loyal to my family know about it. You'll be safe there, and I can see you as much as I want. Don't say no before seriously considering my offer."

"Mustafa, you're crazy. I can't just run away and leave my life, my job. I know you probably don't think much of a woman who works, but I'm a professional, and I've worked hard to get this far. Besides, I don't walk away from danger. I never have, and I'm not going to start now."

"*Habibi*, I know you work for the DGSE, Nasrallah told me. I know your job as a journalist is a cover."

Disbelief and denial were written on her face, but Mustafa knew better. He knew her first response would be to deny she was a spy. He didn't care. If anything, he admired her for it. He was fascinated by a woman who cast aside her traditional role and yet managed to retain her femininity. "He's going to blackmail you and force you to become a traitor to France. You'll end up working as a mole in the service of Hezbollah."

"I won't do it."

"You won't have a choice. It won't last long because you're a threat. I'm almost certain Nasrallah and his henchman, Amir Haddad, will eliminate you after all of this is said and done. You must listen to reason. They've already made one attempt on your life."

She arched a delicate brow. "Why don't you want to eliminate me? After all, you claim to know the truth."

"I can't. I have deep feelings for you. Besides," he added with a grin, "I saved your life once. I believe Allah has placed your future in my hands."

"I know you believe that now, Mustafa, but you may live to regret this. Your world, for good or bad, worked perfectly well before I came into your life."

"It did, but meeting you changed everything. I can never go back to who I was." He wrapped his arms around her, forcing her to meet his gaze. "Come with me."

"And what happens once you've accomplished your mission?"

"I will have fulfilled my promises to my father, uncle, and brother. I don't want to end up as they did. I have bank accounts in Switzerland and the Cayman Islands. There is a plastic surgeon in Switzerland who will alter my face." He smiled. "Of course, I might not be quite as handsome as I am now, but who knows, maybe I'll be better looking."

"Are you saying you'd give everything up for me and disappear? You'd never return to Lebanon and Hezbollah."

"Yes. My family has given enough blood for Hezbollah. Hezbollah and my path have diverged, we are no longer in alignment. I want more from this life than a trail of dead bodies. I want you, Zara. I love you."

She broke from his embrace and turned her back to him. He hoped she wasn't searching for a way out. Turning, she challenged him. "This is crazy. Why not leave now?"

"I can't. I must fulfill the promises of the past."

Her frown expressed disbelief. "What could be worth continuing in this madness when you know it will put us both in danger?"

How much could he share with her? He had no intention of letting her out of his sight. Could he afford a mea culpa? "Zara, I told you what I'm working on could change the world as we know it. It will eliminate our enemies. I have to see it through."

"I see. And this thing you are planning will mean the death of millions of innocents."

He shrugged. "Wars are not won by the meek. It is Allah's will."

She stared at him, her face an unreadable mask. Then she turned and began to pace.

"Think of the children, Zara. The oppression inflicted on them by the Israelis."

"By whom, Mustafa? Who oppresses them? Hezbollah and Hamas do. Your Hezbollah uses them as human shields. Your Hezbollah teaches them to hate and to dream of an endless war."

"Don't you understand it all stops when our enemies are gone?" He was weary of the conversation. "We have to leave. We'll go to your place so you can pack what you need. Every minute we procrastinate puts you in more danger. A week from now, you and I will disappear. Your career as a spy is over either way. Hezbollah will use you and then make you disappear."

The look on her face mirrored the fear of an animal caught in a snare. Mustafa took hold of her shoulders, stopping her pacing. "Come with me. Trust me."

"I don't seem to have any other option," she whispered.

He kissed her forehead. "Get your purse. We need to go."

Zara looked around the apartment that had been her home for the last two years. She couldn't believe she was going to walk out the door and never set foot in it again. She'd told Aryeh that Mustafa had fallen under her spell, but things were moving faster than she'd imagined. She should be reveling in her success. Mustafa had fallen completely into her trap and was taking her with him to the Beqaa Valley. If all went according to plan, she'd be able to figure out where the missiles were being staged. It was so unlike her to harbor any feelings for her target, but for some reason, Mustafa had stirred something inside her. She chided herself on her insanity. He was a terrorist, and she was a compromised spy. Where the hell could this possibly lead? *All his confessions of love are getting to me. Weakening my resolve.* She thought of Jacob and gathered her strength.

Don't think about it. Stay focused on the mission. This is the breakthrough you've been waiting for, you've reached the eagle's nest. But what good was it? She couldn't stop Mustafa or the EMP deployment alone. She needed Aryeh. She needed to let him know what was happening, where she was going.

Most importantly, she needed a few minutes alone to text him. "*Mon amour*, sit and relax while I make us some tea. While you refresh, I'll pack a bag."

"We have to hurry, *habibi.* The sooner we leave Beirut, the better."

She caressed his face. "A few minutes won't matter." She took his hand and led him to the sofa. He grabbed her about the waist and buried his face in her neck.

"I want you to know I'm fighting my desire to make love to you right now. I want you."

She cupped his face in her hands and met his gaze. "Don't tempt me."

He pulled her onto his lap and kissed her. When their lips parted, he smiled. "Go make the tea, *habibi.*"

She returned with a tray and placed a teacup with a plate of honey biscuits in front of him. "I'll go pack." Taking her tea with her, she disappeared into the bedroom. She kneeled and pulled a suitcase out from under the bed. She pulled clothes from the drawers and began packing. Every few minutes, she paused and listened but could hear no sound from the other room. Grabbing her satellite phone and her gun from the drawer, she slipped into the bathroom, closing the door behind her. She put her toiletries and makeup into a cosmetic bag. When finished, she turned on the faucet and let the water run. She texted Aryeh: *Leaving with Mustafa for the Beqaa Valley to a vineyard. He knows I'm an agent. I'll try to tell you where I am. Things have escalated. Time is running out.*

"Zara?" Mustafa was at the door.

"Coming." She threw the phone and gun in with her toiletries and zipped the bag closed.

The door opened, and Mustafa entered. "Are you ready?"

"Nearly." She grabbed the toiletry bag and hurried past him. She threw it into her suitcase. He followed her and watched as she continued to pull things from her closet. Holding a pile of clothes, she managed to hide her phone charger between the folds without him noticing. She buried it beneath the pile of clothing in the suitcase.

He wrapped his arms around her and breathed in her ear. "Bring something sexy?"

She smiled. Why was she worried? He only had one thing on his mind. When she got to the vineyard, she'd find a way to inform Aryeh of her location. "What should I bring?"

"Surprise me."

She turned in his arms and kissed him. "So, you like surprises, do you? Let me see if I can find something a sexy spy on the run might wear." She slipped from his arms and went to the closet, returning with some frilly garments. She opened the suitcase and added them to the pile. Turning, she bit her lip. "Should we go?"

"Yes. Are you okay? You're not regretting your decision, are you?"

"I'm fine. The adventure continues."

"Yes, *habibi*. We will share this adventure together. I will do everything in my power to make you happy."

She smiled, but inside, her stomach was churning. If she intended to destroy Mustafa, why couldn't she extinguish her dangerous attraction to him? They had no future. He represented everything she'd sworn her life to combating. She needed to get a grip on the reality of their relationship. His words meant nothing, and as stimulating as their sex had been, they were unsuited and held different beliefs and opposing worldviews. She needed to separate herself from all emotional entanglements with him. He was determined to keep his promises to his father, uncle, and brother, and she was just as committed to keeping hers to her murdered brother. In the end, she would kill Mustafa, walk away, and never look back.

CHAPTER 21

Beirut, Lebanon

Shit! Aryeh texted Zara back, knowing she might not be able to answer. *You're putting yourself in danger. You can't trust him. Dammit, Zara, why didn't you put him off for a few hours? We have no way of tracking your movement. Text me as soon as you can. Be careful!!*

He knew going to her place would do no good. She was doing what a good agent should do. She was embedding herself with the enemy. She knew how to take care of herself, but his sixth sense warned him she was in danger.

Cyrus and the team needed to set up in the Beqaa Valley. She said they were going to a vineyard. At least the team had something to go on, a vague location.

He should have waited until nightfall, but there wasn't any time to waste. He needed to get to the safe house and inform Cyrus of what was going on with Zara. They needed to confer with the Ramsad. It was time to kick the operation into high gear. They'd been working outside the grid because of the mole at Mossad, but now the traitor mole was dead, and the worry over the mission being compromised was no longer necessary. The team needed Mossad and the IDF's backup. Intelligence and military cooperation would be instrumental to their success in stopping an EMP explosion.

He took the stairwell instead of the elevator and exited a side door at the hotel. He hopped a fence and cut through the back entrance of a restaurant. He walked through the kitchen and main dining area, then exited and crossed the street. For a few blocks, he meandered—window shopping as if he had no destination in mind. When he was sure he wasn't being followed, he hailed a cab.

Amir had tailed Mustafa to Zara's office building and then to her residence. His car was parked several blocks away. He positioned himself at a bus stop close enough to observe but far enough away not to be seen. When the lovers began loading the car with luggage, he'd made the call to Nasrallah, reporting what was suspected. Mustafa was deeply involved with the journalist spy, and his trustworthiness might be compromised.

"I do not believe Mustafa's behavior is treasonous," Nasrallah said. "However, I am deeply disappointed in his foolishness and share your concern."

Amir knew Nasrallah was unable to give the order to eliminate, but years of working with the secretary-general had taught Amir well how to manipulate Nasrallah. "I think you are right, Sayyid. I cannot imagine Mustafa being disloyal."

"I'm relieved you see it that way, Amir."

"However, Sayyid, if I should discover he is, I would suggest you allow me to take things into my hands and deal with the situation. My desire is only to do what is best for the brotherhood."

"Your loyalty and advice are always appreciated. With great confidence, I entrust you to do what is necessary. Use your best judgment."

Amir resumed his surveillance of Zara's home. He studied the jean-clad journalist as she made her way to the Mercedes. Her dark hair was pulled back in a ponytail. He envisioned wrenching her head back by that tail and fucking her. He felt his blood settle in his dick, and he shifted in his seat. The thought of taking her had made him rock hard, and an image of strangling her when she orgasmed made his balls ache for satisfaction. Shura was beautiful, like a child, wanting to please. She was a child addicted to sadism. But knowing she enjoyed the pain had lessened his pleasure. Zara, on the other hand, would fight tooth and nail and would buck like a horse, which made subduing her ever more erotic.

He stood, feeling the press of his cock against his trousers. He needed to radio his tag team to pick up and follow the Mercedes. There was no time to waste. The drive to Baalbek in the Beqaa Valley was just under two hours, which he suspected was where Mustafa would take her.

Aryeh made sure he was clean of a tail before going to the safe house. He had the taxi drop him several blocks away and walked the remaining distance. The bolts on the door's locks slid back, and he entered. He found a beehive of activity at the hub of the operation in the tech center. "Zvi, everything tight?"

"Totally. You're in a virtual fortress, no breach is possible."

Ash sat in front of a screen, switching from camera to camera, observing the video feed that monitored the exterior of the house. "Street's clear. I don't see anything suspicious."

Cyrus shook hands with his counterpart. "What brings you here, Aryeh?"

"We need to relocate immediately to the Beqaa Valley to the farm Ash purchased. It's near Baalbek, isn't it?"

"Right under Hezbollah's nose. It's stockpiled and ready. Everything but the tech stuff is ready to go." Ash puffed out his chest.

"What's up, Aryeh? Why the urgency?" Cyrus asked.

Aryeh quickly briefed everyone on Zara's sudden departure with Mustafa. "Without the tracking device, we can't pinpoint her location. But her text to me gave us a good starting point, and I know she'll find a way to communicate. We need to be ready."

Cyrus turned to his team. "How soon can we leave?"

"I need a little more than an hour," Zvi said.

Cyrus looked around. "I'm sure the rest of you can be ready in less than that." He looked at his watch. "We leave here at twelve-hundred-hours. Get to work. I want this place thoroughly wiped down. Nothing remains that can ID us."

Everyone except Zvi and Aryeh left to prepare. "Are you coming with us?" Cyrus asked.

Aryeh shook his head. "Not yet. I'll join you once you're set up. I need to facilitate the prisoner exchange."

"Okay." Cyrus turned to the tech guru. "Before you break everything down, Zvi, put through a video satellite call to the Ramsad. We need to bring him up to speed."

Zvi's eyes darted back and forth between Aryeh and Cyrus. "You got it, boss."

Aryeh knew it must be strange to be answering to the present boss in the presence of his past boss, but it didn't bother him in the least. He was happy not to be shouldering the burden of the operation for once. He had total confidence in Cyrus's skills.

In seconds, the feed was up, and the Ramsad's face lit the screen. He looked as if he hadn't slept in weeks, which he probably hadn't. "*Az*, where are we?" He listened while Cyrus and Aryeh took turns filling him in.

"I'll have the Orfek satellite's orbit altered to fly directly over the Beqaa. We'll need those eyes in the sky. I've put the IDF on high alert to be ready for retaliatory actions. If they launch that missile, there will be nothing left

147

of Lebanon but a wasteland. The Iron Dome, of course, is always ready, but they tell me it's useless against an EMP attack. They insist an EMP rocket carrying a nuclear payload cannot be stopped once the booster disengages. The team must do whatever it takes to stop it on the ground. You are our best and last line of defense."

"We'll stop them, Noam," Cyrus assured.

"I know you will, son. In the meantime, Aryeh, the prisoner exchange is approved and ready. Let's get our soldiers out of there before the shit hits the fan. Then you can join the team in the Beqaa."

"How do you want this to unfold?" Aryeh asked.

"Contact Nasrallah, tell him we want this done ASAP, or else it isn't happening. We'll release the prisoners at the Shebaa Farms and take possession of Gideon there."

"They'll expect me to return with Gideon to Tel Aviv. All part of my new designation as their deep cover mole."

"We'll use a body double for you. The double will board the plane with Gideon. Everything will appear to be what they wanted. They will see you leave, but you won't."

"Where the Hell are you going to find another me?"

"Don't worry," he chuckled, "we keep a spare on hand. Could be your twin. A little younger, but what are we going to do?"

Cyrus laughed at the Ramsad's attempt at humor.

"Thanks for the knife in the gut, old man," Aryeh said.

The Ramsad joined Cyrus's laughter. "Cyrus, remember that double of yours who took your place at the Sorbonne?"

"Of course. No one in Iran ever suspected I was shuttling back and forth to Israel and training with the IDF and Mossad."

"Your double gained thirty pounds. He sits at a desk now. You look the same as you did then, he's gone to seed, but still smart as a tack. Okay, Aryeh, you have your work cut out, and Cyrus, I need to hear from you as soon as you're set up in the Beqaa. Aryeh, as soon as you hear from Zara, I want to know. We need to get Mustafa in our sights. It's time for Samson to bring down the temple."

CHAPTER 22

Outskirts of Beqaa Valley

"How much longer?" Zara stared out the window of the Mercedes Benz as it ascended the steep, rugged terrain over the Great Lebanon Mountain range. She was anxious to check her phone and hated the long drive. She'd never enjoyed extended road trips, even as a child. Mustafa had released his driver in Beirut for some reason and had decided to drive himself. The road, rutted and slushy, was poorly maintained. Every time the Mercedes hit a rut or skidded, she expected a flat tire or a broken axle. It was nerve-racking, and her nerves were already frayed. Mustafa also told her they were taking an alternate route, which was longer but safer.

"Don't worry, *habibi*." He took her hand and kissed it. "Soon, we will be out of the mountains." His eyes strayed to the rear-view mirror regularly, and she knew he was checking to make sure they weren't being followed.

"Is that Mount Hermon?" She nodded to a majestic snowy peak towering over the range in the distance.

He nodded. "Lebanon is the most beautiful country in the Middle East. Much like your France, don't you think?"

She nodded. "The views are spectacular, but I'm not overly fond of driving on second-rate roads in the snow."

Zara told herself to be patient. She wasn't in control for the moment, and there was no use worrying about it now. Instead, she focused on the beauty of the landscape. Snow flurries hit the windshield melting on impact. She ignored the squeak of windshield wipers that kept rhythm with the classical Arab belly dance folk music Mustafa had tuned in on the radio. She didn't mind keeping their conversation to a minimum. It allowed her time to gather her thoughts.

When they reached the summit, Mustafa took her hand and squeezed it. "The Beqaa Valley. It won't be much longer."

She gazed at the fertile valley below. It looked like a patchwork quilt alternating between greenery and snow-covered fields. She tried not to imagine what it would look like after a nuclear explosion. "It is beautiful. So, where is your vineyard?"

"Not far from Baalbek. You'll be safe. It's guarded by brothers who've sworn their loyalty to my family and me. Once the missile launches, you and I will leave all of this behind. I will have fulfilled my oath to my father and uncle. A man only needs to leave his mark on history once."

"I just hope there is somewhere in this world beyond the reach of those who will seek revenge." The sickening thought of a nuclear strike only solidified her determination to stop him.

"Don't worry, love, I have planned for this my whole life."

It was all she could do not to strike him. *Planned for what? How do you plan your whole life to become a murderer?*

As they neared the wine-growing region near Baalbek, the soil became terracotta red and terraced slopes bearing row upon row of gnarled grapevine stocks blanketed the landscape.

"For five-thousand-years, the Beqaa valley has produced wine. In fact, it was here in Heliopolis the Romans built their temple to Bacchus, the god of wine. Perhaps we should go to Argentina and buy a vineyard. The land speaks to me, and I would be content to be a farmer." He raised her knuckles to his lips and kissed them. "Growing wine and raising children with you would be more than enough for me."

Zara sucked in her breath. Was he demented? How could he imagine himself blowing up a piece of the world and then settling peacefully into anonymity? "You surprise me, Mustafa, I would never have guessed a man such as you to hold aspirations for such a quiet life."

He held her gaze. "There is much about me you do not know, *habibi*."

"Tell me. Share with me who the secret Mustafa is. All I see is a man willing to sacrifice thousands of innocent lives for some twisted vision of a different world. Really, I don't know what I'm doing in this car with you. I'd be better off cooperating with Nasrallah."

Mustafa swerved the wheel and pulled over to the side of the road. He grabbed her chin, forcing her to look into his eyes. "I told you Nasrallah will use you and then discard you with no remorse. He's a deadly killer."

"It can't be worse than placing my life in the hands of a madman who wants to destroy an entire country."

They stared at each other as if in a Mexican standoff.

"You can't fool me, Zara, I know you are intrigued by the possibility of living another life with me." He paused as if considering what to do next. "Forgive me, but I must be cautious, and it's better if you have no idea of where we are or where we're going." He opened the center console and pulled a black hood out. She drew back at the insult. "I'm sorry, *habibi*, please forgive me." She relented with a sigh, and he dropped the bag over her head, leaving her in darkness. She rewarded him with utter silence. For her purposes, it was better to cooperate, lull him into a false sense of security, make him believe he was in control. *All in good time, he'll learn what I'm capable of.*

He prodded her to converse with him several times, but she refused to speak. The bag felt claustrophobic and disorienting. When he returned to the road and drove on, she was left in limbo, a place she was never comfortable in. She wanted to scream but swallowed her impulse and gripped the door handle instead. She began to count the minutes, calculating the passage of time to give her a sense of distance. Anything to keep her mind off the heat and darkness of the hood.

"I understand, my love. I can't blame you for being angry."

After what seemed an interminable amount of time, he removed the sack, and she blinked rapidly in the light. They drove up a dirt road through olive and citrus groves. "Are we here?"

"We're at our first stop."

"First stop?"

"This is my sister Amal's home. She and her husband Razaan live here with their three children. My mother lives with her. I want you to meet my mother."

"Your mother? Are you insane? I'm a foreigner and a westerner. What will she think?" This wasn't what she expected. She didn't understand him at all. Why would he bring her to meet his mother?

"My mother is very wise, and I need her blessing."

"Her blessing for what? How could she, a traditional Arab woman, bless you taking up with a French woman with a career and a string of past lovers?" She wanted to stir his anger. She wanted him to lash out at her, but instead, he raised her knuckles to his lips. "Whoever came before me is of no interest to me. I consider everything before we met simply preparation for our union. Again, my mother sees things as they are. In some ways, she's like you."

Clearly, he'd lost his mind or was suffering from delusions. How could his mother possibly be like her? His mother, an oppressed woman who had likely spent her life under the thumb of a misogynist terrorist for a husband. A man who was never there for her and probably cheated on her countless times. One thing Zara was sure of, there was no way in hell she would ever share her fate.

The car stopped, and Mustafa vaulted out. The door to a Mediterranean style farmhouse opened and barking sheepdogs, and three children came bounding outside.

"Uncle Mustafa!"

With two boys and a girl clinging to his legs, he made his way around the Mercedes and opened Zara's door and handed her out. The children froze and gaped at her.

"Ismael, Samir, and Assi, this is my friend Zara."

Not knowing what else to do, Zara smiled and bent to kiss the cheek of each child as they chorused their hellos. She'd never been good with children and was relieved to see three adults exit the house. The two women were traditionally dressed in hijabs, which covered their hair. She wished she'd worn something other than jeans and a sweater. She tried not to think of what they would think of the burgundy stripes in her own hair.

"Allah be praised, my son," the older woman proclaimed.

Mustafa embraced his mother, sister, and brother-in-law.

When the pleasantries were fulfilled, their gazes turned to Zara. "This is my friend Zara. Zara, my mother, Merjan."

Merjan's grey-green eyes not dissimilar to Zara's observed her. Zara offered her hand, and Mustafa's mother took it within both of hers. "My son does not often bring friends to our home. I am pleased to meet you."

With his mother's welcome, the discomfort dissipated. Mustafa's sister and brother-in-law invited her into their home.

They sat in a large room furnished with heavy wood furniture and Persian rugs. A fire in the stone hearth warmed the room. Merjan and Amal served tea in the French way from an elegant bone china set painted with roses. A delicate honey cake glazed with a warm apricot glaze accompanied the tea.

"Zara, were you born in France?" Merjan asked.

"No, I was born in Morocco. My family moved to Marseilles when I was a child. My father was a physician. He is retired now."

"You must miss your family."

Zara looked out the window. "Yes, but I visit them as often as my work allows. I'm a journalist."

"You are not married?"

Zara smiled. "No. Allah has not blessed me in that way."

"*Ami,*" Mustafa interrupted. "May I speak to you alone for a moment?"

Merjan rose. "Of course, my son."

Mustafa followed her out of the room. In Mustafa's absence, his sister and brother questioned Zara about life in France. Their interest in Arab life in France was keen. They asked her about education, religious freedoms, and of all things the Eiffel Tower.

"Do you have a desire to visit France?" Zara asked.

"Yes, we are curious about life there," Amal answered.

Zara sipped her tea. "You must go then. It would be a lovely experience for the children." She wondered how safe their lives would be if Hezbollah unleashed Armageddon. Israel would never target the family of a terrorist unless they, too, were terrorists. However, for their children's sake, it certainly would be safer to be in France than here.

When Mustafa returned, he was beaming. His mother's expression was unreadable. Zara sensed she was disturbed by what had passed between her and her son.

"Amal, I hope you've not told Zara any tales about me." He winked at his sister.

"Do you mean the one about you falling down the well?"

Zara laughed. "What well?"

He slapped his head. "Spare me from that tired old story. Isn't it time you put that one to rest?"

"Never. Zara, when we were children, Mustafa always was hearing voices. He believed he'd been chosen to commune with angels. One day he thought he heard an angel calling to him from our well." Amal leaned forward. "He leaned so far over the well he fell in." Amal broke into laughter until tears filled her eyes. "I guess there must have been an angel because instead of falling to the bottom, his pants snagged on the bucket hook. His screams brought *Ummah* running, and she fished him out. I remember you hanging by a thread Mustafa, upside down, your pants torn with your butt bare for all the world to see. You bleated like a motherless goat." Amal bleated, "Maaaa, maaaa, maaaa."

Mustafa spread his arms and hands out. "Where is the justice, Razaan? Can't you control your wife?"

Razaan shrugged. "She's your sister. What would you have me do?"

"Muzzle her." He turned to Zara, offering his hand. "Come, Zara, let us leave these traitors before they fill you with more nonsense. I want to show you the farm and orchards. We can walk down to the river. It's quite lovely." He grabbed a couple of woolen blankets from a stack near the fireplace.

Outside, Mustafa took her hand, and she pulled it away.

"Mustafa, they can see us. What will they think if they see you holding my hand?" To her, it seemed ridiculous to instigate their disapproval.

He grabbed her hand back, holding it firmly in his grasp. "I don't care who sees. I will show affection to whom I choose." He raised her palm to his lips and kissed it. "You still don't understand, Zara. My marriage was touchless, loveless, emotionless. I'm like a man who's lived in the desert alone without human contact. God has led me to you. You are my oasis, and I will never want again."

"You are placing too much faith in me, Mustafa. I may disappoint you."

"Never."

They walked past a pen with a dozen goats. "Maaaa, maaaa," Mustafa bleat back at them as they walked on.

The last of the day's sunshine broke through the cloud cover warming the cold, crisp air. Mustafa swung her hand in his as she did her best to keep up with his long stride. They slipped into an orchard of fig and olive trees and followed a path that descended to a river. Mustafa chattered on about the groves and how farming interested him. He'd been in high spirits since their arrival at his family's home. Zara found herself drawn into his joyful observations. She was fascinated by his desire to own a vineyard and cultivate wine. He was like Dr. Jekyll and Mr. Hyde. She wasn't sure which Mustafa was the real one. When they reached the river, they walked along its bank until they found a secluded spot where Mustafa spread out a blanket.

The sound of gurgling water flowing over stones and the caw of crows calling to each other filled the silence. It felt idyllic and far removed from city life, and even farther removed from a world forever teetering between peace and war. Under different circumstances, his courtship of her would make sense. She was struck by the absurdity of pretending they belonged together, but she was keenly aware he was oblivious to the incongruity. In his mind, they were well matched.

They sat on the blanket, and Zara wrapped her arms around her knees and shivered. He grabbed the other blanket and wrapped it around them both. "What did you and your mother discuss?"

"I told her that you were the woman I was meant to love."

She stared at him, incredulously. "You didn't?" She couldn't imagine what his mother must be thinking. Zara hoped the woman's love of her son was stronger than the hate she must be feeling toward the strange woman who'd swept in and turned her son's life upside down.

"I did, Zara. I needed her to know how I felt." He searched her eyes.

"What did she say?"

"She was worried, but she understood. She told me that she's lost enough loved ones to war. She told me to follow my heart." Mustafa brushed his lips over hers, and she felt warmth travel through her body. He pulled her down beside him, and they kissed. "I've wanted to kiss you for hours. I look forward to a time and place where I can kiss you whenever I want."

He stole kisses from her at every opportunity and felt no hesitancy in telling her he loved her. It was such a bizarre world she'd fallen into. The urgency of his kisses made her gasp. Her heart fluttered in her chest, and her uneven breaths were a dead giveaway to his ability to arouse her. "You'd better stop, *mon amour.*"

He smiled and caught his breath. "No matter how you try, Zara, you can't hide from me." He pressed his lips to her ear. "One day, I will make love to you on a blanket in a vineyard."

His romancing of her was having an effect. It reminded her that all her past relationships were based on falsehoods. Bringing her to meet his family was having an impact. It separated him from every man that had come before. It proved he was serious about their relationship. Meeting his family humanized him. If the truth of what he planned to do wasn't staring her in the face, she could easily picture herself falling in love with him. Rather than deal with her mixed emotions, she wrapped her arms around him and kissed him. *Fight fire with fire.* Like a mantra, she repeated. *I'm not in love with him. I'm not in love with him. I'm an actress in a play. When the curtain falls, the play must end with his downfall.*

CHAPTER 23

Beqaa Valley, Lebanon

Zara and Mustafa bid farewell to Mustafa's family. Zara said nothing when he again pulled over to the side of the road, and the sack was dropped over her head. The feeling of not being able to take a proper breath paralyzed her into silence.

Approximately thirty minutes later, Mustafa removed the black hood. They'd stopped at an imposing iron gate. A man holding an AR-15 saluted and stepped back. The gate swung open, and the car entered a treelined road that wound through row upon row of planted vines. After about a quarter of a mile, they approached a sprawling farmhouse. From the outside, it seemed nothing special, and Zara wondered what modern amenities the house might have. By the look of the security fence and guardhouse, she'd been expecting a fortress of some kind. The house needed painting, and there were tiles missing from the roof. An architectural deception. It had to be technologically and defensively state-of-the-art. The risk would be too significant to be otherwise.

Whatever was lacking on the exterior was more than made up for in the interior. A large brown leather sofa along with two matching recliners faced a wall-to-wall hearth with a crackling fire. Everything was comfortable from the colorful Persian rugs on the floor to the floor lamps giving off a warm glow. Again, it wasn't what Zara expected. The only thing missing was a pair of cozy slippers in front of the easy chair. The scent of simmering spices wafted in the air. Food. In all the commotion of getting out of Beirut, all they'd eaten was a piece of cake at Mustafa's mother's house. She was hungry.

"We'll have some lunch, and then you can get settled. I have to check in on the project and will leave you for a time."

She yawned and smiled. "I think I'll take a nap while you're out. A lot has happened in such a short time. Am I free to take a walk through the vineyard?"

"Zara, you need to know the property is secured by an electric fence, which is monitored and guarded, but you are free to go where you wish. I only ask you not to leave the compound. I warn you that all the communication systems are checked regularly and unbreachable without a system code. By the way, it's the reason I haven't searched you for a phone. It won't work here. It's not that I don't want to trust you, Zara, but unfortunately, I don't." He took her in his arms and kissed the tip of her nose. "Forgive me. Eventually, I will."

She relaxed in his embrace. "I wouldn't trust me either if I were you. I'll abide by your rules, for now." Did he really think she couldn't hack into his system and get past his firewalls if she chose? He probably had no idea how typical he was of Arab men. He knew she was a spy, yet he had no concept of what she was capable of. *Just as well, she thought. It makes everything so much easier for me. Big mistake mon amour, you should have taken my phone.* Her cellphone worked on technology that didn't require Wi-Fi, it routed directly through a satellite.

He laughed. "And one day, I promise you, I'll abide by yours."

After lunch, Mustafa took his leave of her. From the bedroom window, Zara watched the Mercedes drive away. As soon as the car disappeared, she turned her cell phone on and was relieved to see it had held its charge. Service she wasn't worried about, but she needed it to be charged. Because she didn't want to get into a text battle with Aryeh, she would hold off texting him until she had some concrete evidence for him to focus on.

She slipped from the room and tiptoed downstairs. She was determined to find something that would lead to the missile site. Hearing laughter and voices from the kitchen, she began to inspect the rest of the house, opening closed doors and committing the floor plan to memory. She only passed one guard who eyed her suspiciously. "I was wondering where there might be any books to read. I'd also love some paper and a pen to write some poetry." It was quicker to ask this goon rather than try to locate Mustafa's office on her own in the rambling house.

He looked at her as if she were a freak of nature. He grunted his disapproval, led her to a door, and opened it. "There's an office down this hallway." Without a goodbye, he turned and left. Mustafa must have made it clear she had a free run of the place. She opened every door along the hallway and inspected the rooms. It was a suite of offices. Some monitors were on; their screens switched from camera to camera broadcasting live video of the exterior of the property. There were phones, computers, and scanners, but Mustafa had emphasized that everything was password protected. Of course, it would be. She could have broken the code, she was an expert hacker, but what would she gain? Besides, she didn't want to jeopardize her relationship with Mustafa. She continued down the hallway and opened the door to an office with a large partner desk and a flat screen on one wall. It was uncluttered and appeared to be more fitting for an executive. *C'est bon!*

She entered and quietly closed the door behind her. She turned, resting her back against the door and perused the room. The desk and chair, computer, phone, and framed photos faced her. There was a photo of a young boy who looked much like Mustafa. In another photo, she recognized Mustafa with his father, uncle, and brother, their arms around each other's shoulders, grins plastered upon their faces. She was struck by the incongruity of murderers, frozen in time, expressing love and humanity. Her thoughts were suddenly eclipsed by the memory of her brother. The last time she'd seen him was at a party at the Sorbonne. He'd accompanied her. She smiled, recalling his teasing her that she needed to find a boyfriend because he wouldn't always be there to fill the bill of dinner companion and escort.

Zara closed her eyes, the pain of his loss still as fresh as the day when she picked up the phone and learned of his murder. She shook her head, driving the bittersweet memory of Jacob back into the recesses of her mind.

One more photo rested on the desk. It stood by itself on the corner. Zara froze. Surely, her eyes deceived her. She rubbed them to make sure she wasn't hallucinating. It was a picture of her and Mustafa, taken the night of their first dinner. She didn't recall them taking selfies, but someone, probably a bodyguard, had snapped this candid shot. She looked ahead as if indifferent, and he gazed with utter love and adoration at her. He'd placed this photo on his desk in a place of prominence. Her rejection meant nothing to a man who believed in destiny.

Ignoring her quickening pulse, she focused on what she'd come to find— the location of where they were assembling the missile.

Opening each drawer, she searched the contents, careful not to disturb or move anything to a place it didn't belong. She only found the usual things expected in an office: checkbook, pens, receipts, paperclips, and rubber bands. A lower drawer held files, which looked promising. She extracted each one and thumbed through it, returning it to its hanging folder before taking out the next one. Several contained complete bios and personal information of leaders of the opposing political parties in Lebanon. *Hit lists?*

Nothing she found was the information she needed. There was a credenza against one wall, and after making sure everything in the desk was just as she'd found it, she rose. Sliding open the flat front panel, she found blueprints. *Voila! What have we here?*

She took them out and spread them on the floor. The blueprints were architectural renderings of a building, a remodel. She read the Arabic writing on the back. They were plans for the remodeling of a cannabis greenhouse and auxiliary buildings. She knew Hezbollah, with their Syrian Shiite counterparts, controlled the drug trade in the Beqaa valley. A drug trade that represented more than six billion dollars. A large architecturally altered greenhouse might be the perfect cover for the assembling of missiles. This was it—her heart raced with the discovery. She took her cell out of her pocket and began taking photos of every drawing front and back. She continued to thumb through the drawings, shooting pics. By the time she'd finished, she felt confident this was the proof she needed. Hezbollah had built a hidden missile assembly plant invisible from the sky. Invisible to satellites. She searched but could find no indication on the blueprints of where the cannabis farm was located, but she knew it couldn't be far from Baalbek. Hezbollah's center for the illicit drug trade was Baalbek. Where else would they have total control and no interference from the outside world?

She needed to send Aryeh photos of what she'd found. She put everything back in the credenza, and grabbed a book from the shelf, paper, and pens, and slipped from the office and hurried to her bedroom.

She was anxious to get the pics and her assessment to Aryeh. Rapidly she typed, *Arrived in Beqaa Valley at Mustafa's vineyard. Not far from Baalbek. I know where the missile is. I've attached pics of blueprints I found. Focus on Baalbek cannabis farms. Let me know you got these. TTYL*

She waited a few minutes for Aryeh to reply, but he didn't text back. She wasn't too concerned and told herself he would contact her when he was able to. *He must be busy facilitating the prisoner exchange.* In the meantime, she needed to gather as much info on this place as she could. She changed into sneakers, stuffed the phone in her pocket, and set out on her walk.

She pulled her jacket tight about her, buttoning her collar. It had turned cold, and the property was mantled in a dense fog. She followed a path through row upon row of ancient grapevines. It felt like she was floating through a cloud. Olive trees appeared out of nowhere, their looming presence disconcerting as they suddenly came into focus.

When she reached the perimeter fence line of the property, she removed her phone and snapped a few shots. She explored the path bordering the fence and snapped more photos. She knew the fencing was electrified, but there had to be somewhere she might be able to escape.

She estimated she'd walked about a half-mile around the vineyard when she heard Mustafa calling to her. She stashed the cell in her pocket just as he emerged from the fog.

"*Habibi.*" He opened his arms to her, and she snuggled close to his warmth. He kissed her temple. "You're all wet, my love, not the best day to see my vineyard."

"I needed some exercise and fresh air. I find the fog invigorating. How are things at the job site?"

"Excellent. I'd say two days at best from putting our plans into motion. The North Koreans are tireless workers."

"You probably shouldn't have said North Koreans, you know?" She placed her finger in the dimple on his chin.

He grinned, stealing another peck on her lips. "Did I say North Koreans? Well, I'm sure you suspected they were involved, as are the Iranians. It doesn't matter. You're my prisoner." It was a casual throwaway line.

She frowned, pulling out of his embrace. "I do not care to be a prisoner, Mustafa. You should know the last time I was held prisoner, the villains paid dearly."

"I'll keep that in mind. Right now, all I want is to get out of this cold and relax with you, my queen."

"If I am your queen, then you should do as I say," she said.

"Ah, you are the queen of my heart, but I also have my duties."

"And what would be so wrong with you abdicating your duties and becoming my king in truth?" she whispered.

He caressed her cheek with the back of his hand. "You mean stopping the missile launch?"

"You have the power to do it. Don't you see Mustafa?" She blinked back the tears in her eyes. "How can love and hate co-exist in your heart? How can you condone the death of thousands of innocent lives?"

He turned away from her. "And what of my wife and child and all the other innocent Muslim lives that were destroyed?"

"My brother was also an innocent life lost to this ongoing violence. But you and I, we have the power to end it here and now." She reached out and placed her hand on his shoulder.

He turned back to her and pulled her into his arms once more. His lips claimed hers in a kiss so deep and filled with yearning that she almost wept. She held him close clinging to him.

How did I get here? How can I stop this madness and heal this man from the demons haunting him and his own broken sense of loyalty to his cause?

She didn't hate him as she should. She found herself drawn to him, to who he could be if only he would let go of this darkest of deeds.

And what if he doesn't let go of the past and this horrific mission? What if he doesn't put a stop to this missile launch?

She would have no choice. She had a duty to uphold, as well. A duty that went beyond any feelings she had for this beautiful, passionate man standing before her.

She would pull the trigger when the time came.

It was what she'd been trained to do what she was programmed to do. She'd done it countless times, but deep down in her heart, she knew this was going to be the most painful kill of her life.

She'd checked her phone several times to see if Aryeh had answered her text, but he hadn't. It was annoying and increased her sense of isolation. Now she'd have to wait until Mustafa fell asleep. It seemed reasonable to assume a meal with plenty of wine, and a heated sexual encounter would do the trick.

In all probability, the team was now in the Beqaa Valley, setting up a mobile base from which to launch their attack on the cannabis farm and shut down the nuclear EMP threat. She desperately wanted to know what Aryeh's thoughts were and what he and Cyrus had determined as their course of action. Time was running out, and her role in this was crucial, Zara needed to be in sync with the team. It was likely, she'd need the team to free her from the vineyard. She'd begun to take Mustafa's jest as a real possibility.

The truth was inescapable.

She may have been Mustafa's queen, but she was also his prisoner.

CHAPTER 24

Beqaa Valley, Lebanon
Baalbek Farm

The team members stood with bated breath as Ash slid back the massive doors to the barn revealing a cornucopia of weapons, ammunition, delivery systems, and vehicles. There was a staging station well supplied with chemicals and plastics, everything a bomb-maker could wish for was at their fingertips.

Only Zvi was missing. He was busy bringing everything up to speed in the van that would serve as their mobile tech center during the attack. The equipment needed to function without any glitches. Zvi needed to have his eyes on everything during the assault. He would be transmitting the operation to Tel Aviv. Everything would be live and routed through the satellite Mossad had ordered into position.

Cyrus inspected the set-up and couldn't help grinning. What Ash had procured was impressive. Ash hadn't been kidding when he'd boasted he had enough high-tech and cutting-edge equipment for a small army. But when Cyrus caught sight of four Kawasaki Ninja H2R motorcycles, he let out a low whistle. "How the hell did you get your hands on four of these?" The Ninja was the fastest production motorcycle in the world, with recorded speeds exceeding two-hundred-forty-nine miles per hour.

Ash folded his arms over his expansive chest. "My arms dealer flew them in from Japan. I had them modified to my specifications. They're fitted with sound suppressors, which dampen the performance a little, and I had enlarged storage compartments installed for ammo. Not too shabby, huh?"

"It's going to break my heart to leave these babies when we make our escape."

"Don't sweat it, boss. You want one of these?" He laughed, turning on a thick Yiddish accent. "I can get it for you wholesale."

"I'll bet you can. May have to take you up on your offer, although Layla will probably cut my balls off if I do."

"Ah, the joys of marriage. I suggest you keep your balls and get a Vespa motor scooter."

"Are you suggesting I'm henpecked?" He laughed. "Because if you are, I'll be the first to admit it. It seems I'll go to no end to please my muse. But if you're challenging me on motorcycles, how about we have ourselves a race, wise guy?"

"Anytime, boss."

His cell vibrated in his pocket. The text was from Aryeh. *The prisoner exchange set for tonight at midnight. I need to talk to you ASAP when Zvi has communications secured.*

Cyrus texted *Roger that* and put his cell away. "Listen up everyone, I just heard from Aryeh. The prisoner exchange is tonight. We need to be ready to roll on a moment's notice."

"No problem, boss," Cyrus noted the man who rarely smiled, Daniel, was grinning at him. *Well, I'll be damned, he's coming around.*

Nira picked up an assault rifle, her muscles tautly defined when she assumed firing stance and held the scope to her eye. "You did good, Ash. This AK-12 is as sweet as a rifle gets."

"So," Ash's eyes gleamed mischievously, his tone was suggestive and taunting, "what do you like best about it? Is it the recoil control or the firepower?"

It was a man's kind of gun, but Nira was no ordinary woman. She ignored Ash's sexual innuendo and adjusted the stock to fit her diminutive shape and again assumed a shooter's stance. "This baby is mine."

"Yeah, it's your color for sure," Ash teased. "Matches your eyes. Are you sure it's not too heavy? I have girlier guns for you. Couldn't get my hands on a purple Tinkerbell, but I did find a gray .22LR."

She turned and aimed the rifle at his chest. "Where'd you say the safety is, Ash? I might need to release it and have me some target practice."

Ash put his hands up in surrender and grinned. "Didn't mean to ruffle your feathers, sweetheart."

She let the muzzle drop down to aim at his genitals. "I don't think you'd miss these jewels if I removed them, do you? They're not worth much."

"I'd miss them for sure, but there's a whole lot of ladies out there who'd be missing them even more."

She lowered the rifle with a humph. "I'd be doing them a favor."

"Yeah, but what if I'm the future father of your children." He raised his brow.

"Do you think I'd choose brawn over brains for my mate? Think again."

Daniel snorted. "Enough! I wish you two would get it over with and fuck. All the back-and-forth is giving me a headache."

Both Nira and Ash glared at him.

Cyrus laughed. "Okay, lovebirds and not so loving birds, let's get to work."

The sun was setting by the time they'd all chosen their weapons of choice and body armor. Nira and Ash would be riding on the back of the motorcycles driven by Ben and Daniel. They'd be free from encumbrance to fire weapons at will. Aryeh and Cyrus were riding their motorcycles solo. Yitzhak would drive the armored van loaded with explosives and additional weapons. From inside the van, Zvi's job was monitoring satellite feed and coordinating Tel Aviv's instructions to the team. They'd all be wearing helmet cameras that would televise their movements to Tel Aviv and Zvi live.

The plan was to infiltrate the compound and place enough explosives to blow the entire place to kingdom come. It sounded simple, but everyone knew the complex would be heavily fortified and guarded. Being outnumbered meant it would not be a cakewalk by any means. The decision to kill everyone within the compound walls had come from the Prime Minister himself. No surviving witnesses—a clear message to Israel's enemies. Israel would not stand for Hezbollah's nuclearization and would do whatever it took to ensure the safety of its citizens.

Determined and ready, the team headed back to the main house to prepare some dinner and take turns grabbing an hour or two of sleep before go-time.

Cyrus left the chattering bunch in the kitchen and hurried to the living room, where Zvi was adjusting and testing the last equipment to be loaded into the van.

"Hey, Zvi, everything good to go?"

"Purring like a Ferrari. The last thing to load is the computer system."

"Good. Can you put me through to Aryeh? I need to talk to him before the prisoner swap."

"You got it, boss." The tech guru worked his magic, and seconds later, Aryeh's face popped up on the screen. Zvi waved as he headed to the kitchen.

"Hey, man, how goes it?" Cyrus asked.

There was a wariness in Aryeh's eyes. Cyrus knew from experience it was the intense look of a man about to head into the eye of the storm.

"I'm going to cut to the chase," Aryeh said. "I just picked up a text from Zara. For some reason, the damn phone wasn't working, but now it is. Mustafa has her at his family's vineyard slash compound. She only had a minute to text, but she sent me these blueprints, which I've forwarded to Tel Aviv. It's for the conversion of a cannabis greenhouse into a rocket building facility. I've checked with headquarters, and our satellites have detected unusual activity at a particular location." He held up a map pointing to a circled area, which looked to be in the middle of nowhere. "Tel Aviv has uploaded everything to Zvi's computers. Everyone agrees this is our target."

"I'll have Zvi pinpoint the coordinates, and he and I will prepare the attack plan," Cyrus said. We'll be ready whenever Tel Aviv gives us the go-ahead."

"Our timetable is as follows. I'm on my way to you as soon as we hang-up. Once we know Gideon is safe, our operation begins. There's just one problem."

"And what might that be?"

"Zara. She's vulnerable. She's unarmed, and whether she realizes it or not, I believe she's a prisoner. I need to get her out of there."

"I have a killer Kawasaki and plenty of ammo and guns waiting for you. I'm sure the team will want to help. What's your plan?"

"Perfect. But I'm going on this one alone. I'll rescue the princess from the castle, and we'll join you before you're ready to lead our army in its attack."

"You sure you won't need help saving the damsel in distress?"

"Nix that. Zara also sent me photos of the compound and the interiors. She's like a Ninja. I won't be fighting alone. She and I will rendezvous with you. We'll need as many feet on the ground as we can muster. I expect the missile facility to be crawling with soldiers. No big deal—we're always outnumbered."

"Okay, as soon as you and Zara get back here, we'll launch. My guestimate is zero-two-hundred hours. Whatever they have on the ground there, I'm confident they're no match for the team."

Aryeh nodded. "One thing is for sure, Hezbollah should be well distracted by their celebration of the release of seventeen of their deadliest from jail. Once we've taken out the threat, the Stealth Hawk and the RQ-170 helicopters will swoop in and pick us up. We'll be on our way home before the first light of dawn."

"Let's put this baby to sleep for good," Cyrus said.

"Amen."

CHAPTER 25

Baalbek Vineyard
Beqaa Valley, Lebanon
11:45 P.M.

Zara had spent most of her life since her brother's death believing in nothing. Since she'd become a spy, her sole purpose had been to stop the next killer before someone else had to suffer the loss of a loved one like she had. Mustafa represented the antithesis of everything Zara believed in, and yet she couldn't stop the way she felt about him. Now she found herself in an impossible position. She felt alive in the arms of a man who meant to kill, and for some reason, she believed she could change him.

She, a trained operative, had done this before. Entrapping a male adversary to reveal secrets were the tools of her trade. But unlike every time before, the thought of killing Mustafa made her sick to her stomach. He wasn't like the others. He wasn't a man in heat who wanted to satisfy an impulse. He wasn't a man cheating on his wife. In fact, he was a widower who'd barely had sexual relations with his wife before her death and had lived like a monk afterward.

She believed him when he said he loved her. Why? In her mind, he'd risked everything for her, even the condemnation of his family. He'd saved her life and gone against Nasrallah when the easiest thing would have been to burn her. He was willing to give up everything for her, his family, Lebanon, and his powerful position within Hezbollah. She would run away with him if only he'd stop this missile launch.

Was it possible love could obliterate hatred? *If a terrorist could love, could he also have the capacity to change?* In Judaism, she knew the concept of *tikkun olam* meant repairing the world in action. The idea of changing the course of a life, Mustafa's life, had taken hold of her and rekindled her belief in

167

something good and pure. Her heart told her she could change him if only she had more time. But time was running out.

It was no wonder she couldn't keep the mission in mind. When Mustafa made love to her, every part of her answered. She fought to separate her emotions and just go through the motions of sex. But she couldn't. He kissed her, and she forgot everything else.

"We are probably totally unsuitable for each other, but I don't want to live my life without you. Together *habibi*, we can change the course of our lives."

He was inside of her. Making love to her. Was he reading her mind?

His hands caressed her face as he stared into her eyes. "You are mine, Zara, Allah's gift. You hold my heart in your hands."

"*Mon amour*," her nails dug into his back, her back arching. She trembled like an exposed electrical wire, wildly she sizzled beneath him, catapulting him into release.

Their hearts clamored thunderously against each other, their gasping breaths filling the silence. Mustafa held tight to her as they lay drenched in each other's sweat. "Zara, Zara," he moaned as if the repetition of her name was a magical incantation. "What have you done to me? You're all I think about."

And then to prove his words true, he delved in kissing her as if this were their last moment on Earth and their lovemaking divine.

Breathlessly she pulled away. "I'm exhausted, *mon chéri*, you've worn me out. I need to sleep. Today is a day without end."

"*Habibi*, sleep in my arms. It is my dearest wish."

She rolled over, and he wrapped himself around her. Zara took deep breaths, fighting an almost irresistible urge to sleep. She needed to text Aryeh. She needed to know what their plan was.

The last thing she remembered was listening to his breathing.

A series of pings woke them both. Mustafa picked up his cell and read the message. He sat up, squinting, fine lines wrinkling his eyes.

She yawned rising on her elbow. "What's wrong?"

"I have to go. Nasrallah has decided to make an unplanned appearance."

"Is there anything wrong? What time is it?"

"Nothing is wrong. I'm sure Nasrallah only wants to see the progress we've made. It's only ten p.m. You stay here, *habibi*, go back to sleep. I shouldn't be too long."

"I am still sleepy," *Damn, I overslept*. All Zara could think about was checking her cell. Aryeh must have texted her back by now.

He leaned over and brushed his lips over hers. "Of course, you are my love." His eyes twinkled with satisfaction. "What you do to me fills me with power and endless desire. I am a man who knows no limits when it comes to loving you."

She placed her hands on his scruffy cheeks. "You are a formidable lover, *mon chéri*. Go and come back to me."

He bent and kissed her nipple. "I can't bear to leave you, but I must."

She pulled the sheet up, covering herself. "Go before I pull you back into this bed."

He dressed and stopped, turning at the door. "Zara, I'm taking some men with me for protection, so there will be only a minimal crew on duty. Only the gate and the perimeter of the house will be manned. Please don't leave the house. You're safe here."

She waved dismissively. "Mustafa, the only place I'm going is back to sleep."

He smiled. "I'll be back to join you soon, *habibi*."

Zara waited and listened for the sound of the Mercedes' engine turning over. Once she heard the car recede in the distance, she got out of bed and grabbed her cell phone. She sighed a breath of relief when she saw Aryeh's text. The prisoner exchange of his nephew and the Israeli held Hezbollah prisoners would take place at midnight.

Located the missile facility. Elimination tonight. Coming to get you now. It's time to get out. We need you. You've accomplished and delivered. Mustafa no longer important. I'll text you on arrival.

The text had come in fifteen minutes ago. Aryeh was right. There was nothing she could do to save Mustafa, and even if she could, would she be able to do it? He was the enemy. All those feelings she'd been fancying had twisted her reason. *We have no future.* What they'd shared was already in the past, a sweet memory, but nothing that could withstand the harsh light of day. This is where their paths diverged.

She texted Aryeh.

Meet me quarter-of-a-mile east of guardhouse. A narrow road borders property. Old oak tree where I can jump the fence. Stay away from guardhouse. Mustafa gone to cannabis farm to meet Nasrallah. Bon chance.

The house was quiet and seemingly deserted. When she and Mustafa had returned from their walk, they'd eaten their meal alone in the dining room. Mustafa had ordered everyone to their quarters. He wanted nothing to interrupt his time with her.

Zara dressed warmly and pocketed her phone and her gun. She braced herself against the cold, turning up the collar on her coat and slipped out of the house. She walked past an out-building, her shoulders hunched up against the chill. She was taken by surprise when a large hand clamped over her nose and mouth, and her legs were kicked out from under her. Her assailant dragged her a few feet, cursing her in Arabic.

She kicked wildly to free herself, and then a sickly-sweet smell accosted her senses, and she knew her attacker was drugging her. Nausea filled her. Bile rose in her throat. She heaved, gagging on the drug that saturated her reason. In a last-ditch effort, she drove her elbows into the monster's gut, hoping to dislodge his hand, but it was like slamming her elbow into a steel door, he was solid and massive. She grew weaker with every breath and kicked and flailed desperately to dislodge him. But he pressed the cloth tighter against her nose and mouth causing her vision to blur. She was spinning. Wave upon wave of dizziness left her weak and unbalanced. The last thing she heard before she slipped into unconsciousness was a man's heated whisper in her ear, "Now, the fun begins, *eahirat faransia*." He'd called her a French whore in Arabic. Fear gripped her as darkness claimed her.

CHAPTER 26

Shebaa Farms
Beqaa Valley, Lebanon
11:45 P.M.

Abe Harel, head of Unit 8200 checked his watch for the umpteenth time. Generally, as the head of the IDF's most formidable intelligence-gathering arm, he wouldn't be participating in an active mission. However, the Ramsad had requested he personally oversee the prisoner exchange.

The Ramsad wanted to track the released enemy combatant terrorists. The plan was to eliminate them should they ever choose to fight against Israel again. Each of the Hezbollah prisoners before leaving the prison had been given a last meal containing a newly developed isotope, a radio-nuclide, which would remain in their body indefinitely. The scientists had explained to the Ramsad that it was like being permanently tattooed from within. With new secret gamma technology, the released prisoners would be tracked, and their activities monitored by Abe's Unit 8200. Already work had begun to build a satellite bearing a gamma camera with the ability to identify these terrorists on the ground. It was a dangerous new technology, and if it fell into the wrong hands, it would be deadly, but to release a deadly combatant to come against you again was an unacceptable proposition. If the prisoners again attacked military or civilian Israelis, they would not be given the luxury of a prison sentence a second time. Repeat offenders would be eliminated.

Three Blackhawk helicopters crossed the Golan Heights flying in formation to the narrow strip of disputed territory called the Shebaa Farms.

The prime minister had symbolically chosen the Shebaa Farms for the prisoner exchange to remind Hezbollah that the Shebaa was now annexed along with the Golan Heights and belonged to Israel. The narrow parcel of land had been a point of contention between Hezbollah and Israel for years. Hezbollah used the disputed land as one of their reasons for ongoing warfare.

The Blackhawks were accompanied by two Longbow Apache attack helicopters, armed with electronic warfare systems and AGM-114 Hellfire missiles. At 11:45 p.m., all five helicopters touched down at Shebaa Farms. The prisoners were unloaded and stood surrounded by IDF soldiers. Abe stood among them, waiting for Gideon Reise and two other prisoners to emerge from a line of Hezbollah armored vehicles. There was tension in the air, and even the prisoners shuffled nervously, probably fearful their nearness to freedom might be deprived.

Finally, a figure supported by two Hezbollah soldiers emerged and stumbled forward. The man was being half dragged, and even from a distance, Abe could see he was in terrible condition. Two other gaunt men followed. He couldn't bear to see what they'd done to the young men. He nodded to the soldiers surrounding the seventeen prisoners who were tied to each other and signaled them to move the men forward.

Slowly the two sides moved toward the middle where they would meet. Abe glanced back at the helicopters, noting the gunners with their sights and machine guns aimed and ready to attack if anything went wrong. Gideon was hefted onto the back of one of the IDF soldiers and carried back to the Blackhawk, where he was immediately taken in hand by the medics on board.

From the Hezbollah side, there was joyful shouting, hugs, and thumps on the backs of the returning warriors. Their laughter made Abe's stomach turn. These men had been returned fit and healthy, while Gideon looked barely alive. The prisoners were loaded into Hezbollah's armored vehicles, and without further ado, they reversed the vehicles and drove back toward Lebanon.

As soon as they were gone, the Blackhawk with Gideon in it took off racing back to a military hospital where the Israelis would be assessed and treated. The other Blackhawks and the two Apaches remained on the ground. Abe texted the Ramsad, *Exchange successful. Gideon safe.* The Ramsad could now notify Cyrus.

The assault on the Hezbollah cannabis farm was approved to commence.

Moments later, a Stealth Hawk, designed to avoid radar detection, swooped in and landed next to the Blackhawks. Abe climbed aboard the military owl in the sky and waited for the signal.

The clock had begun to tick on the operation. For Abe and the helicopters under his command, the night's work had only just begun.

CHAPTER 27

Mustafa's Vineyard
Beqaa Valley, Lebanon
1:00 A.M.

Zara woke with a dry mouth and nausea. Her hands and feet were tied behind her. Horrified, she stared down at her nakedness. She pulled on the knots, trying to break free, but the ties only cut deeper into her wrists. The only thing she succeeded in doing was making herself dizzy. She closed her eyes and breathed deeply. Her vision cleared, and the world around her came into focus. She was lying on the ground on her side. Across from her, a huge behemoth of a man with his back to her was spreading a blanket over stacks of hay. It was bizarre. It appeared he was arranging props into some semblance of a bed.

"You bastard, what the hell are you doing? Untie me!"

He turned, and she shuddered. The look in his eyes resembled a predatory animal. He grinned, and her blood turned to ice as his eyes surveyed her naked body. "Ah, the French whore has awakened. Good. I want you awake to enjoy what I have planned for you."

"Who are you? What do you want from me? Mustafa will kill you for this…" Vaguely she recalled his face. He was one of Nasrallah's henchmen.

He roared with laughter. "Mustafa? Mustafa is a boy, a fool. He took the bait like a fish. He's at this minute pacing around the cannabis farm, waiting for the arrival of Nasrallah, wondering where the secretary-general is. In the meantime, his whore will enjoy the pleasure of a real man." He rubbed the large protrusion straining against his pant leg. "And I will have the pleasure of fucking and then ending your life in the most erotic way imaginable."

She spit at him. "You're a pig. I wouldn't fuck you if you were the last man on Earth."

"Oh, *mon amour*, you have no choice in the matter." He waved his hand toward the arrangement of hay and blanket. "Soon, I will introduce you to Goliath." Again, he rubbed his member. "Goliath will be the last cock you will ever know. Take comfort in the fact that because you are so beautiful, I've decided to immortalize you forever." He walked over to a camera mounted on a stand. "In a way, you will be mine forever. Perhaps one day, I'll show the video to your lover Mustafa. I think it will be an excellent lesson for him on how to fuck like a real man."

"Mustafa will kill you, as will I if you come near me." Her bravery was waning. She knew her only hope was to stall the deadly madman.

"Believe me, you've never known such pleasure as I plan on giving you. It is the least I can do for you before I kill you."

"And who do I owe this unbelievable pleasure to?"

"Amir Haddad. General Amir Haddad."

"Does Nasrallah know what you are planning to do to me?"

"Our holy leader need not know everything. So long as he gets the results promised him, he will not inquire further."

"Nasrallah has ordered me murdered? I don't believe it."

"He has not ordered it, but he has not forbidden it either. He's left the matter in my capable hands."

How long had this sick sociopath had her in his sights? Her thoughts raced through everything that had happened since she'd met with Nasrallah. "In Beirut, the near hit-and-run attempt on me, was that you?"

"Yes, my men failed when your boyfriend pulled you out of the way. It was meant to be a warning to you both, but in retrospect, it was lucky for me. In Tel Aviv, I killed a woman in the same exquisite way I intend to kill you. I haven't been able to get it out of my mind. To be given the same pleasure twice is beyond my expectations."

"You're a sick animal, Amir. Allah will curse you. You are an abomination. A freak of nature—"

The huge monster lunged at her and slapped her so hard her head snapped back and she saw stars. She was lucky he hadn't broken her neck. She couldn't stop the flood of tears that rained down her face.

"Shut up, bitch! The name of the sacred is not to be uttered by the likes of you. You are a traitor to your faith and people. You are nothing more than a whore in the employ of the French. The same corrupt French who colonized Lebanon draining her of her wealth and resources. I intend to make you pay dearly for your treachery."

For the first time in her life, Zara felt real fear. Amir was a brutal killer. He was the embodiment of evil, and he would revel in squeezing the life out of her in the most macabre way. The only option left to her was to die fighting him to the end. Maybe she could anger him enough to snap her neck and end her life quickly. "Doesn't your wife satisfy your sick sexual perversions?"

He glared at her. "My wife does what she's told to do. She knows her place. Do not sully her name by speaking of her. You are a whore, and she is the mother of warriors."

"She's the mother of pigs. And your daughters? Have you introduced them to Goliath, you sick fuck?"

He grinned. "Are you trying to instigate my anger? Are you hoping I'll kill you before I stick my cock inside you?"

"No. I figure a sick prick like you with no moral boundaries wouldn't hold any compunction against fucking the unfortunate female offspring of his loins."

"Tsk tsk, *habibi*, I like your fire. It's something lacking in most women. It is no wonder Mustafa fell under your spell."

"The only kind of woman who would put up with the likes of you is a dishrag, a submissive with no backbone. But then your wife probably prays your dick is anywhere other than in her cunt."

Amir's face reddened, and his hands fisted. "You are going to pay dearly for your words, whore."

"Touch me, and you will know what it is to rattle a tiger's cage." Her bravado gave her courage, but courage wasn't going to save her. She needed to get free. She needed a weapon.

"As much as I've enjoyed our verbal foreplay, I'm far more interested in what comes next." He strode toward her, and she shrank back. With little effort, he swooped her up and carried her writhing and cursing to the haystack.

She screamed at the top of her lungs. "Help me! Somebody help me!" He threw her down on the blanket and reached down and squeezed her nipple between his fingers so hard she nearly passed out. She screamed at the top of her lungs, and fresh tears rained down her face. The cries stuck in her throat as she gasped, gulping for breath.

"No more screams, or I'll cut your nipple off, which would be a shame since there are so many more pleasing things I want to do to it." He leaned down and glided his tongue over and around her nipple. Then he suckled her humming with pleasure as she tried to twist and turn away from him. He growled, "Your body was made for sex. Why would Allah give such perfection to a whore?"

Dear God, kill me before he touches me. Don't abandon me in my hour of need.

As Amir continued to maul her body with his mouth and hands, she tried her best to remove herself from what was happening. If there was ever a time she needed Aryeh to show up, it was now.

And then God answered. The depraved psychopath placed his ear within reach, and in a flash, she struck, sinking her teeth into a vulnerable bit of flesh as hard and deep as she could go. Shaking her head like a rabid dog, she tore a piece of his ear from his head. He screamed and reared back as a stream of blood dripped down his neck and onto her. Disgusted, she spit the chunk of flesh from her mouth and closed her eyes, knowing she would pay for what she'd done.

His fist slammed into her cheekbone. The pain ricocheted through her body. She smiled as she slipped into unconsciousness.

CHAPTER 28

Mustafa's Vineyard
Beqaa Valley, Lebanon
1:15 A.M.

Aryeh killed the engine and pushed his motorcycle up the road toward the guardhouse. When he was within a hundred yards, he put the kickstand down and left the bike. He kept to the shadows and the trees on the side of the road. The moon passed free of the clouds and cast a silvery light on the gate. *Open? Where are the guards?*

He approached the gate and peered into the window of the guardhouse. The moon disappeared behind another cloud, but his night goggles made everything crystal clear. Inside the guardhouse were two bodies lying in a pool of blood.

He retrieved his motorcycle and pushed it up the road toward the house. His heart thundered in his chest. All he could think about was Zara. Near the entrance to the house, he found another man dead, his throat slit. He left the bike under a tree and walked the perimeter of the house. Nothing. No movement. No sign of life. Was Zara dead too? He didn't dare imagine it.

"*Laenat Allah ealika!* You bitch, you whore!" An angry male voice pierced the silence.

Aryeh pulled his gun and ran toward the sound. He burst through the doors of the outbuilding, his weapon drawn. Zara was lying naked and unconscious—or possibly dead—on a pallet. It reminded him of a sacrificial offering table you'd see in some B-rated horror movie, where the beautiful virgin is sacrificed to satisfy some bloodthirsty god.

Fucking sicko!

The man turned, and Aryeh immediately recognized him. This was the man who'd set off the bomb in Tel Aviv and left a trail of dead. This was the man who'd ruthlessly tortured, beaten, and starved his nephew, Gideon. The thought of killing the bastard gave him great pleasure.

Aryeh glanced at Zara again. Thankfully he saw the rise and fall of her chest. *She's still alive.*

The man barreled into him, knocking the gun from his hand. The giant's fingers slipped around his neck, cutting off his air. Aryeh attacked frontally, driving his fists into the man's solar plexus. It was enough to loosen the iron grip on his neck. Aryeh was brawny and muscled, pound for pound an equal to his assailant.

Aryeh used his hands as blades, chopping into Amir, but the giant was giving as good as he got. He, too, was trained in hand-to-hand combat and used his massive strength with every blow, knocking Aryeh nearly senseless. One punch caught Aryeh near the eye, splitting the skin. Blood oozed down his face. With a flat palm punch, Aryeh retaliated and broke Amir's nose.

The bear of a man toppled, and Aryeh jumped on him, fists flailing. The two men rolled over several times as they each tried to get the upper hand. They hit the straw pallet where Zara was lying. The shouts and curses must have awakened her because from the corner of his eye, he glimpsed Zara struggling to break free of her bonds. Like a contortionist, she'd managed to slip her arms forward, and she sat gnawing on the zip tie binding her wrists.

Spinning like a top, the brute managed to gain the upper hand, pinning Aryeh beneath him. His thick fingers wrapped around Aryeh's throat. Aryeh grabbed at Amir's hands, trying to dislodge them. His vision blurred, and his ears rang. He hovered on the edge of blacking out as Amir's fingers closed tighter around his neck. All he could think about was what this monster would do to Zara if he didn't kill him. He tried to rally, driving the point of his elbow into Amir's gut. Amir howled, but his fingers remained firm. It seemed the harder Aryeh fought, the more strength the monster gained.

And then a shot rang out, and Amir's hands squeezed. His face bore a look of surprise. Blood gurgled up from his mouth, dripping on Aryeh's face and chest. Amir's hands lost their grip, and Aryeh gasped as his windpipe was freed.

With a final death rattle, Amir collapsed on top of him.

Aryeh wheezed, gulping air like a fish out of water.

Zara's voice sounded distant, eclipsed by the pounding of his heart. "Go to hell, you bastard."

With a groan of disgust, Aryeh rolled the dead terrorist off him and just lay there trying to breathe. He croaked, "Thank you, *mon amour*. I owe you one."

She kneeled beside him. Tears welled up in her eyes, and her shoulders shook. She tried to wipe them away. "Thank God you're okay. If you hadn't shown up when you did—I was so scared—God only knows what that monster intended to do to me."

He took her face between his hands and held her gaze. "*Mon chéri*, I've never seen you cry like this."

"I've never been afraid before tonight. Forgive me. I owe you my life."

"We are human, Zara. You saved my life too. Let's call it a draw, *oui, mon chéri?*"

"*Absolument.*"

He caressed her swollen cheek. "Get dressed, Zara, we have bigger fish to fry. The team is waiting for us."

Looking down at her naked body, she quipped. "I forgot I was nude, *merde*." She grabbed her clothes and began dressing. "Fill me in on where we stand."

Aryeh stood, brushing the dirt from his clothing. "The prisoner exchange was successful, Gideon's safe and on his way back to Tel Aviv."

"Oh, *mon ami*, that's wonderful news. You got my text, and Mossad has confirmed my information?"

"Yes, thanks to you, they're in our sights." He looked at his watch. "We attack tonight. I have a motorcycle outside. We need to leave."

She nodded. "Let's go. This place gives me the creeps."

They exited into the cold evening air. "Where's Mustafa, why did he leave you alone?"

"He got a call telling him to report to the cannabis farm. The text said Nasrallah had decided to see the operation for himself. The pig," she nodded back toward the barn, "told me it was a lure, a text from him to get Mustafa away from here."

Aryeh studied her face in the moonlight. "You care for him, don't you?"

"Who, the pig?"

"No. You know who I mean."

She shrugged. "Yes, I care for Mustafa, but it won't prevent me from doing my duty."

"Zara, are you sure you're all right?"

"I'm fine."

They reached the bike, and he pulled a leather jumpsuit and the extra helmet out for her. She slipped the jumpsuit on and donned the helmet. She winked at him. "You're a good personal shopper. A perfect fit."

He was glad she couldn't see his face redden. He ignored her comment and pulled a first aid kit out. He broke an ice-cold pack and handed it to her. "Hold the ice to your cheek. It'll bring the swelling down." He began to clean the cut near his eye.

"Let me help you." She cleaned the area with an antiseptic wipe, applied ointment, and sealed the split skin with a suture butterfly bandage. "*Voila.* I don't think you'll need any stitches. Let's fly, *bébé.*"

Zara was about to climb on the back of the motorcycle when she suddenly stopped. "Stay here, *mon ami.* I'll be right back." She grabbed a gun from Aryeh's arsenal.

"Where are you going? We need to get out of here." She ignored him and ran back toward the main house.

She called over her shoulder, "I'll just be a minute." Without making a sound, she opened the door and strode to the back offices. Not a floorboard creaked. If there was anyone in the house, they weren't interested in revealing themselves. She made a beeline to Mustafa's office. During her earlier visit, she'd noticed a laptop in a briefcase. Just as she remembered, it was still there beside the desk. She grabbed it and retraced her steps out of the house. She ran across the grounds to Aryeh and shoved the briefcase into the storage compartment on the bike. "I think Mustafa's laptop might come in handy. Zvi should be able to break the security code. I bet there's a bonanza of secret Hezbollah business on it."

"A bit risky, *mon amour,* but you're right. It could contain valuable information." He mounted the motorcycle. "Can we go, please?"

She threw her leg up and straddled the seat behind him. Wrapping her arms around his waist, she held tight as he swerved in a tight circle. Aryeh gunned the motor and tore down the road through the gates.

The motorcycle was a rocket ship, fast and responsive. The late hour and empty roads were a gift. Zara couldn't help but wonder what Mustafa would think when he returned and found her gone and bodies everywhere. A part of her wanted to text him, but then she'd be tipping the team's hand and risking their success.

She tried to reason like the man she'd come to know. If Mustafa returned to his vineyard and found the body of Amir and the grotesque stage set, he would assume Amir had gone rogue, and she was his targeted victim. But wouldn't he wonder whether Nasrallah had approved the plan and how she'd gotten away? If Nasrallah had okayed her assassination, who was to say that he wouldn't okay Mustafa's assassination. She told herself it didn't matter because Mustafa was still at the missile facility awaiting Nasrallah's arrival. Zara tried not to think about the last time they'd made love or his tender words to her. She resigned herself to the likelihood that he would be dead before the night's end. Aryeh had told her there were to be no survivors.

Mustafa would die as he should, and there was nothing she could do to stop it.

CHAPTER 29

Beqaa Valley, Lebanon
Cannabis Farm
1:15 A.M.

One hour and still no Nasrallah. *Where the hell is he?*

Mustafa paced the perimeter of the missile assembly plant. His patience was wearing thin.

For the past thirty minutes he'd watched the North Koreans arguing over the loading of the ten-kiloton bomb into the cone of the missile. The bomb was relatively small in comparison to most nuclear warheads. But in the deployment of an electromagnetic pulse implosion, the size of the bomb was less important than the altitude at which the bomb detonated. An explosion at four-hundred kilometers in altitude would be enough to spread the resulting gamma rays far and wide before they hit the Earth's atmosphere. The result would cripple all of Israel, shutting down their ability to wage a responsive attack allowing Hezbollah to realize their dream of driving the Jews into the sea.

He'd received a text from Nasrallah claiming the secretary-general was on his way, but so far, the leader of Hezbollah was a no-show. Everyone but the night watch security team unit had gone to bed. Mustafa's thoughts strayed to Zara as he waited. The minutes that ticked away brought him closer to what he hoped would be a new lease on life for him. But his impatience to begin the countdown to the missile launch, and afterward disappear with Zara, had him chomping at the bit. He paced and checked his phone every few minutes. It was more than a man in love could bear. Again, he dialed the guardhouse at his vineyard. The phone rang and rang. A dark premonition crawled up his spine. He suppressed his mounting panic. There were a million logical explanations for his men not to answer. It took a supreme effort, but he waited five minutes and dialed again. The outcome remained the same. He listened to the endless ringing of the phone.

Gruffly, he told his men to remain at the cannabis farm and await Nasrallah's arrival. Overriding their protests, he took the keys to the Mercedes and left by himself. He had an AR-15 and a pistol, more than enough to defend himself.

He drove with reckless abandon, barreling over ruts in the road and ignoring the screech of tires as he accelerated through tight turns. His driving grew more erratic as his worst fears seized him.

The Mercedes bounced over the unpaved road that led to the entrance of the compound. His pulse pounded in his temples when he saw the gates were open. He stopped the car and grabbed the AR-15, running to the guardhouse. Seeing the gruesome carnage of his murdered men made the bile rise in his throat like mercury in a thermometer exposed to heat. Unable to control his revulsion, he threw up. He wiped his face and ran toward the main house.

With his gun raised, he barreled in. "Zara!" The house echoed back with silence.

From the second story, he heard the creak of a floorboard. He ran up the stairs, his rifle aimed and ready to shoot. Aisha, his servant girl, stepped out of the shadows with her hands raised and trembling.

He lowered the muzzle of the AR-15, and she ran to him. Tears poured down her cheeks as she pressed her face into his chest. "*Sidi*, a man, dressed in a military uniform, attacked us. He slaughtered everyone, it—" She broke down sobbing.

Mustafa rubbed her back. "Thanks be to Allah, you are safe. Where is Zara?" His voice broke. *Please, Allah, let her be safe.*

The girl looked up at him with eyes brimming with tears. "I do not know, *Sidi*."

"Go back to the safe room and stay there until I call you. I need to find the French woman."

She ran to her hiding place, and he retraced his steps down the stairs. He walked the perimeter of the house and found another guard's body. A light burning in the outbuilding where they stored tools and farm implements drew him. He kicked open the door with his foot, holding the assault rifle in the ready position. When he saw the body lying face down on the ground, he lowered the muzzle.

With his foot, he flipped the body onto its back and stared. *Amir.* Swiftly he looked around and tried to make sense of what he saw. The bed like bales of hay, the camera, the cut zip-ties, and the blood on the ground baffled him. When it finally dawned what must have occurred, his stomach knotted. *Zara couldn't have killed Amir without help.*

He inspected the body more closely and could see the blue, black bruises inflicted by punches and Amir's broken nose. A bullet had passed through Amir's chest. He didn't pretend to care about the ugly brute's well-deserved fate.

Her rescuer had to be Mossad, which meant they were here in the Beqaa. *But why? Do they know about the missile and the planned EMP implosion?*

His thoughts were running wild. Had Nasrallah ordered the hit? *Wait. Was I duped?* It was like putting the pieces of a jigsaw puzzle in place... *Nasrallah isn't coming, he never was.* Amir had lured him away so he could get to Zara, and Nasrallah had cooperated by texting him and keeping him at the cannabis farm. *But who rescued her, and what is he doing in the Beqaa Valley? Unless?*

Mustafa ran back to the house and yelled up to Aisha, "Go home to your family. You are safe." Then he ran from the house and tore down the road to the Mercedes. With his lungs bursting, he spun the car around, reversing direction. With tires squealing, he sped to the main road, back to the cannabis farm. There wasn't a minute to waste. Mossad knew about the missile and the planned EMP attack. He had to stop them from destroying everything he'd planned, but mostly he had to find Zara. As much as he hated to admit it, she might have double-crossed him. He prayed he was wrong. The last thing he wanted to do was kill her, but if she betrayed him, he would have no choice.

CHAPTER 30

The sound of the Kawasaki's arrival brought Cyrus and the rest of the team outside. Everyone had been on edge awaiting Aryeh's return. Their relief was palpable when Aryeh and Zara pulled in.

"What the hell took you so long?" asked Cyrus.

Lithe as a gazelle, Zara dismounted, removed her helmet and shook out her hair. Aryeh cut the engine and swung his leg off the bike. He lowered the kickstand and removed his helmet.

"I ran into an unexpected problem."

Cyrus's gaze swept from Aryeh to Zara. "Man, that problem must have packed one hell of a punch. Looking at the two of you, I'm not sure who was the winner."

"Trust me," said Aryeh, "he ended up in a far worse place. Zara made sure he'll be dancing with the devil in Hell from here on in."

All eyes turned to Zara.

"*Mon amour,* I only did what you've done for me a thousand times," she said to Aryeh with a quirk of her lips.

Yitzhak furrowed his brows. "Who did this?"

Aryeh turned to Cyrus. "You owe Agent Zayani a debt of gratitude."

Cyrus laughed. "Me? It's your ass she saved."

Aryeh nodded, a big grin spreading across his face. "I do, but she avenged someone near and dear to your heart."

"Care to enlighten me as to what you're talking about?"

"She put a bullet through Amir Haddad, the man who blew up the bus in Tel Aviv, the man who nearly put an end to Layla and Cerise. Yeah, I'd say she's the one you should be thanking."

Cyrus stared at Aryeh and then fixed his gaze on Zara. "You took that son of a bitch out?"

Zara smiled and curtsied. "It was my pleasure, Cyrus. One less monster is walking the Earth tonight."

He would have loved to be the one who pulled the trigger, but it didn't matter. Aryeh was right. The news of Amir's death was music to his ears. He took Zara's hand and held it tight between his. "Thank you. I welcome you to take your place among us as part of the team."

She smiled. "So, what's next, boss?"

He released Zara's hand, his gaze shifting to each member of the team. "It's time for us to do what we came here to do." He glanced at his watch. "Let's wrap this up."

Like a gang of outlaws, they rode from the farm—three motorcycles in front of the van, and two behind. Inside the van, Zvi navigated their course with a GPS system and communicated with them through their earpieces. The night was cold and quiet, but Ash had been spot on with his choices of transport and the alterations he'd made to them. They rode toward the cannabis farm, a small army in virtual silence.

They chose a hill on the outskirts of the property with a commanding view of the facility. The farm, surrounded by a chain-link fence with coiled ribbons of barbed wire at the top, would discourage most invaders. However, it presented no problem for Ash and Daniel. With wire cutters, they cut a hole in the fencing giving the team entry.

Zara's swollen face had affected her vision. Cyrus decided she'd be most useful guarding Zvi and the mobile command center. It would keep her away from what he knew would be active combat. She'd already done more than her part.

"I'd prefer sticking with Aryeh and the team and heading into the eye of the storm," she protested.

"Zara, protecting the mobile center is protecting our flanks. Without Zvi communicating with the satellite and Tel Aviv, we're goners. We both know you remaining here is better for everyone." Cyrus stopped just short of ordering her to remain, but he'd gotten his point across, and reluctantly she agreed.

One at a time, the team members crawled through the gap in the fence, pushing their loaded backpacks and automatic weapons in front of them. They were all dressed in black and wore face camo as cover.

Moonlight streamed in and out of the clouds, but occasionally for what seemed an eternity, it lit the ground, causing them to freeze in place.

Inside the compound, they held to silence. Cyrus motioned his commands with hand signals. The team spread out. Unless it became necessary to talk, they would keep to radio silence. However, each member had a computer watch with which to communicate. The watch also had a tracking system that emitted the location, heartbeat, and pulse of the wearer. If activated, an alarm would send out signals leading to the wearer's position. The devices also sent the data to Zvi, who could track them in live time. All of this information simultaneously transmitted to Tel Aviv. Cyrus could easily imagine the Ramsad sitting on the edge of his seat, listening to their heartbeats.

Cyrus ran in a crouched position toward the main gate of the compound. His infrared heat-sensing goggles registered two guards in the gatehouse. His attention shifted back and forth to his watch as each member of the team's position, condition, and their communications began to scroll in. Nira and Daniel, working from opposite sides of the building where the scientists, engineers, and Hezbollah soldiers slept, were planting plastic explosives. When the action started, the building would consume itself in a fiery inferno.

His attention shifted, as a car was barreling up the road toward the gatehouse. He texted—*Speeding green Mercedes approaching guardhouse.*

Zara answered. *Mustafa! He went to vineyard. Knows Amir is dead. Knows I'm gone. Knows Mossad is here. Operation in danger!*

Mustafa hit the brakes and stopped within an inch of the gate. One of the guards ran from the gatehouse and identifying him, nodded to the guard inside.

"Sound the alarm for high alert," Mustafa yelled as the gates swung open. In an instant, lights flooded the compound. The wheels of the Mercedes screeched as Mustafa pressed the gas pedal to the floor and raced toward the greenhouse where the missile waited ready for launch.

He jumped out of the car and raised the AR-15 scope to his eye, turning in a circle surveilling the area. He froze at a sudden movement on the ground, but it was just a rabbit hopping in a frenzy to get away from the commotion.

Determined to see his plan through, he ran past the armed guards at the greenhouse. "No one gets in here," he shouted. He opened the steel doors and locked them behind him. The North Koreans had finally loaded the payload earlier in the evening, and the missile was armed and ready. He'd been briefed on the procedure and felt confident he could launch the rocket himself.

He would be doing it without coordination or confirmation from Nasrallah and the Mullahs in Iran. In all likelihood, Iran would scrub their attack against the United States because of retaliation from the superpower. Mustafa had never believed Iran would follow through anyway. It would be easy for the Mullahs to deny culpability with Hezbollah and let their surrogates do the dirty work. But Mustafa wasn't interested in Iran or what they would or wouldn't do. He was focused on only one thing, launching the missile and finding Zara.

An explosion resounded outside as he typed in the codes to enable the launch.

Mossad.

He activated the control panel, and it lit up, indicating all systems were a go. He pressed the button, opening the electric roof above the missile. He groaned at the slow process—like standing over a pot and waiting for the water to come to boil. Ignoring the amplification of gunfire outside, his finger hovered over the launch button. Finally, the roof was open. He looked up into the night sky and, for a moment, hesitated. Was he unleashing Armageddon or freeing the Muslim world from its greatest threat—Israel? Seconds were all he had. His hand shook. Everything in his life hung in the balance. Zara would never forgive him, but then Zara had most likely betrayed him. He didn't care about Nasrallah or his likely treachery—this wasn't about Nasrallah. Mustafa wanted revenge against those who had destroyed his father, his uncle, his wife, and his son.

Taking a deep breath, he pressed down and felt the Earth tremble as the boosters fired.

Cyrus ran after the Mercedes that sped toward the greenhouse. He made it about a hundred yards when the dormitory building exploded. Concrete, brick, and debris rained down, forcing him to take cover. With the explosion, the team's silence ended. He could hear Aryeh calmly ordering everyone to check-in. Nira shouted above a barrage of gunfire. "Daniel and I have taken cover," static and machine-gun fire broke up her words. "We're fifty yards east behind some tractors near where the dormitories were." Again, the line sizzled with the whiz of bullets, cutting in and out. "We're in a gun battle with approximately thirty combatants. We need back up!"

"Roger. Yitzhak, Ben, and Ash, did you hear? Over."

"Read you clear," Ash answered. "We're on our way. Roger."

That left him and Aryeh. "Aryeh, meet me at the greenhouse. Mustafa is on his way there. We have to stop him before he launches that damn missile. Over."

"Roger. On my way. Over."

Cyrus shook off the dirt from the explosion and took off at a sprint. His heart pounded in his chest, and adrenaline surged through his veins as he zigzagged, avoiding bullets that pounded the dirt around him. Cyrus returned fire as he made it to within fifty feet of the heavy steel doors of the greenhouse when he began to take heavy fire. He rolled in the dirt, avoiding a steady barrage of bullets that flew around him. He steadied himself and aimed at the two men shooting at him, and then he saw them topple to the ground.

Aryeh.

Cyrus leaped up and threw his weight against the doors, but they didn't budge. Taking a quick glance around, he saw Aryeh barreling toward him, and then he heard his worst nightmare, the sound of rocket boosters.

Aryeh shouted, "Stand back. I've got this." Aryeh removed his backpack and pulled out a yellow-orange brick of Semtex and deftly molded two pieces to each of the door hinges and inserted the fuses. "Stand back." He lit the fuses, and both men covered their ears and flattened themselves against the building on either side of the steel doors. The boom blew the doors off their hinges, and both men rushed in through the smoke and froze.

The missile was rising through the opening in the roof. Cyrus and Aryeh stood helpless.

Zvi's shouts in their earpieces snapped them out of their dazes. "What the hell is going on?" he yelled. "The missile is taking off."

"Mustafa locked himself inside the greenhouse. He only had a few minutes, but it was enough," Cyrus fired back.

"Headquarters saw everything. Tel Aviv is mobilizing a response. We're ordered to proceed as planned to the extraction rendezvous. You need to clean up the mess. Our orders have not changed. I repeat our orders have not changed. No survivors. Over."

Cyrus's voice filled with frustration. "How the hell are they going to stop that rocket?" All he could think about was Layla and Cerise. He fought back the guilt that threatened to eviscerate his ability to perform his duty. He wouldn't be there for his family, and there wasn't a damn thing he could do about it.

"They have a plan B. Over," Zvi shouted through the earpiece.

"What did you say?" His worry was already beginning to alter his effectiveness. He needed to pull himself together.

"I said they've switched to Plan B. Over."

"What's Plan B?"

"I have no idea."

CHAPTER 31

Ash ran with his Colt M4 assault carbine raised and aimed. Bouncing on his back was his Barak, HTR sniper rifle. He glanced at his watch, following the GPS to where Nira and Daniel were bogged down and ran in that direction. He needed to find some high ground where he could take out enemy combatants and even the score so Nira and Daniel would have a fighting chance. They were heavily outnumbered and were under immense fire from Hezbollah forces. Ash figured the enemy consisted of about thirty to fifty armed men. He needed to pare the number down and stop an all-out assault on the two trapped Mossad agents.

When Ash halted, Yitzhak and Ben stopped behind him. "Why are you slowing down? Didn't you hear Zvi, Daniel's wounded, and Nira's holding off the barrage by herself? I don't think she can hang on much longer."

Ash had been so focused on figuring out a plan of action he'd missed Nira's SOS. He scanned the area and hissed. "Damn-it, I need to find higher ground."

The deafening sound of machine-gun fire hitting metal assaulted them. "Over there," Ben yelled, "behind the tractor. That's where they are."

Ash adjusted his night goggles. The tractor where Nira and Daniel had taken cover was inadequate. Their precarious position could be quickly overrun. He took a few seconds to scan the area surrounding the machine. He pinpointed where the bulk of the assault against them was coming from and made up his mind. It was a metal storage shed of some sort. He could see the muzzle flash of rounds fired coming from inside and around it.

Running in the opposite direction, he gave a wide berth to the enemy. He'd spotted a tower. It would have to do.

Ash calculated the tower was about a thousand meters from where Nira and Daniel were holed up. The Barak rifle was accurate at eight hundred meters. Ash knew he was the best sniper the IDF had produced, but he also knew to be accurate at a thousand or more meters was going to be a challenge. The biggest problem was he'd be out in the open and an easy target for the enemy. The tower offered no cover, what it did offer was a birds-eye view.

Yitzhak gave him a leg up, and he hoisted himself up to the lower level of the tower. He jumped and grabbed the metal bar above him and did a pullup lifting his weight up. He was loaded down with arms and ammo, and he could feel his muscles straining as he climbed higher.

"*Mazel tov*," Yitzhak called up to him, before taking up a position of safety in a drainage ditch. Ben took cover behind a cypress tree. Between their two machine guns, they'd keep the Hezbollah combatants busy.

Ash would need the traditional Hebrew wish of good luck, *Mazel Tov*. He climbed the tower hoping the moon would remain behind the cloud cover. Even in his black ninja suit, he'd be a sitting duck if the night sky filled with light. He was on the third rung when his fingers on his left hand slipped. Barely able to hold on, dangling precariously thirty feet above the ground he was holding on by his fingernails. Grunting, he swung his legs and managed to grab onto the bar with his free hand. He hung for a moment, catching his breath, and then with an adrenaline-fueled determination, he resumed his upward climb.

He refused to dwell on his close call, and he sure as hell didn't have time to dwell on his personal feelings, but he couldn't help it. Everyone knew how he felt about Nira, except for Nira. Their back-and-forth bickering was his only outlet when it came to his feelings for her. She considered him a womanizer and a pest and had made it clear she had no interest in him. Ash had long ago accepted her rejection, but it didn't stop him from incessantly teasing her. He was like the teenager who picks on the girl he likes because it's the only way of getting her attention. Nira could hurl all of the insults she could muster at him, but when the time came to make the ultimate sacrifice, nothing would stop Ash from giving his life to save her. Thinking of her made him fight harder.

He reached the midway platform. Below with his night-vision goggles, he could see the lay of the land. He knew if he climbed higher, he'd lose accuracy. He brushed aside the thought that at this distance, he was completely vulnerable. Keeping Nira in mind kept him focused.

He lay on a narrow slat of metal and removed his goggles. The sighting-scope attached to the Picatinny rail would give him perfect night-vision. He lowered the bipod that hinged under the forend and balanced the rifle on the rail. It was precarious, but when Ash focused his powers of concentration, he would be steady as a rock. He quickly attached a sound suppressor to the muzzle. From firing thousands of rounds, Ash knew suppressors didn't affect accuracy or velocity but, on the contrary, increased both. He'd trained to compensate for any deviations affecting point of impact.

Pressing his eye to the scope, he scanned the open ground between the storage building and the tractor. A group of four men crept from the building. They inched toward the tractor where Nira and Daniel were pinned down by enemy fire.

Ash aimed.

Holding his breath, his finger curled around the trigger, and he slowly squeezed.

In his head, he knew the expansion of propellant gasses drove the bullet through the muzzle at fifty-thousand pounds per square inch. The round exploded from the rifle, and he saw his first mark hit the ground. He inhaled, and the world fell away from him.

Training, practice, and talent had transformed Ash into a killing machine. Barely aware of his surroundings, the killing machine was unleashed. He fired round after round, seamlessly reloading a new Magnum cartridge as he emptied them. One after another, he took out each combatant who made the mistake of trying to get to Nira and Daniel.

Bullets cracked by him, and the enemy made a concerted effort to bring him down, but Yitzhak and Ben kept up a steady stream of machine-gun fire, which disrupted their attempts to get to him.

Ash had no idea how much time had passed, but he kept a count of his kill. By the time he'd reached thirty-two, the gunfire had all but ceased. Ash looked down and could see Yitzhak waving an all clear. Climbing down from the tower, he reached the lower platform and froze. The sound of rocket boosters firing, and then the sight of the missile lifting out of the greenhouse made him freeze. It seemed impossible. The team, his team, had never failed before. *What the hell's gone wrong?* He jumped down, and Yitzhak and Ben joined him. The three men stared with disbelief as the rocket ascended into the night sky.

———— ◆⊰◦⊱◆ ————

Zara stood outside the van with her assault rifle held limply in her hand, its muzzle to the ground. Zvi climbed out of the van and stood beside her. Both of their gazes were fixed on the rocket climbing into the skies over Lebanon. The look on their faces mirrored their fear. The missile launch was perfect thanks to the know-how of the North Koreans. Because of Lebanon's proximity to Israel, the trajectory of the missile had been straight up. She wondered if the EMP would affect Lebanon or Syria. Her neck craned backward as she watched the projectile ascend through the cloud cover, disappearing. "What have they unleashed, *mon ami?*"

Zvi clenched his fists. "My mother and sister are at home alone. I should be—" He stopped, his words hanging in the air between them. The truth was too painful to voice.

Tears crept down her face as she imagined the outcome of a nuclear explosion in the upper atmosphere. *Worthless tears,* she scolded herself. She'd cried enough tears over the years, mourning every attack where an innocent life was lost or ruined. Angrily, she wiped away her emotional reaction with her sleeve. The resulting chaos that would follow an EMP strike filled her with anger.

"Who did this? How did they get past Aryeh, Cyrus, and the team?"

"Mustafa launched the missile. He locked himself inside the greenhouse."

Zara felt her mouth go dry. She'd hoped he wouldn't go through with it. All his professions of love and devotion and starting a new life. In the end, he was still a terrorist. "Where is he? Did they get him?" She should have killed him when she had the chance.

The butt of the rifle came down like a hammer on Zvi's head and knocked him out cold. Before Zara could lift her AR-15 to respond, the muzzle of the rifle that knocked Zvi out pressed against her back, and the man who claimed to love her said, "Don't move Zara."

She froze. "Mustafa…how—"

"Never mind how. It's not important. Start walking, we need to get away from here. The rest of your cohorts will be here momentarily."

"But where—"

He pelted her with a harsh, brittle reply. "Stop your bullshit, Zara. Drop the rifle, put your hands in the air and start walking."

There was no arguing with him. Zara did what he ordered. The AR-15 slipped to the ground, and she put her hands up.

"Now move. We're heading west back to Beirut."

She stumbled ahead with the muzzle of his assault rifle pressed hard to her back. "Mustafa, this is ridiculous. We can't walk all the way to Beirut."

"Who says we're going to walk? I have a motorcycle stashed at a farm not far from here. Don't you think I would have prepared for every eventuality? *Mon amour*, how little you know me."

They walked in silence for a quarter of a mile. She waited for Mustafa to initiate a conversation with her. *What he doesn't know is probably eating away at him.* Her silence paid off.

"Tell me what happened at the vineyard, and don't lie to me, Zara. If you do, I swear I'll kill you right here and finish it."

She turned and looked at him, thrusting out her chin in defiance. "If you've made up your mind already, why should I answer? Just shoot me and get it over with."

He smiled. "Always the show of bravery, Zara. I suppose it's why I fell for you. You wear that mantle of iron will and unbreakable righteousness. Your beauty and bravado have been irresistible to me since the moment I first laid eyes on you."

She huffed indignantly. "You see what you want to see Mustafa. You have from the beginning."

"I see the woman I love. The woman who betrayed me."

"I never betrayed you."

"Tell me what happened at the vineyard. I have to know."

"Can we sit for a moment? I've been through a lot tonight." She raised her swollen face to him so he could see the blue-black marks left by Amir's fist.

He hissed under his breath. "The bastard."

"You have no idea what a monster he was."

"Tell me. It is important for me to know."

She told him everything, beginning with his beating her when she'd baited him. "You saw the video camera. You must suspect what he intended to do to me."

"It made me sick."

"He was going to film his rape of me and then strangle me as he filled me with his disgusting sperm. He bragged about doing it before."

"How did you get away, who helped you?"

"Mossad figured out everything you were planning and sent a team to stop you. My friend is part of the team. I've worked with him before. He warned me to leave. He came to get me."

"Didn't you trust me?"

"Being held prisoner doesn't work for me. And that is what you did to me. Thank God Aryeh came, or Amir would have gotten away with all of it. Aryeh and Amir were in a fight to the death. Amir was winning. I got free and shot and killed him. He deserved a much worse death. He blew up a bus in Tel Aviv and brutally murdered a Palestinian girl the same way he intended to kill me. He killed all of your men at the vineyard." She spit. "Good riddance to garbage."

Mustafa paced back and forth. "So, you didn't betray me to Mossad?"

She looked at him without expression and answered. "No."

He scrutinized her.

She wondered if he would believe her. "Mustafa, did you even hesitate for a moment before launching the missile?"

His eyes clouded. "For a moment, I considered not pressing the button. But then I thought of my father, uncle, and brother, and the promises I'd made to them. When I saw my son and wife's face before my eyes, I was filled with a hatred you could never understand. I pushed the button."

"Did you think of the destruction you would unleash on other innocent women and children? The elderly? Good people who live simple, honest lives?"

"Do they think of us when they send their bombs?"

"This is why we can never be. Two wrongs don't make a right. We see the world through a different lens."

He ignored what she said. "We need to go, *habibi*. I've done what I set out to do. It's time for us to leave this valley, to leave Lebanon. No matter what occurred, nothing has changed the way I feel about you."

"I can't, *mon amour.*"

"Why not? I know you love me. We can make a life together away from all of this."

She shook her head. "Mustafa, for a time I believed it was possible, but no more. When the missile climbed into the sky, it took with it any possibility of you and I sharing a life. I can't live with what you've done."

"With time, you'll forget. With time everything will be as it should be. We can make a new life together."

"No. With time I will grow to resent you. I will grow to hate you, and I don't want to hate you."

He studied her face as if memorizing it. "You will never hate me, my love. You are only trying to convince your heart, but your heart will never listen."

"You may be right, but I can't come with you now. I won't."

"I will wait for you to come to your senses. One day I will reach out to you, find you, and you will come to me."

She didn't answer because she wasn't sure whether he was wrong or right. Her feelings ran deep for him. She prayed with the passage of years, she would forget him. "You'd better go. My friend will be looking for me. He won't rest until he finds me."

"He loves you?"

"No. But we've shared a lot. We saved each other's lives in the past. It's a bond neither of us will ever break. If he finds you, he will kill you, Mustafa."

"I could stay and kill him, ambush him."

"I won't let you. I'll throw myself in front of your bullets if you try. You'd better shoot me now because there's no way I'll let you harm him."

He studied her face. It took less than a second for him to make his move. Before she could push him away, he embraced her pinning her to his chest, and his lips claimed hers. He kissed her, and she didn't have the will to refuse him. He broke the kiss, releasing her. "This doesn't end here, Zara." Without another word, he walked away and disappeared into the darkness.

Zara stared into the night. Her lips wet from his kiss. Tears pricked her eyes. She fought them, but she might as well have stuck her finger in a dam about to overflow. There was no way to stop the flood of feelings. Her life had become an abyss of emptiness and loss.

The minutes ticked away, and the tears finally subsided. A branch crunched, and Zara turned. Out of the darkness came Aryeh, his rifle ready and his finger on the trigger. She put her hands up. "Aryeh, thank God you're safe."

"Where is he?"

"Gone."

"Where, Zara? You know what he did, he has to pay."

"I can't help you. I have no idea where he's gone. He didn't trust me with that information."

"He didn't harm you?"

"No. He tried to convince me to escape with him, but I refused. When he realized I meant what I said, he left."

"You could have stopped him. Delayed him until I got here. You knew I'd come for you."

"Aryeh, leave it alone. I couldn't play a part in his death."

His face reddened with anger. "Let's go, the helicopters is on its way. You're endangering the team, or don't you care?"

Her cheeks filled with heat, but she swallowed her outrage like a bitter pill. "I will pretend you didn't say that to me." She walked past him back toward where the team was assembling.

CHAPTER 32

Mossad Headquarters
Tel Aviv, Israel
2:31 A.M.

Noam Levi stood, his arms rigid, his hands fisted behind his back. He wasn't a large man, but his power filled the situation room. His attention was riveted on the large video screen dominating the room. The live satellite feed from the team was being monitored and analyzed by twelve computer stations. Eight video screens were projecting live action as it took place. A command table was in communication with each branch of the IDF. Smaller monitors carried both domestic and foreign news feeds. The back wall held a row of clocks displaying different time zones around the world.

Security systems and the Orfek satellite had picked up the missile launch. In less time than it took to take a breath, everyone in the situation room froze as they watched the missile with its deadly payload rise through the roof of the greenhouse.

The notion of the team failing to stop the missile launch had always been a possibility. Plan B—an unacknowledged plan—had simmered on a back burner in the hopes its implementation wouldn't be necessary. The grim reality of the situation activated the alternate solution.

Weeks ago, the Ramsad had been briefed on new strategic defense technology that Israeli scientists had been working on for the last year. The premise of it was well known, Airborne Lasers, better known as ABL, could be used to destroy a nuclear missile threat.

Staring at the big screen, the Ramsad and everyone else in the command center held their breaths as the UAV drone lifted off from Tel Nof Airbase on a course to intercept the missile. They all knew this drone was their last hope of defense against an EMP attack.

It was hard for Noam Levi to wrap his head around the fact that the fate of the nation was in the hands of a twenty-year-old video gaming genius who probably didn't shave yet. Israel had an arsenal of computer geeks and gaming geeks serving in every branch of the IDF. The commanders of all branches of the military knew that tech brains as much as brawn controlled the future of defense. Aggressively they targeted these teen prodigies for the military.

The Ramsad's gaze shifted between the screens displaying the drone and the missile. He knew the rocket was stoppable only in the booster phase of the launch. Once the booster fell away, the missile would be impossible to disarm. Its speed and trajectory beyond their ability to neutralize. Beads of sweat formed on his brow as he watched the missile climb into the night sky.

The technology being used to stop the missile wasn't new. For years, earlier versions of ABL had been tested by the Americans. The problem was the oxygen-iodine lasers they'd used had always been too burdensome. These enormous lasers mounted on the nose of a large aircraft were ineffective. Using scientific ingenuity, Israeli scientists had come up with a solution. Megawatt solid-state lasers were miniature in comparison to oxygen-iodine lasers. Now without endangering pilots or aircraft, the new laser was mounted on a drone. They'd named the armed drone, *Hakela shel David*, David's slingshot.

General Samson stood shoulder to shoulder next to the Ramsad. "Don't worry, Noam, so long as the missile is still in the booster phase, we can stop it." The general's gaze was locked on the screen. "The drone using infrared sensors is calculating and transmitting at lightning speed the missile's course, speed, aimpoint, and simultaneously measuring atmospheric turbulence."

The data sped across one of the computer screens so fast Noam wondered how the analyst monitoring could even begin to make heads or tails of it.

"When, General, when will the drone engage?"

Noam had barely uttered his question when the drone fired the laser at the missile. The bursts lasted only a few seconds. It seemed impossible those few bursts of energy could bring down a missile.

"What's happening?" the Ramsad asked, struggling to remain calm.

"Watch, sir. The laser's concentrated power needs only a few seconds of pulses to be effective. The outside shell of the missile is heating to such a degree it will structurally fail."

The missile did seem to be wobbling. And then without warning, it tilted. Right before their eyes as if by magic, the missile burst into flames—the heat radiating off its metallic skin had set the missile ablaze. Then in an about-face, the missile upended and plunged toward Earth.

"But won't the nuke explode?"

"No, sir. The nuclear device and the missile are disintegrating together. The EMP threat is over."

Applause broke out in the situation room. Even the Ramsad who had fought to maintain a stoic calm blinked back tears. "Thank God, we have prevailed."

"Yes, sir. We have won the day. David has slain Goliath again and saved the Israelites."

CHAPTER 33

Beqaa Valley
Beirut, Lebanon
2:45 A.M.

Ash, Ben, and Yitzhak found little resistance as they zigzagged across the open ground to where Nira and Daniel had made their stand. Ash ran with his rifle slung behind his back, his eye pressed to the AR-15's night scope. Sweeping the weapon back and forth, he sprayed bullets shooting any combatants who got in his way. Yitzhak brought up his flank, and Ben ran beside him. As per their orders, they killed all enemy combatants in their path, but their main desire was to get to Nira and Daniel.

Yitzhak radioed, "Nira, don't shoot the milkmen, we're almost to you. Over."

Instead of her typical feisty reply, they heard a decidedly weak and tired voice. "Daniel needs attention, and I…never mind you'll see when you get here. Over."

Ash listened to the communication between Yitzhak and Nira and replied. "Hold on, baby. We're coming for you. Over." He knew she'd rip him a new asshole for calling her baby, but he didn't care. All he cared about was making sure she was safe, and right now, he was plenty worried. Her voice told him something was wrong. Worry and anger only made him a more deadly killer. He ran like a madman firing bullets in every direction.

"Slow down, damn-it," Yitzhak yelled. "She's going to think you're the enemy and shoot your ass."

Ash finally stopped and grabbed a breath. "Nira, don't shoot."

Nira's voice rattled in his ear. "*Meshuganah*, have you lost your mind?"

Ash released a sigh of relief. Nira calling him crazy sounded more like the woman he knew. The three men walked around the tractor. Daniel was lying on the ground in a semi-conscious state, moaning. Yitzhak ran and dropped his pack in the dirt. He pulled out his medical kit and immediately began triaging. Daniel had taken a bullet on the right side of his chest and was bleeding profusely. "He's lost a lot of blood, but it doesn't look like anything vital was hit. I'll do what I can and give him some morphine, but we need to move."

Ben, who'd taken up a position of defense, called, "Do whatever you need to get them stable. No one is getting past me."

"I've only the basics, but Zvi's got provisions in the van, and the pick-up point isn't far." He turned to Nira, "Are you all right?" Then he saw her stagger, and Ash caught her in his arms before she hit the ground.

"No, you big ape, I've been hit."

"Where?"

"My thigh…" She groaned, her features scrunching up from the pain. He looked down and could see her pants drenched with blood. "Take it easy, baby." He gently laid her on the ground.

"Don't call me baby, or I'll…" Nira's words were cut short, and her features twisted in pain as Ash used his knife to cut away her blood-soaked pant leg. Yitzhak was packing Daniel's chest wound. Neither Ash nor Yitzhak was a doctor, but they'd all received training in the treatment of battle wounds. They knew how to stop the pain and stop the flow of blood until medics could take over.

He ignored Nira's reprimand. "Lucky for you, it's not the femoral artery, or you'd be dead." He eased her onto her side. Using an auto-injector, he administered a dose of morphine. The effect was almost immediate. Her eyelids fluttered, and she sighed.

He grinned. "Feels better, doesn't it, baby."

She glared at him, but he remained focused on cleaning the area where the bullet had entered. He tied off her leg with an Israeli bandage, designed with a pressure applicator to staunch the flow of blood. He wrapped it tight around her thigh, bandaging her up. "This should hold until we get you aboard the helicopter. Do you think you can walk? If not, I'll carry you." He knew she couldn't walk, but he wanted her to ask for his help.

"I'm going to try," she growled.

"Suit yourself." He offered his hand to help her up. There was no sense in reminding her that he'd saved her life. Nira was Nira, and the thought of owing him would only exacerbate her more.

She took his hand without comment, but when she put weight on her leg, she cried out and collapsed. "Good try, but I'll take it from here." He swooped her up in his arms. "Yitz, can you manage Daniel on your own? I've got my hands full." He held back his grin.

"Yeah, I'll carry Daniel on my back."

"I'll cover you both," said Ben. "Yitz, we can take turns carrying Daniel."

"Nira, you can hold my AR-15 just in case Ben needs backup. It'll give you something to think about other than being helpless in my arms." The grin that had threatened to make an appearance spread across his face.

"When this is over, I'll teach you a thing or two about being helpless," she snarled.

"I think I might enjoy being at your mercy."

Yitzhak radioed Zvi. "Zvi, we've got Daniel and Nira, they're both wounded. We could use back up. Over."

Cyrus answered. "Zvi's indisposed, but I'm on my way to you. Over."

"Roger that. What about the EMP missile?" Asked Yitzhak.

"It's been eliminated. I'll fill you in later. Over."

Carrying Daniel on his back, Yitzhak fought for every breath and every step forward. Nira fell in and out of consciousness, mumbling incoherently.

A bullet whizzed by Ash just missing his temple. He hit the ground with Nira. She cried out. Ash yelled, "Damn it, Ben, do something," Yitzhak gently lowered Daniel and grabbed the AR-15 from Nira.

Ben and Yitzhak crawled forward on the ground. Two minutes later, the air crackled with gunfire. Ash angled his body in front of Nira, protecting her from the retaliatory fire. His eye pressed to the scope of the rifle, he stilled. He blew out a breath of relief when he saw Ben and Yitzhak walk back, smiling.

Nira was moaning. Ash gave her another shot of morphine. She quieted. Ben hoisted Daniel back on Yitzhak's back, and they pressed slowly forward.

Cyrus met them when they reached the fence. It seemed like hours since they'd initially cut and crawled through. "How are they?" He helped Yitzhak with Daniel.

"Daniel took a bullet in the chest, and Nira's got a bullet lodged in her thigh. They'll both need surgery and blood transfusions," said Ash.

"What happened to Zvi?" Yitzhak asked, bending forward with his hands on his knees, trying to catch his breath. Carrying Daniel's dead weight had left him exhausted.

"Mustafa knocked him out and took Zara, but she managed to talk him into letting her go. I suspect Zvi's going to be nursing a hell of a headache. We're set to go as soon as we get Daniel and Nira in the van." He glanced at a semi-conscious Nira, her head resting against Ash's chest. "She's pale. Doesn't look so good."

Ash stared down at her colorless face, worry lines threading across his brow. "I know. She's lost a lot of blood. She's been mumbling a whole lot of gibberish. The sooner we get her to the medics, the better."

They made it to the van and loaded Nira and Daniel inside. But when Ash kneeled to lay Nira down, she cried out, "Ash don't leave me." Her arms locked around his neck.

Ash brushed his lips over her forehead and whispered. "Don't worry, baby. I'm here. You couldn't drive me away if you tried."

She whispered in a delirious state, "I need you, Ash."

The last thing he ever expected to hear was Nira saying she needed him. She drifted off with a contented smile on her lips. Ash stood, his gaze fixed on her as Zvi got an IV with hypertonic fluids flowing into her arm. Zvi sporting a bandage on his head worked feverishly to stabilize both Daniel and Nira. When he'd done what he could, he gave the okay for the team to move.

They raced back to the farm. The Stealth Hawk that had crossed into Lebanese airspace ten minutes before landed. The first rays of sunlight warmed the eastern horizon. Daniel and Nira were loaded first so the medics could start immediate treatment. Then the rest of the exhausted team climbed aboard. The rotors had never stopped silently turning, and the invisible bird lifted off on command from Abe.

"You should know the Ramsad believes you performed well."

Cyrus frowned. "We failed, Abe. You don't have to sugarcoat the truth."

"You didn't fail. Without your efforts, the missile wouldn't have been stopped. We wouldn't have been ready for it. Believe me, we're all grateful. Last night the people of Israel slumbered peacefully, without knowing how close they came to Armageddon. As far as I'm concerned, you should all be decorated."

Yitzhak laughed. "Decorated? That's pretty funny. How do you decorate a team that doesn't exist?"

"You thank them behind closed doors and hope it is enough." Abe reached out and shook hands with each member of the team. "Thank you."

CHAPTER 34

Cyrus sat through each team member's debriefing, except for Daniel and Nira, who were taken to Hadassah Medical Center.

As soon as Ash finished with his debrief, he grabbed his gear. "I'm going straight to the hospital. I want to be there when she wakes up."

"Ash, call me as soon as she's out of surgery."

"Will do, boss." He grinned. "Nira's tough. I figure when she sees me hovering over her like a mother hen, she'll want to kick my ass. If I know my girl, getting pissed off at me will speed up her recovery."

"Give her a kiss for me."

"I plan on giving her a lot of kisses." He gave Cyrus a thumbs up and left.

Zara's interview was quick. She was commended for her contribution and then escorted to the airport. The DGSE apprised of the situation recalled her, and she left to board a flight to Paris. Her career as a spy was at an end. What should have been a proud moment for her had culminated in tragedy. In retaliation for her collaboration with Mossad, Hezbollah had executed Faiz, her photographer. Cyrus tried to console her, but she was devastated. She left for the airport as if she was on her way to the guillotine.

During Zara's accounting of the events, Aryeh leaned against a wall but said nothing. The old comrades in arms had exchanged few words since their return from Lebanon. Zara tried to give Aryeh a hug before departing, but he pulled away. Once she was gone, Aryeh disappeared without a word. As usual, the elusive spy kept his thoughts to himself.

The rest of the team parted with handshakes, eager to reunite with their families. For the time being, they were all given a leave of absence.

Before they left, the Ramsad stood before them. "I know you all blame yourselves for the missile being launched. You think you failed, but in reality, there was nothing you could have done. The important thing is that we were successful—without your efforts, the attack could not have been stopped. Enough said. Take this time and seek renewal. Go home to your families and forgive yourselves. The enemy still plots, still plans, and we still need you to stand against them in the future."

The sly fox who headed Mossad didn't lavish praise or scorn. He was a realist, not an idealist. With a nod, he left the room.

Cyrus arrived at the safehouse in Ramat Hasharon. The driver punched in the security code, and he walked through the gate. Even though Cyrus was running on borrowed fuel, having not slept in more than twenty-four hours, he couldn't wait to see Layla and Cerise. Not that he needed reminding of what they meant to him. Everything Cyrus had been through only reinforced how precious they were to him. He heard voices coming from the kitchen. His beloveds were safe, and he couldn't wait to see them.

He dropped his bag in the entry and brushed back his hair. When he strode into the kitchen, Cerise shrieked, "*Aba*," and threw herself into his open arms. He lifted her up, smothering her face with kisses. Across the room, he saw Layla turn. She stood frozen, unaware that the spoon she held dripped oatmeal on the floor.

As if waking from a dream Layla ran to him wrapping her arms around both Cerise and him. She wept, "You're safe. You've come home." she repeated over and over.

"*Eshgham*, my love, I promised you I would."

"I've been so worried about you. Is it over?"

"For now, it's over. I wish I could say it was over forever."

"I don't care." She pressed her lips to his neck. "Having you home safe is the answer to my prayers."

Amused, he pulled away so he could gaze into her eyes. "As you can see, Superman did everything in his power to come home to you."

"He certainly did. And I promise you'll get a proper Superman welcome later." She pressed against him until there was no space between them.

He bent to claim her lips, his love for her filling all the empty space in his heart.

"Daddy, you're crushing me." Cerise interrupted oblivious of the fire that raged between her parents. "Stop kissing. *Ima* and I have a surprise for you."

He sighed, reluctantly ending the kiss. "A surprise? What kind of surprise?" He tweaked Cerise's chin, eliciting a string of giggles.

Her eyes grew wide with excitement. "Let me show you."

"Cerise, let Daddy rest a bit before you show him." The smile on Layla's lips meant she was hiding something.

"No! Now, Daddy! You have to see her now."

"Her?"

Cerise's brows drew together in exasperation. "Yes. I can't tell you anything more. It's a surprise!"

"Okay, okay." He put her down, and she grabbed his hand, pulling him behind her. He smiled, thinking what his life would be like without this child of his heart. She was as impatient as he and never backed down. Layla rarely won an argument with her.

He knew a teenage Cerise was going to give him gray hair. It reminded him of how close he'd come again to losing everything that mattered most to him in the world. Cerise led him upstairs to her bedroom and pushed open the door. He looked around, but he didn't see anything in the room resembling a "her."

"Are you playing a joke on *Aba*?"

"No, silly." And then, like a general, she ordered, "Norit, come." From behind the pillows emerged a yellow ball of fur. Norit yipped at Cerise and sat, her tail thumping on the bed.

Cyrus hid the look of consternation on his face when Cerise turned to him. "Isn't she wonderful, *Aba*? Just like the dog we met at the beach. Do you like her name? Doesn't she look just like a buttercup? *Ima* helped me name her."

Cyrus cleared his throat. "Is she housebroken?"

"Not yet, but we're working on it. Norit's a smart puppy, and she's trying very hard to learn." She turned to him. "Do you want to hold her?"

The look on her face told him he'd better say yes. "Sure. She won't bite me, will she?"

"*Aba*, of course not." Cerise filled her arms with the yellow fluff. Norit slathered Cerise's face with wet kisses. "Hold your hands out and be careful not to drop her. She's still a baby."

Awkwardly, he took the puppy Cerise reverently placed in his hands. He held her at arms distance. "Daddy, you have to cradle her to your chest like a baby and let her kiss you."

Cyrus could see no way out of his daughter's request. He brought Buttercup to his face, sniffing her. The smell wasn't unpleasant. The puppy wriggled and then lathered his face in a wet, tickling tongue. He couldn't help but laugh.

"Oh, *Aba*, she loves you." Cerise clapped her hands together with delight.

"Well." Layla stood at the door. "Cerise, I think Daddy is going to be Norit's favorite. What do you think?"

"*Ima*, I'm Norit's favorite."

"Yes, baby, you are, but look at the way Norit is kissing Daddy. I think she likes him."

"Does she ever stop," he asked, barely able to conceal his concern.

"No, Daddy. Isn't it wonderful?"

Cyrus released a breath. He was done for, and he knew it. The funny thing was he didn't mind. He felt a spark of pleasure holding Norit. He smoothed his hand over her fluffy coat. The puppy was already endearing itself to him. After all, the once cold-hearted spy had succumbed to a feisty redhead, and Cerise had wrapped him around her finger from the moment he laid eyes on her. What would be so bad about having a dog?

EPILOGUE

6 Months later
Buenos Aires, Argentina

Zara sprinted down the steps and lost herself among the crowds of Friday afternoon strollers. Buenos Aires, like Paris, was a lively city at all hours. She turned a corner, and the Rio de la Plata came into view. The widest river in the world she'd learned wasn't really a river, but an immense estuary where the Paraná and Uruguay rivers emptied their freshwater and merged into the Atlantic Ocean. One of the things Zara missed most about Beirut was its proximity to the Mediterranean Sea, and the Rio de la Plata now filled the bill for her need for a water view.

Her assignment to Argentina by the DGSE was about as far away from Beirut, and her former life as a spy as the French intelligence agency could find. It was a routine assignment in a relatively safe capital working with a close ally and trade partner. She'd just finished a lunch meeting with the Argentine trade commissioner. She'd schmoozed and played her role, which was what her duties with politicos required. Her greatest difficulty was fending off the unwanted attention of those same politicians and government officials, both Argentinian and French. The trade commissioner's suggestion of dinner next week was an easy rebuke. There was nothing about the paunchy man she found even remotely appealing.

Only minutes away from the embassy, her apartment was in the Chico Palermo neighborhood. The apartment was small, but the luxury neighborhood was close to *Los Bosques de Palermo*, the most beautiful park in Buenos Aires. Every afternoon it became her destination of choice. It was so like the Bois de Boulogne in Paris. It reminded her of home.

Zara opened the door to her apartment and called "Lulu." A small French poodle came running, the silver ball of fur on her tail wagging exponentially with her excitement. She'd been lonely when she first arrived and had rescued the dog from a shelter. In her previous life as a spy, it would have been unthinkable to have a pet. Lulu made up for Zara's separation from family and friends.

"Lulu, *mon cheri*, shall we take a walk?"

Lulu rose on her hind legs and danced in a circle, her paws clapping together. She'd come with this particular talent and several others that made Zara wonder if she'd been abandoned or lost by a circus.

She picked Lulu up and cuddled her. "Where shall we go today? The Rose Garden with its scent of a thousand varieties of roses, or should we go to the Japanese Garden." The image of the red bridge straddling a diminutive lake and Koi pond settled in her mind. She sighed, admitting the truth to herself, the forest within the city was the only thing keeping her sane these days. Her life had narrowed to anonymity in a park and Lulu.

Since her reckless affair with Mustafa, she had no desire to become romantically entangled with anyone. For a woman who enjoyed the excitement of being chased and conquered, this produced a particularly stressful repetitiveness to her days. The passage of time had never held any sway in a life filled with purpose, but now she felt the years and wondered if she was destined for spinsterhood. She, who'd driven men to risk their lives for the chance to possess her, should end up alone. She chuckled at the thought.

She kicked off her heels and changed into jogging sweats and sneakers. July in Buenos Aires is the coolest month of the year, but Zara supposed fifty degrees was better than the ninety-plus degrees and high humidity of Beirut in July.

Attaching Lulu's leash to her collar, she stepped out the electronic door of the apartment house and down the three steps of her building to the sidewalk. Her route rarely varied. She headed to the Japanese Gardens, and then she'd supper in her favorite Japanese restaurant and eat sushi, sashimi, and drink sake while watching the world stroll by.

Stepping into the park was like entering another world. Her cares melted away when she passed through the gate to an immense expanse of greenery. The park delivered a sense of peace after the hustle and bustle of the noisy horns and chaotic rhythm of the city. She loved the vast array of trees. In her effort to fill the hours of her life, she'd taken to studying their genus and botanical names.

She strolled with Lulu past a Jacaranda tree alive with a cacophony of squawking parrots. The birds kept up a steady stream of caws amid a splash of colored blooms. She laughed to herself and wondered if they thought they were invisible. Their vivid blue, yellow, and red feathers stuck out like a sore thumb, clashing with the pink and lilac flowers on the trees.

A breeze blowing from the La Plata lifted the fallen petals, scattering them across her path. She felt them decorate her hair—taking out her phone, she took a selfie of her dark hair adorned with the colorful crown. She'd text it to her parents who were always complaining about her postings in far off places. Having lost a son, they wanted nothing more than to keep their wayward daughter close. It seemed to her parents when they lost Jacob, they lost Zara too.

The light dappled across the walking path as she strolled to a bench. Mothers pushing strollers and joggers out for their evening run made her feel less alone. She tried not to contemplate what a disappointment her life had become. It made her realize how much she missed the excitement of never knowing what the day held in store for her. Now her days were predictable and mundane. She'd tried reaching out to Aryeh several times, but he'd never texted back. She wondered if she would ever see her former lover and trusted friend ever again. Life was full of so many regrets. And the life of a former spy even more so. In truth, she held the hope that one day Aryeh would forgive her. Eventually, he would come to his senses and miss their friendship. For ten years, their lives had been entwined. When he lost Esther to a sniper's bullet, Zara had been the one to help him pick up the pieces of his life and forgive himself. *He's punishing me right now, and I must be patient that he will forgive me in time.*

Zara let Lulu off her leash to sniff the grass and explore. She took a moment to email the selfie to her parents. Glancing up, she saw Lulu running away in the direction of a teenage boy who walked toward her. She stuffed her phone in her purse and ran after Lulu. The dog had never ventured more than a few feet from where she sat, and she couldn't understand why now she'd chosen to make her escape.

Breathless, she came to a halt. Lulu was doing her circus dance around the boy, vying for his attention. "*Lo siento,* she's never done this before. She's usually timid with strangers."

"*No hay problema.*" The boy smiled, unable to take his eyes off Lulu.

"*Sentarse,* Lulu." Lulu yipped and planted her rear in the grass. Her tongue slipping in and out of her mouth with each breath. Dragging his gaze away from Lulu, the boy handed her a folded piece of paper.

"What's this?"

The boy turned to look behind him. "A man asked me to give it to you."

She felt the hairs on the nape of her neck rise. Her gaze swept across the park to search for the man. It could be anyone, but her sixth sense set off an alarm. The only reason someone would enlist the help of a teenage boy to deliver a note was because he didn't want to be seen by her, or if he knew she wouldn't welcome his approach. "Did he pay you?"

The boy nodded shyly.

"Where is the man now? Did he tell you to wait for a response from me?"

"No, Senora. He just told me to wait ten minutes and then deliver it." She could see the boy was now uncertain whether he'd done the right thing.

She smiled. "It's okay. You did nothing wrong. *Gracias*, you've accomplished your task." Reaching in her wallet, she grabbed a hand full of pesos and handed them to him. "For your trouble."

She bent and picked up Lulu and walked back to the park bench. She attached Lulu's leash and sat, ignoring Lulu's whines to be set free.

She opened the note and read:

Zara, I have someone that belongs to you. Someone close to your heart. If you want him back, meet me at the Muelle de los Pescadores at 6 p.m. Come alone.

Her heart pounded in her chest. She had no idea who was close to her heart. Had she somehow put another life in danger? All she could think about was Faiz, and she knew he was dead. There was no one in Buenos Aires she truly cared about enough to want back.

She glanced at her watch. It was 5 p.m. If she did go to the fisherman's pier, she'd need to take a cab and leave now. The traffic was horrific at this hour, and fear crept up her spine. If she was late, would someone's life be in danger? She picked up Lulu and walked at a brisk pace to the main gates where taxi cabs congregated.

How did the mystery note writer know to find her at the park? She, an ex-spy, had always had a sixth sense about being followed. How long had this man—she assumed it was a man— been following her? What else did he know about her? She shuddered, her mind racing to find answers.

As expected, the traffic was awful, and by the time the cab dropped her off, she was five minutes late. *Late for what?* She wondered. On the pier were numerous fishermen, catching and filling buckets with small fish. Dinner, she supposed.

Her eyes warily searched for a familiar face or body type. Was she five minutes too late? *Impossible*, she thought, *five minutes is nothing*. Lulu pulled at the leash, wanting to investigate the bucket of one of the fishermen.

"Stop, Lulu…" and then she saw a man standing at the end of the pier. He leaned casually against the railing. Was he watching her? It was too great a distance to tell. Slowly she began walking. She didn't have a gun, and he'd managed to find an isolated spot. *At least, I'm not entirely alone.* She looked around again and was buoyed, knowing there were several groups of fishermen laughing and congratulating each other when one of them pulled a line with a dangling silvery fish from the river.

She kept walking. Even as he came more fully into view, she felt no recognition. He wore a fedora, and it was pulled down, shading his face. She could see the reflection of dark sunglasses. He wore jeans and a black leather jacket, which revealed nothing about him. Buenos Aires was the capital of leather goods in Argentina, and most everyone had a closet full of leather.

She stopped about five feet from him and waited. Lulu danced around her legs, and she shushed her without ever taking her eyes off the man who raised his head to look directly at her. She broke the stand-off, pulling the note from her pocket. "Recognize this?"

He smiled. There was something familiar about his smile that made her heart race. She needed to hear him speak. "I asked you a question."

Instead, he took a few steps toward her until he was barely a foot away. Before she could back away, he reached out and cupped her shoulders, pulling her closer. His face was inches from hers, but she still couldn't identify who he was. *Could he hear her heart beating wildly in her chest?*

His voice was heavy with emotion when he whispered, "Zara…*habibi*… it's been so long."

She felt her knees grow weak, and if his hands weren't holding on to her, she might have collapsed. His name escaped her lips, barely a whisper. "Mustafa?" She was lightheaded, the world spinning around her. "How did you find me?"

He lifted his sunglasses so she could see his eyes. The way he looked at her was like standing beneath the rays of the sun. Warmth spread through her limbs, awakening all the passions that had lain dormant since they'd last made love. *How can this be happening?*

"Finding you was easy, figuring out how and when to contact you was more difficult. I was afraid you'd stubbornly refuse to see me. I'm sorry about Faiz. I never wished him harm."

She scrutinized his face to see whether he was sincere. She remembered how jealous he was of her photographer. "It wasn't your fault, it was

Nasrallah. I'll always be heartbroken about Faiz's murder. More than anyone, I'm the guilty one."

"No, Zara, he was a professional. He did what he'd been trained to do."

Pausing, she let the memory of Faiz find its proper place in her thoughts.

"Your face—I didn't recognize you. Everything is different about it, yet everything is the same."

He smiled. "I told you about the Swiss plastic surgeon. After I left you, I went to Switzerland, and the doctor created a new me. What do you think?"

She studied his features. His nose, once flat and spread across his face, was now aquiline. His forehead was higher and gave him a brainy look. The forehead lift had also lifted his brows and straightened them, giving them an upward tilt. His previously dark chocolate brown eyes were now hazel thanks to contact lenses. The most profound difference, however, was the implants of cheekbones and jawline, which squared his features and made him look exotic like the gypsies of Spain. It was no wonder she hadn't recognized him, nothing about him resembled who he'd been. Even his lips had been altered, with a bowed indentation that made her envious. "Truthfully, I thought you were handsome before."

He frowned.

"But, I must admit your face is more interesting now."

He grinned. "Zara, I've missed you in every way imaginable."

She pulled out of his grasp. She had questions, and his body pressed against her made it hard to think. "Where are you living, and what are you doing in Buenos Aires?" She was annoyed at herself—she was still attracted to him. She needed to hide her true feelings, and the best approach was nonchalance.

But Mustafa wasn't buying in. "I'm in Buenos Aires only for you. I want to show you my new home. Do you remember I told you I had a desire to live off the land, to farm?"

"Yes, and I couldn't imagine how such a sedentary life could ever replace the drama of terrorism."

"Ah, but you are wrong, my love. There is nothing sedentary about working the land. It's humbling but never dull. I bought a vineyard in Mendoza. A thousand acres in the eastern foothills of the Andes. From my ranchero, you can see the snowcapped peaks of Mount Aconcagua. We grow Malbec grapes, and I'm producing a high-quality vintage Malbec wine that I hope will please even the smug French woman I hope to marry."

Her response froze on her lips. "Did you say marry?"

"If you would do me the great honor. I'm a changed man, Zara."

She was speechless. Was it possible a man could change so radically? Could he change not just his appearance, but the very clay he was molded from? Could a leopard change its spots? And why did she care? "You launched the missile, Mustafa. If the Israelis hadn't miraculously stopped it, you might have killed millions. How can I forget what you did?"

"I'm sorry, Zara. I wish I could have stopped it back then. I have tortured myself with the knowledge of what I did every day since. I was wrong, Zara. I know it's not an excuse, but I did it in the heat of anger. I thought you'd betrayed me. I did it with a vengeance in my heart for my wife and my son and for the misguided loyalty to the cause for my father, my uncle, my brother—all lost. But afterward, I only felt worse. I was lost as well. I thank Allah every day that he stopped the missile. But I realized I was done. I was finished with the past. I want to live in the present. To appreciate each day that Allah gives me. I can only atone by being a good man, and I hope—a good husband and father." He lifted her hands to his lips and kissed her palms. "Zara, I'm begging you to forgive me. Give me a chance, *habibi*."

"You ask a lot, Mustafa."

"I love you, Zara. I know that you love me. I know how you live here in Buenos Aires. Alone." He looked down at Lulu, who'd curled up in a ball. He kneeled to pet her and looked up at Zara. "Don't reject me because of what I've done in the past, or who I was. We have both done things that will haunt us for the rest of our lives. But we can also choose a different path. Give me a chance to prove to you I've changed. Come with me to Mendoza."

"There's something you need to know, Mustafa. It may change what you feel for me."

Mustafa searched her face, the look on his face was one of patience.

"I'm Jewish, Mustafa. My mother was a Moroccan Jew, and my father was a Tunisian Arab, but I was raised in the faith of my mother. I am a practicing Jew."

"I know. I've known for some time."

"But how?" She scrutinized his face. "Doesn't this bother you?"

"Zara, I love you. I don't care about anything else. If you love me, everything else will work itself out. Come with me to Mendoza."

"So, you want me to just drop everything and go with you to a mountain in the Andes."

"Yes. I want you to try it. I know once there you'll never want to leave, but if you decide you don't want to stay..." His voice broke.

She finished his sentence. "You'll let me go?"

He nodded. "I'll let you go." He stood and pulled her in, wrapping his arms around her. She could hear his heart pounding in his chest, and then everything went to slow motion. He raised her chin, his gaze locked on her, and he pressed his lips to hers.

Zara stiffened, her instincts telling her to stop it while she could. But Mustafa's tongue sought hers, and his moan of desire and passion surged through her, setting fire to her world. Losing control, her heart and body betrayed her. With a will of their own, her fingers entangled in his hair. When finally, their lips parted, she breathed. "I'd like to sample some of this extraordinary Malbec you're producing."

The depth of his vocal register vibrated inside of her. "There's a bottle waiting for you, and a lifetime of love waiting for both of us."

It was crazy, but she couldn't deny her feelings for him. She believed him. But most importantly, she knew he was her second chance, and considering what he'd been through, she knew she was his. *If I don't follow my heart, who am I?*

"It would be interesting to see this vineyard of yours. I can't promise I'll stay, but when would we leave?"

"Now." He took her hand and kissed it.

They walked together with Lulu trotting ahead at the end of the leash.

"I'm afraid. What if this is a mistake?"

"There are no mistakes in life, *habibi*. There are just lessons to be learned and wasted opportunities. We've wasted enough time already. It's time to believe anything is possible. It's time to believe in love." His fingers tipped his hat as he greeted the fishermen.

"You think it will all fall into place. That it's possible you and I can just pick up where we left off."

"It's just a matter of time and perspective." He squeezed her hand in his.

"Time and perspective," she repeated in a whisper. It was impossible to ignore or forget the carnage they'd seen. There was no forgiveness for the lives they'd both taken. Could she ever trust him? It would take time, and the road would not be without its bumps and setbacks. Could she build a life with a man like him, a man with blood on his hands? She thought of her twin, Jacob. Jacob was the most forgiving person she'd ever known. She listened to the sound of the river lapping on the pier pilings. For a moment, she felt Jacob's presence and warmth fill her.

"I think with time we'll find forgiveness in our hearts," she said. "Perhaps we can start by forgiving each other." She turned her head to look at him. The setting sun surrounded him in a halo of light, blinding her.

Maybe he's right. If we try, it just might work.

He handed her into a black Mercedes with dark tinted windows and got in beside her. Behind the wheel, a mustached man observed them in the rearview mirror. Mustafa held her hand and met the man's gaze. "*Vámonos. Es hora de que nos vayamos a casa.*"

He turned to her. "It's time for us to go home, *habibi*."

EXPOSED: TIP OF THE SPEAR THRILLER SERIES BOOK 4

SNEAK PEEK

London, United Kingdom
February 1st
6 pm

He wants to kill me.

Jasmine Amin choked, swallowing the vomit that filled her throat. She didn't dare make a sound as she crouched beneath the outside windowsill of her family's home. The bitter taste of bile coated her tongue, and more than anything, she wanted to curl into a fetal ball and die. She couldn't think beyond what she'd seen, couldn't breathe beyond her next breath. Jasmine looked up, unable to see the assassin, but sensing his face pressed to the window, she could feel him squinting, searching through the gloom of night, intent on finding and eliminating her.

Do murderers dream? Do they have families? Do they love?

She had no answers, only the horrible images that replayed in her mind. The assassin uttered a curse, and she shuddered. She thought about standing up tall in front of the window and screaming loud enough for the entire neighborhood to hear, "Kill me, too, you bastard!" Instead, she closed her eyes, hoping this was just a nightmare. Praying that when she opened her eyes, everything would be just as it had been…Tonight was meant to be a family dinner celebrating her upcoming wedding. Tomorrow would have been her wedding day—marrying the man of her dreams, Darien Amani, an intern specializing in cardiology at Royal London

Hospital. Their future had seemed so bright. Jasmine soundlessly swallowed the thickness in her throat. In an instant, Darien and their life together was gone.

How will I go on?

The minutes ticked away, her thighs burned, and her stomach cramped. If she didn't move soon, she'd soil herself. It was beginning to drizzle, and she could feel her hair frizzing in the cold moisture. How could she possibly think about her hair at a moment like this? Would she ever see past the blood and bone spattering the white walls like a Pollack painting? What would Pollack name such a painting? *Death of a Family.* Insane thoughts even for an art major. But how could she focus on the truth that everyone she'd ever loved had disappeared in the blink of an eye?

I must survive. I'm the only one who knows what happened. The dead will never rest unless I live. "Inna lillahi wa inna ilayhi raji'un," she whispered, leaning her head against the brick in exhaustion. "Indeed, to Allah we belong and to Him we shall return," the Muslim prayer for the dead, its mournful song echoed in her mind.

The front door slammed shut reverberating through the bones of the house. Instantly alert, Jasmine strained to hear footsteps—anything that would alert her to the whereabouts of the assassin so she could make her move—but all was silent except for the voices of the dead who called to her for vengeance. Now was not the time to listen, she needed to ignore their cries echoing in her head. She stood paralyzed. *What should I do?* Should she force herself to go into the house and call the police? *No, I can't. I can't see them dead.* The gruesome thought made her double over. Her stomach convulsed, and she heaved up everything until there was nothing left. Tears and snot streamed down her face. *Oh, God, Oh, God. Please, God, this can't be real. Don't let it be real.*

Jasmine ran to the stately old sycamore tree in the backyard, its branches leafless and barren, she crouched behind it. She stared at the ground and grabbed a handful of dirt. She crushed it in her fist, squeezing the damp, moist, earth through her fingers. She rose on shaky legs and leaned back against the tree; her slender body dwarfed by the massive tree trunk. She gulped the frigid air, filling her lungs, fighting to calm her rampant emotions.

Unprepared, the explosion caught her off-guard and flung her to the ground. She covered her head, protecting herself from the ballistic projectiles that flew through the air, slicing into the tree. Blazing fireballs rained down on the lawn. Black smoke billowed, and the roar of fire, incinerating everything it touched, sounded like horrified screams. The bodies inside the house burned, forever silenced.

Rage swept through her, and the blue vein in her temple throbbed. There would be nothing left, no evidence of their having lived, no bodies to bury and pray over, nothing but ash.

My life is ash.

There was nothing left inside of her, only hatred and the desire to expose and bring whoever did this to her family to justice. Taking a last look at the home that was a towering inferno of flame, she stumbled across the yard and left through the back gate. She had to get away, but where would she go?

Was there any place on earth that was safe for her?

End of Sneak Peek

Like what you've read? You can order *EXPOSED* by Belle Ami on Amazon.

ABOUT THE AUTHOR

Belle Ami writes breathtaking international thrillers and compelling romantic suspense with a touch of sensual heat. A self-confessed news junky, Belle loves to create cutting-edge stories weaving world issues, espionage, fast-paced action, and of course, redemptive love.

Belle is the author of the ongoing international espionage thriller series *TIP OF THE SPEAR*, which includes the highly acclaimed *Escape*, *Vengeance*, and *Ransom and Exposed*.

She is also the author of the ongoing bestselling *OUT OF TIME* thriller series, which includes the #1 Amazon bestseller—*The Girl Who Knew da Vinci* and #1 Amazon bestseller—*The Girl Who Loved Caravaggio* and *The Girl Who Adored Rembrandt*.

Belle is also the author of the romantic suspense series *THE ONLY ONE*, which includes *The One*, *The One & More*, and *One More Time is Not Enough*.

Recently, she was honored to be included in the RWA-LARA Christmas Anthology *Holiday Ever After*, featuring her short story, *The Christmas Encounter*.

A former Kathryn McBride scholar of Bryn Mawr College in Pennsylvania, Belle, is also thrilled to be a recipient of the *RONE, RAVEN,* and *Readers' Favorite Awards*.

Belle's passions include hiking, boxing, skiing, cooking, travel, and of course, writing. She lives in Southern California with her husband, two children, a horse named Cindy Crawford, and her brilliant Chihuahua, Giorgio Armani.

Belle loves to hear from readers—you can contact
her at: belle@belleamiauthor.com

Connect with Belle Ami online:
belleamiauthor.com
BookBub
Amazon
Twitter: @BelleAmi5
Facebook
Instagram
Newsletter Signup